HIDDEN WITNESS

HIDDEN WITNESS

Nick Oldham

This first world edition published 2010
in Great Britain and in 2011 in the USA by
SEVERN HOUSE PUBLISHERS LTD of
9–15 High Street, Sutton, Surrey, England, SM1 1DF.
Trade paperback edition first published
in Great Britain and the USA 2011 by
SEVERN HOUSE PUBLISHERS LTD.

British Library Cataloguing in Publication Data

Oldham, Nick, 1956–
   Hidden witness. – (A Detective Superintendent Henry
   Christie novel)
   1. Christie, Henry (Fictitious character) – Fiction.
   2. Police – England – Blackpool – Fiction. 3. Intelligence
   officers – United States – Fiction. 4. Murder –
   Investigation – Fiction. 5. Organized crime investigation –
   Fiction. 6. Witnesses – Fiction. 7. Detective and mystery
   stories.
   I. Title II. Series
   823.9'14-dc22

ISBN-13: 978-0-7278-6964-7 (cased)
ISBN-13: 978-1-84751-293-2 (trade paper)

All Severn House titles are printed on acid-free paper.

Severn House Publishers support The Forest Stewardship Council [FSC],
the leading international forest certification organisation. All our titles that
are printed on Greenpeace-approved FSC-certified paper carry the FSC logo.

Mixed Sources
Product group from well-managed
forests and other controlled sources
www.fsc.org Cert no. SA-COC-1565
© 1996 Forest Stewardship Council

Typeset by Palimpsest Book Production Ltd.,
Falkirk, Stirlingshire.
Printed and bound in Great Britain by the
MPG Books Group, Bodmin, Cornwall.

*This book is dedicated to the memory
of Dave Briggs*

ONE

They were the first of the killings.

No one was expecting them to happen, especially not 'off-turf', and consequently their guard was down. They were relaxing, smiling, enjoying the lack of tension in the air, able to breathe easily for once whilst discussing expansion plans with the American who'd flown in just for the meeting.

The weather was cool, but warm enough to sit out in the evening on the terrace of the restaurant in the Calle de Nanses in Can Pastilla, overlooking the tiny bay which was essentially the start of the huge curve of man-made beach, the Cala Estancia, stretching about six kilometres east as far as El Arenal. During summer this whole expanse was a throb of interconnected holiday resorts, but at this time of year in that lull between Christmas and New Year, Can Pastilla was nothing more than a sleepy suburb of Palma, Majorca. Few establishments were open, apart from the big hotels catering for ageing Spaniards from the mainland, or Germans, and even the tat shops were mostly closed for winter.

That said, there was still a lot of people about, and the Somali immigrants continued to ply their trade along the front by trying to encourage people to fork out for fake Rolexes and poorly pirated DVDs and CDs.

But this restaurant was open, caught a decent trade, served good Spanish food, a change from the pasta that three of the four men usually ate in Naples, excellent though it was. The men also knew a club for later, open all year round and run openly, blatantly, by the Russian Mafia.

Not that the men minded. They had no quarrel with the Russians in this neck of the woods and looked forward to an evening of debauchery, Soviet-style. The drink, drugs and girls had been pre-ordered, and all would be exquisite.

There were four men at the table, and to celebrate their arrival on Spanish territory they ordered paella and were now in that pleasant delay between placing the order and its arrival. A gap, usually, of about twenty minutes. They picked on tapas, including olives, *patatas bravas* and garlic-fried prawns.

The waiter, sensing the danger these men oozed, hovered attentively, wringing his hands together. But for the moment, the guests were content. Each had a large cold beer and the three Italians languidly smoked pungent cigarettes, blowing out rings of thick smoke.

Cars drove along the one-way Calle de Nanses, slowly, only feet away from the table at which the men lounged. Some were big, four-wheel drive monstrosities with smoked windows and unseen occupants. The men eyed each car but stayed chilled. After all, no one knew they were here. The Italians had covered their tracks well they thought, and the interest in the passing vehicles, whilst inbuilt, was only cursory. It wasn't like being on show in a pavement café in Naples, where every time anyone of the Italians appeared in public they were in danger of being mown down in a hail of bullets from rival factions.

Here, for the moment, they were safe.

Although there was no head of the table as such, it was obvious that of the three Italians, the one sitting with his back to the restaurant, enjoying a view out across the small bay, was the boss. He was only young, maybe thirty-four, with pinched features and a pockmarked face, but with body language that exuded confidence and superiority. It was in the way he sat, the way he exhaled cigarette smoke, how he picked up an olive and dropped it into his mouth. How his hooded eyes examined the other men. The two Italians with him were down the pecking order. One was a man older than the first, who gave advice when asked for, but never offered it, and the other, a slim, reptilian guy just out of his teens, was the bodyguard. The most relaxed of the three, he should have been the most alert.

The boss was called Carlo Marini.

He said to the American, 'What was your route?'

The American, a man with very obvious Southern European blood that showed in his dark, brooding features and jet black hair, said, 'Miami, overnight New York to London, by car to Liverpool, then to Palma . . . I was careful,' he finished.

'That is good,' Marini said. 'I'm impressed by your professionalism.'

The American sipped his lager, his eyes moving from one man to the other. He smiled thinly at Marini.

'So you think you can help us?'

He nodded, but rejoined, 'No, *you* think I can help you,' he said, correcting Marini, but with due deference in the tone of his voice. Deference was vital, respect everything. At the very least a lack of either could cause offence, at most it could be fatal. It was a fine line to tread.

'Yes, yes, true,' Marini agreed. 'But even so, you do know we have to be so careful.'

'In what way?' the American asked.

Marini's evil eyes half-closed. 'We need to be sure.'

The American guffawed, understanding. But some resistance was acceptable, so he said, 'I've flown halfway around the world to meet you – for the fourth time. Doesn't that say something?'

'It does, it does . . . however . . .' Marini left the rest unsaid with a lazy flick of the hand.

The American said, 'OK, have it your way.'

'*Grazie* . . . then go with Paulo.' Marini indicated the young bodyguard who took a long draught of beer and stood up, politely waiting for the American to do the same. The two men then went into the restaurant and to the *Senor's*.

The toilets were cramped, space tight.

'You know the drill,' Paulo said.

The American turned to the wall, placed the balls of his hands high on it, something that went unnoticed, and spread his feet, allowing the Italian to frisk him lightly but thoroughly. He didn't flinch when Paulo jabbed the blade of his hand up into his crotch to check there. Too many concealed weapons had been missed by a searcher's reluctance to squeeze a guy's balls.

'OK, hands down,' he was instructed. He turned back to Paulo. '*Finito*?'

'*Benito*,' Paulo grinned.

'Mind if I have a piss?'

'Just so long as you use the urinal,' Paulo clipped with a smile, patted the American on his shoulder and left him to do his business.

'Sorry about that,' Marini said to the American when they were all seated back on the terrace.

'It's business, I get it,' he said, looking up as the waiter arrived with a large steaming pan of blind paella, so named because all the shells had been removed from the seafood, and the bones from the meat, to make eating it less messy. The pan was placed on a folding trestle table next to them and served immediately, a wonderful mountain of food they forked into with the gusto of Mediterranean people. A smooth Italian wine and sparkling mineral water accompanied it.

A Lexus four-by-four cruised slowly past, the occupants virtually hidden by the dark glass.

Paulo watched it suspiciously, a forkful of hot rice hovering at his mouth. It drove on; he pushed the food into his mouth.

'So,' Marini said sitting back after his first sustained attack on the paella, 'you think you can help us?'

'I do.' The American wiped his mouth with a serviette.

'We've had some discussion, I know . . . edging here and there . . .' Marini moved his body as though he was describing a football move. 'But let me warn you, if anything you say doesn't fit with what I know, the deal will become shaky.'

The American nodded. 'It's simple . . . I have a business that can connect up with yours to our mutual advantage . . . it's wholesale and retail and continually expanding.'

'How does it work?'

'You provide me with the goods, I sell them.' He shrugged.

'On what terms?'

'Sale or return.'

Marini shook his head sadly. 'Too hit and miss. No commitment from you. You're asking me to give you something for nothing and if you manage to sell it, you'll pay me a percentage.'

'A proper business model.'

'I incur all the costs of production and exportation, and only get paid if you manage to sell?'

The American wanted to exhale and show annoyance. But he didn't.

'Let me paint a picture . . . I now have forty retail outlets in the US, in shopping malls from Orlando to Memphis, right across the panhandle. Forty,' he reiterated. 'I already supply over two hundred more right up the eastern seaboard. This time next year, I'll have sixty outlets and be supplying two-fifty more. I need good quality merchandise at cheap prices. The market snaffles them up like vultures, credit crunch or not.' He spoke earnestly and persuasively.

Marini nodded. 'And my percentage?'

The American sat back and considered the question, as though he didn't know the answer already. 'A thirty-three per cent mark-up, which is good. And don't forget, we're talking a lot of output here.'

Marini's head nodded from side to side thoughtfully.

'And I can start selling as soon as you start providing – but

I cannot wait forever.' He scooped up more paella and chomped it noisily, savouring it. 'This is excellent,' he said.

Marini went into deep thought. This venture could be his making, his break from the constraints of the past. He hadn't rushed things, done it all very slowly and carefully. Built up his contacts, spoken quietly to people he thought were disaffected and downtrodden, and now he was ready to move. Trusted allies surrounded him and all he needed to do was strike the blow that would release him. His dark eyes glistened as he imagined the future of power and wealth in the palm of his hand, which would also help to crush his rivals who had been getting out of hand recently.

Even so, that profit margin could be higher.

He nodded finally and, stone-faced, he said, 'It needs to be thirty-seven per cent.'

The American didn't actually care. Marini could have asked for fifty per cent. However, for the sake of appearances and not to raise suspicion, he would not go over forty.

He mulled over Marini's demand as though it mattered – then he nodded.

'We have a deal.'

The men reached across the table and shook hands, and for the first time their faces cracked into grins. The other two men breathed out with relief, also, and the American offered his hand to them. Marini beckoned the waiter across and ordered champagne.

'You won't regret it,' the American promised. 'This is the start of something very big . . . yeah, sounds corny, but it's true . . . now, Jeez, sorry guys, I need to pee again . . . if you'll excuse . . .'

Marini waved him happily away, still doing the sums in his mind. Immense amounts of money. He leaned to the man who gave him advice for an ear-to-ear whispered conversation. There was much nodding and agreement and shoulder touching.

'Many people will be glad of this, but there may be some personal times ahead.' They were talking in Italian now, having conversed in English all night for the American's benefit, who, though of Italian blood, hardly spoke a word of the mother tongue.

'You will need to be strong,' the adviser cautioned.

'I know – but with you beside me, we can surmount the attrition.'

They clapped each other's shoulders again.

'Success!'

Marini raised his champagne glass as the American returned from the toilet.

Just then, the same Lexus four-wheel drive that had trundled past earlier, cruised by again. This time the men tensed up, lowered their glasses. Paulo rose slowly from his seat, his right hand snaking underneath his jacket to reach for the pistol tucked into his trouser waistband at the small of his back.

The Lexus stopped.

Marini began to rise now, his instincts clicking in.

Then the front passenger window opened smoothly to reveal the face of the guy sat there.

'Hey fuckers! When you coming to my club?' the big, round-faced Russian bawled.

Marini relaxed, gave the guy a wave.

'Girls queuing up for you all!'

'An hour, give us an hour,' Marini said after consulting his watch.

'Yeah, yeah – beluga on ice, vodka on ice, girls on heat.' The window slid back up and the Lexus jumped forwards quietly.

The American was still standing. 'Jesus,' he breathed.

'Yeah, man, I thought I was back in Napoli for a moment,' Paulo laughed nervously, his hand coming back into view and sitting down with relief.

Marini covered his nerves with a hand gesture telling everyone to keep cool. In Naples, eating al fresco meant having men up and down the street watching for danger. 'Just the Russians trying to shit us.'

They all laughed.

The American was still on his feet.

Marini looked up at him. 'You sitting, or what? C'mon, chill. Discussion time . . . a deal to make.'

The American had spent his time with the three men carefully weighing them up. Paulo being ordered to search him had been a good thing. It meant that finding nothing had put him off guard and also that by getting so close to each other in the toilets, the American had been able to brush up against him and make a judgement about his fire power. The passing of the stupid Russian just confirmed what he already knew: one gun, a pistol, probably a Glock in the waistband . . . a knife in the jacket pocket.

Having assessed the other two – meeting them earlier, shaking their hands, patting shoulders, being effusive, touchy-feely, told him that Marini was unarmed and that the adviser was armed similarly to Paulo.

It was going to be a big kill, but it had to be done.

He actually thought about giving some sort of retort to Marini's remark about the deal, saying that, actually, the deal was off . . . but that was the kind of silly display that shaved valuable seconds off your time and gave people the opportunity to react.

Instead, he moved fast and picked his moment with precision – the seconds just after the Lexus had disappeared.

All three had had a surge of adrenaline – was this going to be a drive-by shooting or not? Each would still have that bitter taste in his mouth: fear. But it was short-lived and as soon as the possible danger had passed, they were all telling each other to relax, cool down, remember where we are – in a foreign land where they were safe. Internally their bodies were also telling themselves that, too.

The American moved as Paulo made himself comfortable, as the adviser shook his head at their stupidity, as Marini reached for his glass and the bottle of champagne.

The gun had been left for him by another guest at the restaurant. He did not know who, didn't want to know, but who had been into the toilet just after he and Paulo had left following the body search.

He was standing at ninety degrees to Paulo, who was first to go.

The American's hand appeared from underneath his jacket holding the pistol. He hadn't checked it. He'd been told it would be ready for use: one bullet chambered, safety off, gun ready to fire.

The move was smooth, seemingly unhurried.

He touched Paulo's temple with the muzzle and squeezed. The noise was deafening, disorientating, as it was meant to be. Paulo's brained splattered all over the chest of the adviser who, stunned, looked down in disbelief as though someone had just spilled a beer over him.

But he had no time to consider further because as he started to move and react properly, the gun swung at him, was fired. The bullet entered his head through his right eye, twisted sideways and exited through his left temple like a rocket tearing through a warship, the exit wound enormous.

All due credit to him, Marini moved quickly, and threw himself off his chair, starting to scurry-crawl desperately away, but the American shot him in the back of the head, and the exit wound removed most of his face.

In seconds the American had stepped around the table and put another bullet into each of the men, even though in his heart of hearts he knew they were dead, but he was paid not to make any mistakes and a man in a coma can always wake up.

Then he allowed himself his little quip.

'Deal off.'

TWO

Three years later

B y the time the two boys came across the old man that evening, they had already committed three robberies.

Technically, the first one wasn't a robbery, just a theft. This was because to commit a robbery by the legal definition under the Theft Act, there has to be violence combined with stealing.

Simply rolling a drunk didn't count.

However, if they'd ever got chance to brag about it they would have claimed it was a robbery by their own definition. In fact, all they did was trip over an unconscious vagrant in a Blackpool back alley and when he didn't respond to their tentative prod-kicks, other than to groan, they shared a triumphant glance and one dared the other to go through his pockets. The tramp stank of body odour, vomit and booze, and had obviously urinated where he lay, so searching through his trouser pockets took some doing. The younger of the two lads, the least experienced one, took on the task to prove himself. He found a crumpled, wet, five-pound note and some loose change. After helping them-selves to the unopened can of cider in the gutter by the guy, they legged it victoriously through the rain-splattered streets of the resort.

They shared the cider in a shop doorway opposite the entrance to Blackpool Tower, tossed the empty tin at two passing girls, then moved on to find more victims.

They were fired up, brimful of violence, on the rob.

Next time it was a fully-fledged robbery as per the legal definition. Still hyper from their first success and fuelled by the cider that went straight to their heads, they wanted to feel someone fall under their punches. The Goth teenager standing on Talbot Square opposite where Yates' Wine Lodge had burned down, using his mobile phone was an ideal target. Once chosen, they didn't hesitate – simply walked brazenly up to him, unfazed by the number of other people walking about and the older lad said, 'Gimme your phone, badger-face.'

The Goth, his eyes blackened by make-up, his face whitened by foundation, looked quizzically at them, part-way through his conversation. 'Eh?'

It was the younger of the two lads who stepped in and took the lead. The boy with the phone was older than the both of them, but no match physically or aggressively, as evidenced by his terrified expression. 'Phone,' the lad said, as if the Goth was stupid.

'Get lost.' He angled away from them, hoping that ignoring them would make them go away, like covering your face with a bed sheet to stop a burglar attacking. He was very wrong. The youngest lad smashed him hard on the side of his head, crashing his knuckles into the temple. He hit him three times in quick succession, driving the victim down against a building as his legs buckled at the knee and he dropped his phone. As he went down, his attacker continued to strike, and the older lad joined in, kicking him several times on the head with the sole of his trainer, stomping on him as he hit the ground.

The older lad snatched up the phone, which hadn't shattered on impact with the pavement, and the pair raced away from a crime scene for the second time in half an hour. It was an attack that had taken place out in the open on a busy street, on a bustling evening, and though it lasted for less than thirty blurred seconds, there were many eyewitnesses but none brave enough to challenge or intervene. In fact, the bleeding victim crawled unaided to a nearby phone box to call the police, and on that short, incredibly painful journey, at least four people walked around him, one actually stepped over him. The streets of Blackpool could be harsh and unforgiving.

The two boys never even saw a cop car because none was dispatched to the incident. The poor, sobbing Goth was informed that every police officer in town was busy, and if it wasn't too much trouble, he should make his way to the police station to report the crime. His other option was to make an appointment for a home visit by his local beat officer.

Within ten minutes the boys had sold the phone for ten pounds and so, fifteen pounds richer, they treated themselves to a burger and coke each at the McDonald's opposite central pier. Then they decided to keep a low profile for a while in the amusement arcades before selecting their next victim.

But as it happened, they were so hyped up after the Goth robbery and the fast food, they couldn't stop themselves going out on the prowl again. As they stalked through the streets they chanted, 'Vic-tim, vic-tim, vic-tim,' quietly, winding themselves up into some sort of feral frenzy. This time they wanted real money, to really hurt someone, and they needed to make a careful choice.

At nine p.m., they turned into the southern entrance to Bonny Street, which ran parallel to, and one-step back from, the promenade. They were walking north, the multi-storey car park and high-rise police station on their right, and the backs of various premises on their left, such as amusement arcades and the Sea Life Centre. Tucked in amongst those buildings was a pub called the Pump and Truncheon, a hostelry frequented by cops from the station opposite.

With the police station, and its enquiry desk now relocated to ground level, Bonny Street should have been a safe haven.

But it wasn't. It was poorly lit and deserted at that time of day. The backs of the buildings, so inviting from the front, were grim and dark and full of shadow.

The lads quit their chanting as they passed the pub. The door opened and a couple staggered out, obviously the worse for wear, bickering at each other. They turned south, paying the robbers no heed, apart from a quick glance. The boys stopped for a moment, watched the man and woman cross the road and disappear.

Then they noticed the girl. She was walking towards them, not much older than they were, dolled up for a night out, unsuitably dressed to be walking through the drizzle. She was kitted out like someone much older, a tiny silver purse hanging on a thin chain from her shoulder that had to contain her money and phone. Her micro-skirt and skimpy top meant there was nowhere else to stash her valuables. And the boys knew this.

'Vic-tim,' the older one hissed.

'Vic-tim,' the younger one agreed.

They pretended to ignore her, walking along the centre of the road, the police station fifty metres behind them now. The girl was on the pavement to their left, in the shadow cast by the buildings. They passed within feet. Her eyes nervously checked them out, picking up a suspicious feel for the duo, uncertain, wary . . . then relieved as they went past without even seeming to notice her. Even so, she upped her pace on her unsteady high heels. Better safe than sorry.

Two metres past, they turned like hunting dogs on an unsuspecting gazelle. They bundled her into a wide, deep service door. One clamped a hand over her face and pushed her against the side of an industrial size wheelie-bin where the assault began. Neither boy spoke as they kicked and smacked her, pounding her down to the litter-strewn ground. One ripped the purse off her shoulder, snapping the thin strap easily.

Then they were gone, sucked up on to the busy streets of the resort.

The purse contained two folded up five-pound notes, an expensive looking mobile phone, and a lip-gloss. This brought the cash total of three robberies to twenty-five pounds, less the cost of the burgers. They split the money as they walked up Church Street, past the Winter Gardens complex.

The older, more experienced lad said, 'Maybe we'd better just quit for the night now, eh? Don't wanna keep ridin' our luck.' He handed his mate his share of the cash and kept the phone for himself. 'Not much, but I told you it was ace, didn't I?' The older boy – he was seventeen – had deep-green eyes and curly black hair, as though he could have been a descendant from the Romany gypsies. He had a wild, untamed look and a face that mirrored this.

'Yeah, great.' The younger one snaffled the money, but his voice, though enthusiastic, broke slightly, as though perhaps he didn't feel entirely comfortable with their actions. That possibly he found himself doing something he didn't really enjoy. He stuffed the money into his tracksuit-bottoms pocket and zipped it away. 'I probably need to be getting home now . . . my mum'll be wondering . . .' His voice was thin with the lie. There would be no chance of his mother wondering anything about him, but it didn't matter because the older lad wasn't listening anyway.

He'd stopped abruptly, placed a hand on his mate's forearm, then drawn him back into the recess of a shop doorway.

'What?' the younger lad asked.

'I take it all back,' he said excitedly, 'because our luck is still riding high and we need to keep going while we're on a roll.' He jabbed a forefinger, pointing across the road. 'That guy will be freakin' loaded,' he stated, and the younger lad saw what was being pointed out, and just to confirm, was told, 'Victim number four.'

An old man was emerging from a shop across the road, turning to lock up and stepping back as he pulled down the security shutters covering the door, which he fastened with a sturdy padlock, giving it a shake to test it. He was obviously locking up for the night.

The younger lad watched, a worried feeling clawing at his guts.

The shop was a large, but inconspicuous unit selling male and female clothing and associated gear. The younger lad had been in once during opening hours and had seen stacks of designer jeans, tee shirts and dresses, all claiming to be at least half the price of the same goods in department stores. And all still too expensive for him to buy. So he'd stolen a pair of D&G jeans that did not fit him and sold them on for a couple of pounds.

He recalled the shop being staffed by young people, didn't remember seeing an old bloke on the shop floor. 'Must be the owner,' he whispered.

'Which is why he'll be stacked with cash.'

The old man was satisfied the shutter was locked, the shop secure. He stood upright, turned, looked up and down Church Street. He was dressed immaculately in a black Crombie, brown brogues and well-cut trousers. His hair was thick and grey, combed back from his face which was tanned, healthy looking. He had a silver tipped walking stick and settled a trilby on his head that he adjusted against his reflection in the shop window. He looked dapper and sprightly.

Happy that all was OK, he crossed Church Street quickly and entered Leopold Grove, which ran across the top edge of the Winter Gardens. The older boy held his mate back, allowing the old man to get slightly ahead. Then they emerged from their dark doorway and started to follow, keeping to the shadows. As they turned on to Leopold Grove, the old man, walking briskly, was quite a way ahead, picking up momentum with the incline of the street. He went across Adelaide Street towards Albert Road, quiet, badly lit streets on the outer edge of the town centre. Ideal hunting grounds for opportunistic criminals.

They tracked him on to Albert Road where he turned right in the general direction of the seafront, but then quickly cut over into an unlit alley leading through to Charnley Road. He was moving with purpose, but the boys were closing in, the older one already chanting, 'Vic-tim, vic-tim,' under his breath, winding himself up for the attack. The younger one was less certain this time. There was something about the way the man walked, held himself. He might have been old – maybe seventy – but he had a confident aura about him, someone who could take care of himself, was unafraid. Nothing about him said, 'Victim.' If anything, 'Vic*tor*' was more appropriate and the younger lad sensed this.

The alley was dismal, but a streetlight at the far end illuminated the last five metres of it and the boys had to get their assault in before the man reached this pool of brightness.

They closed in, the older boy ahead, picking up the pace. The younger one was in his slipstream, carried along with the moment, heart hammering, legs weak, a taste of something unpleasant in his mouth that he tried to swallow down his dry throat.

With three metres separating hunter and hunted, the old man suddenly stopped, turned around completely and faced the boys. They stopped in their tracks.

'You think I didn't see you!' the old man roared. He had an accent of sorts, but neither boy could say what it was. 'You think I don't know you follow me!'

'Don't give a toss if you did or didn't,' the older boy sneered, but he was now apprehensive. The man seemed to have grown physically and was almost challenging them, his head tilted back and the fluorescent streetlight slashing down across his heavy features.

The man raised his walking stick, laughing harshly. 'You may move quicker than me, but you will come off worse, I promise.'

The boys stood unsurely. The younger one touched his friend's sleeve, a gesture to retreat. The older boy shrugged off the fingers, his anger building at the challenge. 'Give us your cash and you won't get hurt – that's all I can promise you, old man.'

The old man shook his head, amused, unafraid.

'C'mon, Rory, let's leave this one.'

'No chance – he'll be fuckin' minted.'

The older boy launched himself at the old man, hoping to catch him off-guard. He went in with his head low, but the man took half a step sideways, swung his hip and in the same movement brought the walking stick around with incredible accuracy – hard. He cracked it across the side of the boy's charging head just the once. The blow glanced off, but still knocked him sideways into the alley wall. He moved in then and raised the stick, the boy now cowering behind his raised forearms.

'No, please.'

'You have had enough?' the old man demanded.

'Yeah, yeah,' the lad said, scrambling away, backing into his mate, stepping into a pile of dog shit.

The old man addressed the younger boy. 'You, too?' He brandished the cane and the lad backed off, saying, 'I didn't go for you.'

'Mm,' he said doubtfully, gave them both the evil eye, turned and strutted out of the alley.

The boys stood together, side by side, the older one holding a hand over his bleeding head. 'Bastard!' he shouted.

The old man ignored the insult.

They watched him step out of the alley and begin to cross the road.

He was halfway across when the car hit him. Then everything slowed right down.

He was walking at ninety degrees to the car, which was a big Volvo estate, and the heavy vehicle was still accelerating, maybe travelling over thirty miles per hour when it struck. It connected with the old man's right-hand side. It smashed full on into him, instantly shattering his hip and femur. The old man twisted appallingly with the impact, his body contorting out of shape. The car seemed to scoop him up, taking his legs from underneath him, driving on as his right shoulder smacked into the bonnet. His head, hat still in place at that moment, smashed into the windscreen, indenting it, and his whole body flicked up like a frog being thrown from a spade. He cartwheeled across the roof of the car, his right arm snapping, his cane spinning through the air, his legs flipping upwards, the car passing on under him. He cleared the vehicle and from a height of about twelve feet, crashed head first into the roadway.

In the mouth of the alley, the two boys stood mesmerized by the incident. They could see the old man lying on the road, broken, but moving, twitching. They were overwhelmed by the violence of the impact that had taken the breath out of their bodies. They were not prepared for what happened next.

The Volvo braked sharply ten metres ahead of the man. The engine revved. Then suddenly it reversed at speed, swerving wildly, engine screaming.

Raising his head slightly, the old man saw what was coming. The rear bumper of the car struck him and the back wheels crushed him, the car rising as though it was going over a speed hump. And it kept going, the front wheels doing the same, making the man writhe obscenely.

Still it wasn't finished. The engine revved again, the car lurched forwards and mounted him again, front wheels, then back.

He must have been dead by now, his brittle bones and internal organs crushed. The car stopped and for one terrible moment they were certain it was going to reverse over him again.

The older one stepped forward, but the younger one held him back, something telling him it wasn't over.

Why had the car stopped?

If this was a hit-and-run, the driver having made certain there was no living witness to his crime, why hadn't he gone, left the scene? The old man was dead, why hesitate?

The younger boy ducked instinctively, stepping back into the darkness as the questions barraging through his brain were answered.

A man got out of the passenger door of the Volvo – the first realization to the boy that there were two people in the car.

It was a man, casually dressed, zip-up top, jeans, trainers, dark-haired, thirties, maybe. He walked back to where the old man lay in the road, unmoving, and bent to inspect him. Then the boys saw what he had in his hands, the fact registering with them at exactly the same instant.

A handgun of some sort. Neither could have said whether it was a revolver or pistol, but both saw the bulbous silencer fitted on to the barrel.

The gun was held at the man's side and as he bent over, it angled at the old man's head and the trigger was pulled twice. The old man's head jerked as the bullets entered it.

The older boy, Rory, stepped into the light. 'Hey!' he called.

The man bending over the body turned his head and looked in his direction. There was a flash, lighting up his face.

He rose slowly, confidently and the gun came up.

The younger boy grabbed Rory's arm and dragged him back into the alley, screaming 'Run, run.'

They turned and sprinted away in the direction they'd come

from, keeping low in the shadows, both expecting to feel the
wham of a bullet in the back of the head.

THREE

'How many times do I have to tell you? I didn't kill her.'
The prisoner smashed his fist on to the interview
room table and glowered angrily at Detective
Superintendent Henry Christie, his face now a blotchy red, neck
sinews tight as wire. There had been a full day of denials and
an increasingly tense and confrontational atmosphere as Henry
had relentlessly twisted the screw, turning an initially placid
suspect into one who seethed and showed his true colours. A
man unable to contain rage.

Henry was now feeling jaded by the process, but still wanted
to push on, knowing the momentum of an interview was invalu-
able. However, the man's solicitor had started bleating about
periods of adequate rest, as per the Police and Criminal Evidence
Act, and Henry knew there had to be a break in order to comply
with the law.

He leaned on the table and fixed eye-to-eye contact with the
prisoner.

'Mr Twist . . . Dennis,' he began, keeping his voice level and
unemotional, a tool that had managed to wind-up the suspect all
day long. 'Time's getting on and we're reaching a point where
we have to conclude the conversation for the day. But before
we pack up and you go back to your cell for a lovely sleep,
there's a few things I'd like to say.' Henry paused, ensuring he'd
got Twist's attention. 'You are a dangerous and violent man. You
cannot control your temper. You act on impulse and gut feeling,
and a red mist comes down over your eyes when you get angry
– and then you attack. Which is what happened in the case of
your girlfriend, isn't it?' Henry stopped again. 'She wanted to
end the relationship with you because of your increasing levels
of violence towards her – and you suspected, without a shred
of evidence, that she was seeing another man. Despite her denials,
you strangled her with a length of clothesline, then disposed of
her body and tried to destroy her remains by setting them on
fire.

'You then showed yourself to be a man who lies by pretending that she left you, and you continued to use her mobile phone to text her friends after you'd killed her, didn't you? You tried to make them believe she was still alive.' Henry gave a thin smile. 'Maybe you should've got rid of the phone? Awful things mobiles, aren't they?'

Twist's face was a mask of anger. His teeth ground audibly, nostrils flared wide. His breathing was laboured and his fists bunched tightly in front of him. Henry kept up the eye contact, seeing the slight contraction of Twist's pupils as he listened to this summary. 'You murdered Helen Race, then you disposed of her body like you were throwing out trash. Then you covered it up by lying . . . lying . . . lying . . .'

Twist gave an almost imperceptible, but nonchalant shrug.

'Thing is, though, Dennis, you were absolutely right about her. She was seeing someone else.'

The blood drained from his face.

'You only suspected it,' Henry whispered, 'but our investigations have uncovered that she was seeing somebody else.'

Twist's chest drew in air. 'Bitch,' he hissed. 'Who?'

Henry gave his almost imperceptible shrug. 'Not at liberty to reveal that.'

'You don't have to. I know.'

'And that's why you killed her, isn't it? She got what she deserved, didn't she?' Henry was tightening things again. 'I can see how you would feel. Cheated on, treated bad, mocked, laughed at behind your back. Despised. You put two and two together. Didn't have to be a rocket scientist, did you?'

Sometimes it happens, Henry thought, sometimes it don't. He waited for the reaction.

Twist sat back, his mouth contorting. He averted his eyes, which seemed to film over.

'I hit her hard, first. With a hammer I got from B and Q. That felt good. The sound of it hitting her skull. The feel. I felt it sink into her skull. She was still alive when she hit the floor, right next to the ironing board. Handy, huh? She'd been ironing, see? So I used the flex, wrapped it round her throat.' Henry saw Twist's fists bunch up as he relived the moment. 'Couldn't stop myself. Knew it was wrong, but couldn't stop . . . yeah, red mist.'

Henry emerged from the interview room an hour later having got Twist to take him through everything in detail. It was a harrowing sixty minutes, but from the point of view of a detective investigating murder, very satisfying because the confession was all they had. Twist had covered his tracks well, with one or two bloopers maybe, and the case against him had been circumstantial and slightly rocky. Now Twist was screwed.

Henry and the local detective sergeant, who'd been 'second jockey' with him in the interview, walked into the custody office and booked the master copy of the interview tape into the secure system. Then they made their way through Blackpool nick to the CID office on the ground floor. They stood aside to allow a couple of uniformed officers to rush past them on some emergency call-out or other.

In the CID office, all but deserted at that time of night, Henry and the DS discussed the case which would need tying up by the local cops. Henry, a detective superintendent jointly in charge of Lancashire Constabulary's Force Major Investigation Team, had other things to do. He had only become embroiled in interviewing the suspect following a fairly desperate request from the DS whose interviewing team had been stonewalled by Twist. Superintendents rarely got involved in tactical interviews, but Henry had not wanted to lose this one, a murder that was particularly gruesome and upsetting.

The DS thanked him and Henry rose to leave. He was already anticipating a tumbler of Jack Daniel's, a bit of supper with his wife, Kate, and bed. He should have known better than to look forward to the simple pleasures of life.

He'd parked his Ford Mondeo in a public car park at the front of the police station, and to get to it necessitated him exiting by way of the public enquiry desk on Bonny Street. As usual, the waiting area was busy, people queuing for attention. Henry emerged from the door behind the enquiry desk, his eyes taking in the people, seeing the back of the public enquiry assistant busy at the counter. He let himself out through the security door into the public foyer, the eyes of the public playing over him. He didn't want to hang around, but his eyes caught two people in particular.

One was a young girl, mid-teens, sitting forlornly on a bench, holding a pair of broken high-heeled shoes in one hand, and her head in the other. Her tiny skirt rose up high to reveal her shapely legs.

Second was a young man, maybe slightly older than the girl, sitting at the opposite end of the same bench, though obviously not with her. His head was in his hands and blood dripped between them on to a towel laid out on the tiled floor.

These two made him stop. They looked like they'd been badly assaulted. Mid-stride, Henry pivoted towards them and they looked up at him.

Henry recognized the young man as being a Goth because his youngest daughter had been through a Goth phase, which thankfully had been short-lived. On his face, in the white make-up, Henry could clearly see the imprint of the sole of a shoe, undoubtedly a trainer, where he had been stomped. His whole face was swollen, both eyes blackened for real, under the black make-up, and they were swollen, turning purple. He no longer needed the Goth make-up to look like one.

The girl, too, was a mess. Her knees, elbows and skin were scraped, cut, bleeding. Her skirt was torn. She gulped at Henry, lips trembling, tears brimming on the edge of her eyelids.

'What happened?' he asked generally.

The two victims exchanged glances, each waiting for the other to start. Two polite kids, Henry thought, wrong place, wrong time. The girl blurted, 'Two lads jumped me, just out there.' She sobbed, losing composure. 'Stole my purse, my phone, my money.' Her bottom lip quivered like jelly.

'An' I got jumped in town. Two guys, nicked my phone,' the Goth said, 'then kicked the crap out of me.'

'Do you know each other?'

They shook their heads and the lad said, 'No, but we think they were the same two lads who did it.'

Henry acknowledged this. 'Either of you had any medical treatment?'

Again they shook their heads.

'Anyone spoken to you yet? A detective, maybe?' Henry jerked his thumb at the enquiry desk. More head shaking.

'Right,' Henry tutted. He let himself back in behind the desk and sidled up to the Public Enquiry Assistant, or PEA. She was recording the production of driving documents. Henry saw her name badge said 'Ellen Thompson.'

'Who's dealing with the two robbery victims?' he asked.

She glared at him, clearly harassed. 'Who wants to know?'

'I do – Detective Superintendent Christie,' he said stonily, not liking her attitude at all, under pressure or not. There was a slight change in her body language at the revelation of his rank, something he didn't particularly like doing.

'I've phoned up to CID, said they'd send someone down.'

'How long ago?'

'Half hour . . . dunno.'

Henry grunted. He picked up a phone and dialled the office and spoke to the DS he'd just left, told him to get a DC down to the desk and a crime scene investigator for photos. There was nothing so effective as getting snaps of victims before they'd had chance to clean themselves up. Worked wonders in court. He also told the DS to ensure that whoever was tasked to the job came down with a first aid kit.

He hung up the phone, picked it up again and dialled nine for an outside line. Then three nines for an ambulance. He came back out on to the public side of the counter, followed by a very reluctant looking detective constable carrying a green first aid kit.

'Sort 'em,' Henry ordered. 'Properly.'

'Did you freakin' well see that?' the older boy demanded, utterly breathless. 'We . . . we just witnessed a murder, f'fuck's sake.'

'I know, I know,' the younger one gasped. His hands were on his knees and he was bent double, wheezing. He'd recently started smoking and already it was having an effect on his lungs.

They had run through the streets as though pursued by a demon. Run hard, fast and far, arms and legs pumping, bodies screaming for oxygen, until they could go no further and were certain they hadn't been followed. Or at least as certain as they could be, bearing in mind they hadn't dared look back. Just ran.

'Hell, hell, hell,' Rory repeated, stunned by what he'd seen.

They had reached the seafront at Blackpool and hared across the promenade at Talbot Square, near to the frontage of North Pier, where they skittered to a stop to catch their breath.

'He killed that old guy,' Rory continued, terrified but also impressed, his eyes blazing. 'Ran the old bastard over, then backed over him, then over him again, then shot him.' He tried to control his breathing as he paced around in tight circles, his hands on his hips. 'Christ, murdered him. Ah . . .' He put a hand to his scalp. In the terror of the moment, he'd completely forgotten about his injured head, the split in the scalp caused by the old man's walking stick. It was hurting again. 'Bastard deserved to die,' he said, remembering the blow.

His friend looked up at him. 'No he didn't, not like that.'

Rory stopped circling and pulled a face at his mate. 'He did, he effin' did.'

'Didn't.'

'Soft arse,' Rory admonished him.

'We need to go to the cops,' the younger one said.

'You must be joking. You never go to the cops for anything.'

'We've seen a murder, Rory . . . I mean a killing, an assassination. The guys in the car must've been after him. It wasn't an accident. If they'd just knocked him over and driven off, fair dos. But they drove back over him – then shot him. And they saw us, too.'

'Yeah, you silly twat, all the more reason not to go to the cops, yeah?'

The younger boy was still breathing heavily, feeling lightheaded, and now torn between wrong and right, what was sensible and realistic.

'If we get involved in this, that guy'll find us and kill us.'

'Why – d'you think you could identify him?'

'Pretty bloody sure. What about you?'

'I'd know him if I saw him.'

'And he saw our faces, too. Look, we need to keep out of this, for us own good . . . hey, nearly forgot. Got a picture.'

The younger lad squinted at Rory, then remembered the flash.

'Used that girl's mobile to get a shot . . .' He patted his pockets. 'Shit, it's not here. Must've dropped it,' he said annoyed. 'Don't remember dropping it . . . hell, let's go find it . . .'

'Yeah, right – and meet a man with a gun?'

'Yeah – let's go back and see what's happening. The cops must be there by now.'

'To where it happened?' his mate said in disbelief. 'You kidding?'

'Be safe. Let's go see. The killer'll be long gone. And we might find that phone . . . I don't even remember dropping it.'

Rory wrapped his left arm around his mate's shoulder, grappled him down so he had a neck lock on him, then scrubbed his knuckles into his scalp. 'C'mon, Mark, mate.'

Henry Christie lived on a pleasant enough housing estate on the outskirts of Blackpool, near to the motorway junction at Marton Circle. He drove there with some anticipation, looking forward to some time alone with Kate, then bed. It had been a long day, but there was nothing unusual in that. Ten hours was the norm, twelve unexceptional, nothing to whinge about.

The last few months had been a hard slog, though, since he'd

been promoted to the rank of detective superintendent and he
had a lot of plates spinning. He was dealing with a protracted
investigation into a gang that had sprung a prisoner from court
four months earlier, killing a motorcycle cop in the process. He
thought that progress was being made, but even though the gang
members had been identified, proving the offence and getting
them to court was going to be difficult, not least because they
still had to be located as they were lying low in various hot spots
across the world. But he remained optimistic. He was also
searching for the contract killer of an escaped convict, a professional who worked alone, and had still yet to be identified. And
other jobs continued to come in, mostly routine stuff like Dennis
Twist, but still very serious.

Which is why he was happy to be getting home that evening.

That night he was not on any call-out rota.

He was scheduled for two rest days, and then he and Kate
were going for a two-day break to Venice, their first real holiday
since their honeymoon after their remarriage. Gondolas, canals,
a posh hotel, outrageous prices, historic buildings, Italian food
and good hearty sex were on Henry's menu. Bliss.

He smiled at the prospect as he drew up on his driveway,
parking his Mondeo alongside Kate's recently acquired Fiat 500,
a purchase she had not adequately explained to him as yet and
which he could not stop himself from frowning at.

The police were on the scene within minutes. The driver of the
next car along Charnley Road had almost driven over the old
man's body in the middle of the road, mistakenly thinking it was
a bunch of rags. He'd stopped in time, scrambled out of his car,
then, shocked, worked out exactly what was lying there.
Horrified, but still thinking, the driver reversed his own car ten
metres back down the road, flicked on his hazards and called
the police from his mobile.

The first cops on the scene were traffic officers from the Road
Policing Unit. The incident had been called in as a fatal accident,
but it took them only seconds to ascertain this was something far
more sinister. They immediately called for back up – local cops,
CID and CSIs – then cordoned off the road.

Mark and Rory made their way tentatively back, curiosity driving
Rory, caution telling Mark they were doing something silly. They
couldn't get back down along the alley along which they'd

followed the old man, as the full length of it was now taped off and a Police Community Support Officer prevented anyone from entering.

Rory, typically, took umbrage about someone in authority telling him what to do. 'We can go down there if we want,' he protested.

The PCSO, a pasty-faced young man, not much older than the two lads, and a wannabe cop, stood resolutely at the entrance to the alley, not intimidated by Rory, who he obviously recognized.

'There's been an incident on the road at the far end and this is now part of a crime scene – so go away.'

'What happened?' Rory asked. 'Is someone dead?'

'Why would you ask that?'

'Just a question,' Rory said. 'C'mon pal, let's go round,' he said to Mark and dragged him away by the arm. They made their way back down Albert Road, cut across a connecting street and tried to turn up Charnley Road, only to find it blocked by cops and tape, lots of both. People gathered and gawked even though there was little to see, and a fully-fledged constable was on duty limiting comings and goings.

Rory and Mark moved through the growing number of onlookers, trying to get a better view.

'What's happening?' Rory asked someone.

'Bad accident,' a man said.

'Oh, right.' He exchanged a knowing glance with Mark and raised his eyebrows.

Mark took hold of Rory's arm. 'I've had a thought . . . suppose the killer comes back? They do, y'know. Killers come back to the scenes of their crimes, like they go to the funerals of the people they've killed. Suppose he sees us?'

Rory sighed patiently at his apprentice and shook his sore head. 'Not a cat in hell's chance, pal. He won't come back – trust me.' Rory pushed a woman out of the way and peered excitedly down the street. Mark hung back, unsettled, wanting to leave.

As well as being able to appreciate a fine pint of Stella Artois, Henry Christie was partial to a finger or two of whisky. He was no connoisseur but could tell the difference between cheap blended and a decent malt. He actually liked both, mixing cheap stuff with lemonade occasionally, and sipping the more expensive stuff with a chunk of ice. His in-betweener, though, his regular tipple, was Jack Daniel's. He loved its smoky flavour and often imagined the sound of the Mississippi gurgling by as he drank it.

He'd got home, changed into jeans and a tee shirt, put his slippered feet up on the coffee table and had bitten into a baked-ham, Lancashire cheese and piccalilli sandwich on thick bread, prepared by Kate, and was eagerly anticipating the JD to accompany it.

They were chatting about their little holiday, just running through a final check of things they needed to take. Kate seemed to have covered every eventuality, planning to pack as much as possible. Henry was less bothered.

'It's not as though Italy is a third world country if we do forget anything,' he pointed out. 'They've got shops like us, y'know.' He took another bite of the sandwich and sat back. 'We can get HP sauce if we need it,' he teased, but inwardly he liked Kate's attention to detail. It was rare to go on holiday with her and discover something had been forgotten. 'All I need is tee shirts, shorts, money, passports and tickets.'

'You're very basic,' she said huffily and sat down next to him on the settee, thigh to thigh. She was very excited about going away.

Henry turned his head slowly to her and slitted his eyes mysteriously. 'As you'll discover, babe.' He held the look for a moment, then took another chunk out of the sandwich, not having realized how ravenous he was. 'What's on the box?'

'Not much.' Kate sat back and sipped her own whisky and lemonade, made with a supermarket cheapo brand. She sighed contentedly. 'We need to do a last minute shop tomorrow. I need a new dress.'

'OK,' Henry said amiably. He swallowed a mouthful and was reaching over for his JD when his mobile phone rang. It was on the coffee table, next to his drink.

'Bugger,' Kate said under her breath. Her mouth warped into a slightly unpleasant shape.

Henry gave her an apologetic look, knowing the call was unlikely to be from anywhere other than work. The display said, 'Unknown caller.'

'Henry Christie.'

'Boss?' came the first word, making Henry's heart sink with its inflection. It was the detective sergeant he'd recently left at Blackpool police station to tidy up the Twist case. Henry hoped it was a minor query, but he knew it wouldn't be.

'Go on, Alex.'

'Hope you don't mind me calling, but there's a job just come in.'

'I've finished for the day – for five days, actually.'

'I know,' the DS – his surname was Bent – said wearily, 'it's just that the Chief Constable just happened to be here when it came in, doing one of his unannounced "catch you doing something you shouldn't be doing" visits and he wants a quick response to it. The nearest on-call super lives in Blackburn, so he said you'd do it.'

I'll bet he did, Henry thought. His mouth twisted in a similar way to Kate's – whose face hadn't changed its expression. She looked as though she'd been given a bowl of fried whitebait when she'd been expecting Dover sole: very annoyed.

'What's the job?' Henry asked.

The DS, who hadn't yet turned out to it himself, explained what he'd been told. Henry listened, sitting up as he did, paying close attention. He clarified a few points, asked some pertinent questions and issued some instructions. 'I'll be down in fifteen minutes,' he promised and ended the call. He placed the phone down slowly and looked at Kate. 'Sorry love,' he said ruefully, giving her a pained expression. 'Sounds a bit of a messy one. There's no one else nearby to cover.'

She held his gaze, then said, 'This better not screw up my holiday.'

'It won't. I'll just cover it, then hand it over. Promise.'

She closed her eyes and shook her head. Same old story.

Henry stuffed the last of the sandwich into his mouth, glanced sadly at the JD, and was aware that the warm fuzzy atmosphere had just turned cold and icy.

The police moved the public further and further away from the scene until they'd sealed off a good two hundred metres either side of the incident and completely closed the road, as well as the whole length of the alley.

Rain started to fall heavily as Henry, having parked his car almost a quarter of a mile away, pushed his way through the dwindling crowd of onlookers, their enthusiasm for the grisly tempered by a downpour. He always preferred to walk up to outdoor murder scenes. It gave him more time to take in things, assimilate matters, rather than racing up and leaping out of cars like the Flying Squad. He hunched up the collar on his raincoat, ducked under the cordon tape and flashed his warrant card at the on-guard constable, who had scuttled up to him thinking he was a member of the public trying it on. After a close inspection of the ID, Henry was allowed through, pulling a knitted cap out of his pocket and tugging it down on to his head, over his ears, cursing the rain. It was one of the worst things that could happen to an exterior crime scene. Nature's way of swilling away evidence for good. He hoped the first cops on the scene had acted swiftly and professionally to protect and preserve evidence.

The local DS, Alex Bent, the one Henry had received the phone call from on this murky night, hurried towards him, head down against the rain that was now a torrent. Henry looked past him to see a lighting rig and a crime scene tent being erected. Good, he thought. DS Bent briefed Henry quickly, then led him up to the body.

The younger of the two boys had noticed Henry Christie's arrival and slid into the shadow, not wishing to be spotted. Rory backed off too. Both boys knew Henry, but for different reasons, and neither wanted to come face to face with him.

'There's nowt to see now,' Rory said.

'We saw it all anyway,' Mark said.

'Pity we couldn't find that phone,' Rory said. 'Anyway, let's bog off . . . down to the arcades, eh?'

Mark screwed up his face. He wanted to go home, although there wasn't anything to go home for. His mother would be out and there was no one else. He just wanted to get back to his room, curl up in bed and rid his mind of the image of the murder.

Rory took his arm. 'Come on, or we'll get pissed wet through.'

'I don't know,' Mark whined.

'Stop being arsey . . . let's check out what's happening in town and if there's nowt, we'll hike it home. The chippy'll be open – and hey – we can afford the full hit. You could take it home from there.'

The prospect of taking home fish, chips and mushy peas was mouth-watering.

'OK then.'

It was an old adage: you don't get a second chance at a crime scene. So Henry quickly ensured that everything was done to protect it, particularly when its seriousness became apparent when he saw the poor mangled body of the old man, crushed under the wheels of a car, and the bullet wounds to the head that had left horrendous exit wounds. Standing underneath the hastily erected tent against which the rain pounded incessantly, Henry took it all in, his hands thrust deep into his pockets, letting his brain start to work on hypotheses.

He inhaled, asked Bent, 'Any ideas who he is?'

'Not as yet. I haven't allowed anyone to go through his pockets. Didn't want to spoil anything.'

Henry nodded. 'We'll save that for the mortuary. Witnesses?'

'Uniform are knocking on doors, but nothing yet.'

He nodded again, trying to piece it all together. His instinct *was* to go through the pockets for an ID, but there was a lot of stuff to do before that stage was reached. He needed the CSIs and a forensic team to do their job; he wanted the Home Office pathologist on scene, too. He didn't mind speculating, but didn't want to be drawn to any firm conclusions that could lead him down a blind alley. The man had been run over and shot, and though he was pretty certain in which order that had happened, he didn't want to get it wrong, as the sequence of events would have a fundamental bearing on the investigation.

Then the tent flap was drawn back and a rain-drenched constable said, 'Can I have a quick word, boss?' to Henry. He went to him, but stayed under cover.

'Fire away.'

'Might be nothing, but I've been having a look down this alley.' The PC turned and pointed to the alley that ran at right angles to the road. Henry poked his head out of the tent and squinted through the rain into the passageway.

'And?'

'Dog shit – right up by that wall.'

'Dog shit,' Henry said.

'There's a footprint in it, but it's sort of tight up against the wall and not generally in a place where someone would step in it. Just wondered if it was worth preserving . . .' His voice trailed off uncertainly, as if preserving a mound of canine excrement was as ridiculous as it sounded. 'Y'know, before it gets washed away.'

That'll be a popular one to get a cast from, Henry thought, already visualizing the CSIs tossing a coin over who drew the shit end of the stick. He nodded. 'Cover it up. You never know.'

'OK, boss – I already got a seed tray from a resident,' the officer said triumphantly.

'Good man,' Henry said. 'I'll leave it with you.'

The boys ran down to the promenade through the rain and into one of the amusement arcades they frequented, where they mingled with a few of their mates for a while. Rory's head injury caused a stir of interest. He kept it vague as to how he got it, making up a cock and bull story about a cop whacking him with a baton that no one believed, until all interest dwindled and the two lads stood at a one-armed bandit, feeding it change from a fiver they'd cashed.

Finally, they lost it all and decided to call it a night, emerging into the rain and heading back up to the estate they lived on, which was about a twenty-minute walk away.

'We should nick a car,' Rory suggested.

'That would be pushing our luck,' Mark said. 'We've robbed three people, not been caught, and watched an old bloke get murdered . . . nuff's enough,' he went on, clearly uncomfortable with the whole evening. Rory picked up on his friend's tone of voice.

'You can't go to the cops, you know that, don't you?'

'Yeah, course.'

'More friggin' trouble than they're worth. Do not get involved. They hate my family as it is, especially that Henry Christie.'

Mark looked quizzically at him. 'Christie?'

'Yeah, that detective who turned up.'

'I know the one you mean. You know him, do you?'

'Bastard – always mixing our family a bottle. You know him too?'

'He dealt with my sister's death.'

'Ahh,' Rory said sagely, knowing a touchy subject when he came across one. 'What are you having from the chip-hole?'

'Going for pie, chips and peas, me,' Mark said, having reviewed his options, 'covered in that stodgy gravy they do.'

'Sounds good . . . come on.' Rory plucked Mark's sleeve and they ran on in the rain, deliberately crashing through puddles so they couldn't get any more wet if they tried, reverting in many ways to the adolescent carefree kids they really should have been.

They arrived at the fish and chip shop about ten minutes later, soaked and breathless, and bought their food. The shop was on a small row of retail outlets in a block on the edge of their estate. Behind the row was an unlit, underused car park, strewn with debris and the burnt-out shell of a car. The lads had to walk across this piece of land, then cut into a high-walled alley that dog-legged and came out on to the estate proper.

Crossing the car park and going into the alley was the quickest way on to the estate, but as Mark came out of the chip shop, his food wrapped in paper and placed in a thin plastic bag, and walked to the end of the shops, he paused and looked across the dark car park. An unpleasant sensation flitted down his spine. A bad memory came back to him. He shivered.

Rory barged into him purposely. 'Hey, watch it,' he said, elbowing Mark out of the way. Then he stopped and looked into his friend's face. 'You OK?'

Mark snapped out of it. 'Fine.'

Rory scrunched up his face and shook his head. 'You're too much in touch with your girlie side,' he taunted and punched Mark's upper arm. 'Gay boy.'

'I'm not, I'm fucking not,' Mark protested, rising to the bait as only a sensitive teenager can. But his moment of reverie had gone. They set off across the car park, leaving the well-lighted place behind them, plunging into darkness.

Locally, the alleyway they were walking towards was known as Psycho Alley, so named because of the high number of criminal incidents that had taken place there over the years, from rapes to robberies. The council were always promising to demolish it and put some lighting in, but never seemed to manage to do either. It had become a no-go area for law abiding people at all times of day and night, being easier and safer to take the long way around rather than risk becoming a crime statistic.

For two streetwise mid-teens, though, it was a place that held no fear.

And in fact, if they had reached Psycho Alley, real name Song Thrush Walk, it was possible both of them could have survived. As it was, only one did.

'I am really starving,' Rory said, lifting his plastic bag up to his nose, inhaling the wonderful aroma of his supper, that combination of hot chips, vinegar, curry sauce and fish. 'I could eat it now – that new lot at the chippy are really good,' he said, referring to the new owners of the business.

'You'll enjoy it better in front of the telly,' Mark said.

Rory gave Mark a curious glance. 'Not with my lot of grabbing

gits. Be nowt left. I'll have it in my room, unless our kid's there
. . . or, I could always come to your house, couldn't I? Your mum
won't be in, will she?'

Mark hesitated. To have Rory around and inside the house
was perhaps taking things a step too far. Mark wanted to keep
his home life – what there was of it – separate from his so-called
friendship with this lad, at least for the moment. Rory had a
terrible reputation on an estate renowned for bad reputations,
was often known to steal from his mates and then intimidate
them with threats of violence if they complained. It wasn't that
Mark had a lot to protect, but what he had he wanted to keep.

'Mm,' he began doubtfully, wondering how to phrase the rejection tactfully – but before he could say anything, a figure loomed
up in front of him and Rory.

'Hi guys,' the man said. He was in dark clothing, against a
dark background.

The lads stopped.

A feeling of déjà vu – and complete and utter dread – coursed
through Mark's body, like razor wire being drawn through his
veins. History repeating itself.

The man stood in front of them, the entrance to the alley
maybe ten metres behind him.

In that instant Mark knew exactly what this was about.

'Scuse me,' Rory said, not getting it. He split away from Mark,
sidestepping the figure with the intention of simply walking past.
But the man moved into Rory's path.

'Don't think so,' he said.

Rory peered at the man's face and then, even in the dark, just
the slightest glint of light from the lamp posts way back at the
fish and chip shop, a hundred metres behind them, he recognized him.

'Shit,' he uttered, ducked low and tried to run to the man's
left. Not quick enough. The man pivoted. There was something
black and bulbous in his hand. There was a dull double-'thwuck',
accompanied by a silver-white flash as the man managed to
touch the muzzle of the gun on to Rory's temple and fire. It was
as if the teenager had been hit by the right hook of a heavy-
weight boxing champion. He staggered sideways, then his legs
crumpled underneath him.

The man contorted away from Rory, Mark being his next
target. He was moving quickly, but there was something unhurried, calm and efficient in the way he swivelled.

By contrast, Mark moved by instinct and fear, which gave him the slightest of edges as he swung the plastic carrier bag containing his newly bought feast into the man's face. The bag – possibly the cheapest and flimsiest plastic bag ever made – burst on impact, showering the attacker with an inferno of pie, chips and peas. He screamed and reared away, tearing at the hot food with his hands.

Mark ran for the alley, knowing he had only seconds at most.

'Goddam little bastard,' the man bellowed.

Mark reached the first right of the dog-leg in the alley. The brick wall above his head exploded with silent missiles: the man was shooting at him. Mark ducked low, threw himself around the corner, not even allowing himself a micro-peek over the shoulder. That would have slowed him down. Even so, he was aware that the killer had recovered and was giving chase, could hear footsteps pounding.

The young lad ran towards the next corner, a left, just metres ahead. He skidded around it, feet sliding in the gravel, careening into the wall, then pushing himself upright and running hard, arms pumping. He was fast and lithe – a good sprinter – and he hoped that his recent cigarette habit wouldn't slow him down too much.

Still the footsteps were behind him. The man was fast and determined.

The alley opened up on to one of the roads on the estate. Mark did not pause to check for traffic, running across the road, bounding over a low hedge into a garden, then down the side of a house into the back garden, noisily kicking over some tins stacked next to a wheelie bin. They clattered loudly. Mark cursed, then abruptly changed direction by ninety degrees and ran parallel along the back of the house, across a paved area, then leapt across a broken fence into the next garden along, landing awkwardly but using his momentum to keep going.

A dog barked hysterically nearby. Someone shouted an obscenity.

Mark kept going, changed direction again and clambered over a back fence, dropping into another garden, ran through it and came out on another road, this time a cul-de-sac.

He stopped, wheezed for breath, in the middle of the road, his eyes wild.

An engine revved. A car swerved into the street, lights blazing.

Mark knew his cars and instantly recognized it as the Volvo that had struck the old man.

Terrified, trapped by the onrushing car, Mark remained transfixed by the headlights – then his survival gene kicked in. He
spun, ran, the car only feet behind him, catching him, bearing
down, trying to mow him over.

The cul-de-sac opened into a turning circle.

Once more Mark changed direction, cutting across the head-
light beam, his shadow long and distorted. He swooped behind
a parked car, then cut down a tight public footpath running along
the side of a house, hearing the car swerve and stop behind him.

He kept going, never looking back. Pushing himself on, forcing
more out of his being than ever before, using his intimate knowledge of the estate he'd lived on all his life to duck and weave,
to lay false direction in case he was still being followed. Down
alleyways that strangers would have mistaken for dead ends, but
which Mark knew he could cut through. Along streets, through
gardens, on to the fields surrounding the estate, until he reached
the back of his house.

But he didn't just barge in. He secreted himself right at the
back of the garden, sitting on a damp patch of weed. Here he
caught his breath and with the patience of a deer knowing it was
being hunted, waited still in the grass, unmoving, watching until
he was positive it was safe to go home.

Five minutes passed. Nothing moved, other than the usual.
This was one of the quiet avenues on the outer edge of the estate.

Then a car drove slowly past. Mark craned to see. Not the
Volvo, one he recognized as belonging to a guy from the next
avenue.

Another three minutes. Then another car, cruising. This time
it was the Volvo.

His whole being tightened up.

It went by, two shapes inside it.

Then it was gone. He gave it five more minutes before crawling
to the back door, kneeling up to the lock and inserting his key,
letting himself in. He switched no lights on. Moved through the
house on his hands and knees, along the hallway, checking the
front door was bolted from the inside, then slithered upstairs to
his bedroom and locked the door behind him. He edged to the
window where he drew the curtains slowly and then, the light
still off, he flopped on to his bed, exhausted.

Then he began to shake.

FOUR

The old man had been stripped and tagged. His arrival had been entered on to the database at the public mortuary and the computer-generated reference number – there was no name at present – scribbled on to the big-toe tag and in big figures on to his left shin in black felt tip.

Henry, having assisted the mortuary attendant with this procedure, was now wearing a surgical gown, latex gloves and a facemask pushed up on to the crown of his head. He walked slowly around the body, now laid out on a stainless steel mortuary slab. Henry's hands were clasped behind his back as he inspected the body, as though he was walking the beat at regulation pace.

The old man was in a terrible mess, something even more apparent now that he lay there naked and pitiful. The car had done a great deal of damage, crushing his chest, stomach, hips and upper legs; breaking numerous bones as though it had driven over a sack of twigs. The bullets had torn his head open.

Henry didn't flinch. He had seen much violent death over the years, lost count of the number of times he'd inspected a cadaver in a morgue. It was an obvious part of being a detective specializing in murder investigation. He wasn't immune to death, but neither was he upset by it – unless it touched him personally. The luxury of emotion had long since passed, probably since the first post-mortem he had ever attended as a nineteen-year-old rookie dealing with his first straightforward sudden death. He'd passed that test with flying colours – one of the top five dreaded incidents for all new cops – despite the evil machinations of his sergeant who had closed all the mortuary doors, turned up the heating to a swelter, and prayed that the sight and smell of a bloated, three-week-old corpse would cause him to hurl. It didn't. The spectacle had never affected him in that way. He couldn't pretend to be unmoved by the deaths of young people, but his professional detachment had given him inner strategies to deal with such rare occurrences.

The smell always bothered him, though. Never enough to make him physically sick, but enough to know he hated its musty clingy-ness, the way it stuck to clothes and on to nasal hairs for days on end.

But this dead man, mown down and shot, made his arse twitch with excitement. He knew this was no run of the mill Blackpool killing and the prospect of investigating it sent a thrill through him.

'OK, guys, what've we got?'

Henry's observations were curtailed by the arrival of the appropriately suited and booted Home Office pathologist, entering the mortuary blowing into a latex glove until it expanded like a cow's udder, before fitting it.

Keira O'Connell was the locum pathologist standing in for the usual incumbent, Professor Baines, a man Henry knew well. His temporary replacement was far better looking, even though she looked exhausted and her hair was scraped severely back off her face and bunched into an untidy bun at the back of her head. And she was wearing a green surgical gown that did absolutely nothing for her figure.

Her steel-grey eyes regarded Henry as she fitted the second glove and then her facemask. He did not answer her question, which he guessed was rhetorical. O'Connell, like all good pathologists had already been out to the scene of the murder and knew as much as Henry.

She looked at the old man – not Henry – then glanced at the creepy-eyed mortuary assistant, who was precisely laying out the tools of the mortician's trade in a perfect line on a contraption resembling a breakfast-in-bed tray that fitted on runners over the mortuary slab and could slide up and down as the pathologist worked.

'Are we recording?' she asked him.

'Yes, boss . . . sound and vision on.'

'OK,' O'Connell said. Then, for the benefit of the recording equipment, spoke the time, day, date and location, and introduced herself and that she was about to perform a post-mortem on the body of an as yet unidentified male found earlier that evening on a street in Blackpool.

Henry glanced up at the video camera on the wall, and the one attached to the ceiling, both focused on the body.

O'Connell did a recap of what she already knew and gave some general observations such as, 'Male, aged somewhere between sixty-five and seventy-five, five-eight tall – yet to be accurately measured – and perhaps eleven stones, again, yet to be accurately weighed. Slim build, well-nourished, white-skinned but possibly from a Mediterranean background . . .' When she had finished her introduction, she walked slowly around the body, pointing out the various injuries. They were, she said, consistent with having been struck and then run over by a vehicle, possibly a heavy saloon car, and the head injury – massive trauma – consistent with having been shot twice. The obvious always had to be stated.

Henry watched and listened. He admired her professionalism and knowledge, and whilst his professional side nodded sagely at her findings, his less professional man-side cursed the fact he'd once screwed up his chance of ending up in the sack with her. A couple of years earlier, after a post-mortem, they had gone out for a drink. He'd been going through a rocky patch at work and instead of allowing her to talk, he made the fatal error of rambling self-pityingly about his own misfortunes and bored her half to death. When her eyes glazed over she made her excuses and left, leaving Henry mentally kicking the living crap out of himself. She probably didn't even remember it – he hoped.

He glanced at the wall clock: 2.07 a.m. Then his eyes flicked back to the body.

'. . . looks like an old bullet wound,' O'Connell was saying, words that made Henry jerk upright. She was standing along-side the old man, lifting the body slightly and inspecting an area just below the rib cage on the right-hand side.

'What?' Henry blurted.

O'Connell raised her eyes over her mask, tilted her head. 'It looks as though he's been shot before.'

Henry scurried around the slab to inspect the discovery. Just below the rib cage there was an entry wound and an exit wound corresponding to it at the back. It looked as though a bullet had winged the old man through the soft tissue around that part of the body, near to the liver. 'In here,' she said, putting her fore-finger on the entry, 'out here,' and she put her thumb on the exit, taking a lump of flesh between her fingers. 'Obviously didn't do too much damage, not much more than a flesh wound, though the exit is more of a mess than the entry, as they often are.'

'I hadn't noticed it,' Henry admitted.

'That's why we have pathologists,' she responded. Henry saw her ears rise as she smiled teasingly behind the mask.

'How old?'

She shrugged. 'Difficult to say exactly . . . it's well-healed and it looks as though it was treated medically and well . . . maybe five years,' she estimated.

Henry blinked, did the maths. 'So if this guy is at the lower age you estimated, he got shot when he was sixty?' His voice rose incredulously on the last few syllables. O'Connell nodded. 'Not likely to be a war wound, then?'

'Not unless he was in Dad's Army.'

Henry stood upright. 'Can we get that photographed?'

'All part of the service.'

'Thanks.'

'And so we begin.'

Henry retreated a couple of steps, his forehead creased in thought by the wound in the man's side as he considered the possibilities. 'I'll go bag and tag his clothing,' he announced.

When the body had been stripped, the clothing had all been dropped into a plastic basket that was now in one corner of the room. He went across and picked it up, then carried it through to the mortuary office where he dumped it on a desktop. He nipped out to his car parked in the tiny car park at the back of the mortuary and brought back several paper bags, sacks, polythene bags, tags, and a notebook he always had with him – just in case. Most detectives are similarly equipped. You could never tell when some bloodstained clothing or other evidence might have to be seized. He left his portable fingerprinting kit in the boot. That job was going to go to a CSI.

Back inside he began the process of inspecting, recording, describing and bagging each item taken from the dead man, aware that care needed to be taken to preserve any evidence that might be useful, and that such evidence might well be invisible to the naked eye. All the stuff would be going to the forensic science lab for analysis sooner rather than later, so he had to do a good job and not compromise any evidence.

The first item he picked up was the man's sports jacket, which to Henry's untrained eye, looked quite an expensive one. All the clothing, on brief inspection, seemed to be good quality Italian. In an inside pocket was a slim, pigskin wallet, heavily stained with blood. Henry opened it carefully. There was a maker's imprint in the leather and Henry guessed it was an Italian word, something to check on, perhaps. There was no form of ID in the wallet itself, just a hundred pounds in twenties, a hundred Euros, an old thousand-lira note and a faded, bloodied, photograph of a young child. A granddaughter, Henry hazarded. There was nothing else in the jacket, other than three keys on a ring, one mortise, one Yale, and the other possibly a padlock key.

Henry recorded the items, then carried on with what was left in the basket – trousers, socks, shoes (definitely Italian leather), a shirt, silk tie, a vest – and Henry made sure he noted each item and sealed it in the appropriate manner in the correct type of bag.

Finally he was left with two items, a watch and the old man's walking stick. The watch was a heavy Rolex and Henry looked at it longingly. One day, he promised himself, and logged it, tagged and bagged it, then moved on to the stick. It was silver tipped with an intricately carved wooden handle. Henry held it up and his eyes skimmed it, but just as he was about to drop it into a polythene bag, something on the shaft caught his eye, about two-thirds of the way down from the handle. He frowned, then packed and did the paperwork for the stick.

The only things he hadn't recorded were the keys.

He held them up on the simple ring and said, 'But no ID,' to himself. He scratched his ear thoughtfully.

An old man, out and about at night with no form of identification. How weird was that? Well-dressed – slightly dashing if anything – well nourished, a bit of money in the wallet. And a not-so-old bullet wound in the ribs.

Unless something turned up in the meantime – such as, 'My old grandad's not come home,' and here Henry thought that unless grandad was a dirty stop-out, that 'meantime' might well have passed as it was now well into the early hours – one of the first tasks of the morning would be to flood the area with uniforms knocking on doors armed with an artist's impression of the old man's face, as a direct photo might have been a tad too gruesome to shove under peoples' noses at breakfast time. Although Henry realized he was making an assumption, he'd lay odds that the guy was on his way home – but from where and to where?

Already the questions and ideas were starting to mount up and Henry's mind, fatigued as it was, was starting to marshal these thoughts. He sat down at the desk in the mortuary office and jotted down a few ideas about the way forwards with the investigation in the notebook. He'd hardly had time to scribble down three headings on separate pages – 'Victim', 'Location', 'Offender' – when someone came into the office and interrupted him.

It was DS Alex Bent, who tapped lightly on the glass door,

even though it was open. He was drenched, looked exhausted. 'Boss?' he said, quietly but urgently.

Henry squinted at him. 'I was just about to solve this murder by cracking the intricate medieval and religious code I found in this book,' he said seriously, tapping his finger on the notebook.

'Really?' Bent said, Henry's little joke flying right over his head.

'Yeah – so this better be good.' Henry closed the notebook, realizing it was completely the wrong time of day to have a stab at humour. 'What?'

'Well, you being the only SIO in spitting distance – do you want to turn out to another job?'

The shiny, perfectly sharpened dissecting knife was poised above the old man's chest, ready to make the first incision: the classic cut down the middle of the body from the soft skin just below the Adam's apple, all the way down to the pubes. From that first cut, the outer layers of skin and subcutaneous fat would be pared away to expose the ribcage which, depending on its condition, would be removed by use of shears, not unlike those found in a garden shed. It would then be lifted off like the lid on a square biscuit tin. Only difference was there wouldn't be any goodies in this tin, but a squashed heart, lungs, liver and kidneys – organs that would then be hacked out for examination.

'Don't even think about it.' Henry said mock dramatically as he swung through the mortuary door.

The pathologist, Keira O'Connell, paused, keeping the knife hovering just inches above the flesh like the Sword of Damocles. She inclined her head and peered over her facemask. 'And why not?' she asked, voice muffled. 'Has this man actually died of natural causes, meaning a post-mortem is no longer necessary?'

'Would it be possible to delay?' Henry asked.

'Give me one good reason.'

'Another shooting's come in – young lad up on Shoreside. No more details as yet, but I'd like you to come to the scene if possible.'

'OK . . .' O'Connell checked the clock and for the benefit of the recording equipment stated the time and date and that the PM was being suspended for the time being, then asked the mortuary technician to turn off the machine. He obeyed, using a remote control. 'Not much detail you say?' she said, stepping away from the slab and replacing the knife in its position in the line of tools, then removing her mask, 'but you must have something?' she asked Henry. She walked towards him, peeling the latex gloves off, then unpinning her hair, which she shook free and patted into place, even though the expensively cut bob tumbled out perfectly.

Something clogged up Henry's throat as he replied, 'No, nothing,' dreamily.

Ten minutes later the body had been stored on a tray in the chiller, his belongings secured in a locker – Henry taking the key – and they were en route to the scene in his car.

'You know, if this isn't a murder, I'll still have to claim a call-out fee.'

'It's a murder. I have enough faith in my officers for them to be right about that – so you'll be handsomely recompensed for your troubles and you can continue to live in the style to which you're accustomed. How much for tonight? A grand, I'm guessing.'

She guffawed. 'I wish.'

They drove on in silence for a few minutes. Rain continued to lash down heavily, the windscreen wipers trudging manfully against the deluge that was like buckets of water being thrown repeatedly over the car. A strong wind was also getting up.

Henry glanced surreptitiously at his passenger – just as she was doing the same at the driver. Both shuffled uncomfortably as their eyes locked briefly.

'You're a superintendent now?' O'Connell said. Henry nodded. 'Well done. Last time we met I remember you being unceremoniously dumped off an investigation – the Asian woman who'd been set alight.'

Henry swallowed at the memory. Not one of the highlights of his topsy-turvy career.

'Dave Anger, wasn't it?' O'Connell went on. 'Your boss at the time? He'd got it in for you. Your nemesis, I think you called him.'

'Yeah,' Henry growled and added creepily, 'but vengeance was mine.' He raised his eyebrows.

'And we went out for a drink.'

'Mm – and I blew it, as I recall.' So she did remember. He squirmed.

'You did, rather. All me, me, me.'

'C'est la me,' he shrugged. They'd reached the outskirts of Shoreside. He drove to the front of the shop parade and pulled up. There was a lot of police activity.

'And I was in a relationship then, and you were, and then I wasn't, and you were . . . and then I wasn't . . .' Her voice dried up and he yanked up the handbrake. She gulped. 'Still not,' she said and gave Henry a meaningful look.

'Just my luck,' Henry said. He paused, sighed, then clambered out into the rain again. He was almost thankful for the drenching which had the instantaneous effect of dousing his easily aroused ardour. Just the thought of what might have been had been enough to trigger numerous snapshots in his mind's eye of the ways in which a pretty female pathologist might be naughty. He tugged his hood over his head, banished the images, and dashed over to Alex Bent, who, having made to the scene ahead of him, was waiting under the awning that covered the walkway in front of the shops.

O'Connell was right behind, having flicked open her mini-umbrella. She also carried a medical kit with her.

The trio made their way to the rear of the shop parade – although the term parade was a bit of a euphemism. The only two shops left on the block were the chippy and a newsagent. The others – formerly a hairdresser, bakery and launderette – had closed, were 'steeled' up, rather than boarded, victims of the credit crunch and the encroachment of vandalism and intimidation from Shoreside yobs.

Henry's face ticked uncomfortably with the memory of the last serious incident he'd dealt with on the tract of ground behind the shops, which was part car park, part rubble heap, part fly tip. A wild young man had been stabbed to death in a gang feud, a case that not reached a satisfactory conclusion.

Henry had lost count of the number of crimes committed in this area. This no-man's land between civilization and the jungle that was the Shoreside estate. People crossed it at their peril, night or day, to get from the shops to Song Thrush Way. And that did not include the incidents that had taken place in the alley itself. Gangs congregated and sorted out their differences, drug deals were done, rapists and flashers lurked, robbers waited, hiding patiently for their next victim . . . and occasionally, people were murdered. Henry was very much aware of the local name for the alley.

It was such a hot spot that it had the unusual honour of having its own incident location ID in the police logging system. Unusual because most incident locations related to large areas, such as council wards, not mini-no-go areas. Recognizing the problems, the police were constantly badgering the council to get their finger out, but lack of money and willpower were big issues.

'Looks like he was crossing from the chippy to the alley,' Bent was saying as the three of them stepped out of the light and walked towards the scene, heads tipped against the rain. 'Chips everywhere, apparently. Haven't seen myself, yet. Obviously met whoever killed him just short of the alley and was shot in the head . . . apparently.'

Two marked police cars and a police van were parked at skew-whiff angles on the car park, as though they'd just been abandoned. Uniformed cops milled around. An ambulance was parked further away.

Henry said, 'Who was the first officer on the scene?'

'Her.' Bent pointed to one of the constables. Henry stopped and beckoned to the lady, recognizing her but not really knowing her.

'You were first to arrive, I'm told. What happened?'

The officer was as completely soaked as anyone. Even her hat had lost its shape, the brim now corrugated. 'Er, comms got a call on the treble nine saying someone'd been shot here. Caller refused to give details. I took the job.' She shrugged. 'Found the lad there . . . that's about it, really. Drew back, cordoned it off, called the jacks in.'

Henry nodded. 'Do we know the deceased?'

The PC said, 'I'm not a hundred per cent. I haven't been through his pockets or anything, didn't want to spoil any evidence.'

'When you say you're not a hundred per cent, what do you mean?'

'Looks like one of the Costain's.'

The name hit Henry. 'Let's have a see.'

The scene had been cordoned off with tape strung from two broken lampposts, really nothing more than jagged stumps, a stack of bricks and a wheelie bin. A crude but effective first barrier for the time being. Henry, Bent and O'Connell ducked under the tape. The police cars had actually been parked at an angle to each other so their headlights bathed the scene until the arrival of something actually designed for the job of lighting up a murder scene. The lighting wasn't too effective, therefore, but it was better than nothing for the moment and would have to suffice until the circus rolled in.

The boy was lying on his side, facing away from them as they approached him. He looked for the entire world as though he'd just got down on the ground for a sleep. Henry pulled out his mini-Maglite torch and screwed the lens to switch it on. Bent was holding a much sturdier version that he also turned on. O'Connell had stopped and taken a torch out of her bag, one of those wind-up ones.

Despite all the lighting, it was only when they were much closer to the boy that they could see the horrific injury to the head.

Bent whistled appreciatively.

Henry bounced down on to his haunches, his ageing knees cracking loudly, and shone his torch into the boy's twisted face.

'Two shootings on one night,' he muttered. It might have been something everyone was thinking, but still had to be said out loud, although the additional question, 'Are they connected?' remained implicit.

O'Connell was at his right shoulder, seeing the boy from his viewpoint. There was a gaping exit hole on the right side of his head that had removed his ear and upper jaw. The whole face was distorted.

'Do you know him?' O'Connell asked.

The thin beam of Henry's torch worked slowly across the remaining features, open, staring but blank eyes, the mouth contorted horribly, blood oozing out of it.

Henry nodded. 'I know him.' He stood up, knees cracking again, and spoke to Bent. 'He wasn't alone, either.'

He flicked his torch beam around the ground, seeing the scattered and disintegrating chips and other food, and noting the two sets of wrapping paper.

All the lights seemed to be burning in the house, in spite of the late hour. Henry looked up through the rain-streaked driver's door window of the Mondeo, his heart sinking.

It was two hours later, two hours spent at the scene of the boy's murder, ensuring all that could be done was done to secure and preserve evidence. Henry's second murder scene of the night. The second shooting of the night. Blackpool had its fair share of violence, but two brutal acts of gun crime in one night took the biscuit, and even before Henry knew for certain there was a connection between the two, his gut feelings told him there was. He just knew that post-mortems, forensic and ballistic analyses would confirm his suspicion.

O'Connell was in the passenger seat alongside him. She had done all she could at the scene, which was now covered and protected, and would later be combed by CSI and Scientific Support teams.

Henry hadn't wanted her to come with him, had said he would arrange for her to be driven back to the mortuary, but she insisted. She was coming with him.

'You know this family?' she asked.

Henry nodded. 'Oh aye,' he said sourly. He slid his fingers around the door handle.

'You don't want me to come with you?'

'Nothing personal, but not especially.'

'I may be able to help, be able to offer comfort from a female perspective – maybe.'

'That,' he said pointedly, 'is highly unlikely, but suit yourself, you'll be in for a treat.'

He opened the door and climbed out of the car, now hearing the dull thud of music coming from a downstairs room. The rain had abated – slightly – and he steeled himself, getting into the right frame of mind. In terms of murder investigations, the buck stopped well and truly with the SIO in almost every respect. That included the delivery of the initial death message to relatives. It was very much his job, one he would not shirk. The flip side of the coin was that, although he had to tread carefully, be sympathetic, empathetic, firm, caring, supportive and everything else that went with telling someone a loved one had died tragically, he also had to bear in mind that the person he informed, or maybe someone else in the house, could well be the killer. It wasn't exactly unknown for an SIO to tell the actual murderer about the deed they had just done – which was why the SIO needed to do the task. The reaction from the family could be a vital clue to the whole investigation.

It was a tricky balancing act.

Particularly with the Costain family.

O'Connell joined him and they went to the front door.

The house was actually two semi's knocked into one, previously council owned, but now private. They had been big houses to start with – four bedrooms, semi-detached – and now the house was effectively a mini-mansion on a council estate. Henry knew it had been bought for a knock-down price because no one else wanted to buy houses on this estate, one of the most deprived in the country.

Henry paused at the door and rubbed his eyelids.

'I sense hesitation,' O'Connell chirped from behind.

'You always hesitate before knocking on this door.' The sound of laughter came from within. The music pounded away, an incessant, never changing beat. Henry raised his knuckles and rapped loudly. No one answered, so he turned his fist sideways and beat the door again, competing with the bass drum. Briefly the music turned down, then reverted to its original volume. Henry then kicked the door, which was flung open moments later by a teenage girl holding a bottle of WKD. She looked wild and unkempt, and was wearing a mini-nightie, had black hair that looked as though it had exploded in ringlets, mascara that made her look like a nocturnal bird and nothing on under the nightwear, leaving nothing to Henry's imagination.

'Fuck d'you want?'

Henry had no idea from which section of the family this girl belonged, but she was definitely a Costain. She had the looks and attitude.

'I need to speak to a grown-up.' He said, flashed his warrant card and said, 'Police.'

She was an achingly pretty girl and reminded Henry of an actress from a film adaptation of a D.H. Lawrence novel he'd seen years ago and almost forgotten. That said, she sneered contemptibly at Henry's ID.

'Like I said, fuck you want?' She started to close the door, but Henry stepped up like an old-fashioned door-to-door salesman, jammed his foot in the way, and surprised her.

'I want to speak to an adult,' he reiterated, now standing only inches away from her scantily clad body. She smelled of alcohol, sweat, cigarette smoke and cheap perfume – a heady mixture, no doubt. Behind her, the living room door opened and a male appeared, several years older than the girl. He was smoking and drinking from a beer can.

'What's going on, babe?'

'This cop,' she said, 'yeah, wants to speak to an adult . . .' She jerked her head in Henry's direction.

Henry took a steadying breath. It was never – *never* – easy at this household. It consisted of numerous relatives claiming descent from Romany gypsies and therefore stealing and hatred of authority ran in their blood. It was their default position. However, the Costains went far beyond simple theft. They were like a mini-Mafia family that existed by theft, yes, but also burglary, drug dealing, intimidation and violence. The Costains had a very firm grip on the estate, controlling much of the drug trade and acting as fences for stolen property. Henry had a very chequered history with them.

'The first thing I'll do,' Henry said, 'is exercise my lawful right to enter this property and rip the plug out of your hi-fi system, because you are causing a breach of the peace. Next, I'll arrest you both for obstructing me, and then I'll look into under-age sex.' Here he gave a meaningful look to the young man. 'And then, maybe, I'll do what I came to do – which doesn't involve arrests or anything like that.'

'Oh just piss off . . . I can't be arsed with cops,' the girl said, unimpressed by Henry's threats. She put her weight behind the door, crushing Henry's trapped foot.

He uttered a gasp of pain, pushed back hard, caught the girl, sending her staggering back down the hall, where she tripped over her own feet, lost her footing and thumped on to her backside in a very unladylike manner, revealing all.

The young man fronted Henry with aggression, but Henry gave him a withering, daring stare and a tiny shake of the head, and growled, 'If you're over twenty-four you have no defence to having sex with an under-age girl.'

The lad's face dropped.

'What the friggin' 'ell's going on down there?' a huge, booming voice bellowed from the top of the stairs. A man large enough to carry the voice came down a few steps from the landing in a silk dressing gown, his black curly hair in disarray. He saw Henry. 'You, you fucker.'

'Good morning,' Henry said, 'I need to have words with you urgently, please.'

It was old man Billy Costain, the ruthless patriarch of the family, the ruler of the roost, the father of at least seven Costain children, including Rory.

The estate known as Shoreside was one of the most dispossessed, dangerous and crime ridden estates in the country. Many houses were boarded up, others frequently damaged by rampaging gangs. Residents tried desperately to be rehoused. Unemployment was about eighty-five per cent. Drugs were rife. Gang feuds were a constant. A row of shops within the estate was now a pile of rubbish. Cops, generally, patrolled in pairs.

Henry knew it was a very complex social scenario, a build-up of issues over many years and although he couldn't actually blame the Costains for the downfall of society on Shoreside, it was families like them – feral, ruthless and without conscience – that played their part and thrived, whilst other, decent, law abiding ones suffered greatly.

And the master of all the Costain strategies and tactics was now sitting opposite Henry in one of the two living rooms in the interconnected home they owned. Billy Costain was head of the family, although describing him as an old man was not really accurate. He was about sixty-two, but still big and strong, a physical force to be reckoned with. He had a fearsome reputation as a pub brawler that age hadn't diminished.

The family's claim to be descended from gypsies could have had a grain of truth to it. Certainly they had the looks of stereotypical gypsies and no doubt there was some of those genes in their bloodline. In fact their main ancestors were Irish, having come across to the north of England in the nineteenth century to make a living as navvies, digging canals and laying railways.

Henry could not be sure when they came to Blackpool, but he knew they'd been here for at least thirty years and in that time had caused the police a mega headache from generation to generation.

What none of the family knew was that Billy's oldest son, Troy, had been an informant for Henry for many years. Henry had used him mercilessly after he had once arrested him and found that he suffered from severe claustrophobia and could not bear being in a cell. It drove him completely mad, terrified him, and Henry used this knowledge and the threat of incarceration in order to get Troy to pass him information. Unfortunately, Henry had used Troy once too often and the lad had ended up being murdered by a top-line crim Henry was investigating – and the Costains were still seeking answers about how and why Troy had met his untimely end.

Henry glanced around the room. It was plush and well-fitted to the extreme, with a huge L-shaped sofa, a massive TV on the wall with surround sound, a state of the art hi-fi and many expensive looking pieces of garish pottery. He took in all the opulence, juxtaposed against the lack of employment and visible means of support.

'You, pal,' Costain said, jabbing a finger at Henry, 'are the kiss of death to my family.' His jowls wobbled. He looked at Keira O'Connell. 'But you're a bonny thing, lass. You a cop, too?'

'Home Office Pathologist,' she said.

Costain's eyes darkened. He looked accusingly at Henry. 'Fuck d'you want?'

Henry had been to the house on two occasions previously to deliver death messages, not including Troy's. One had been for Troy's brother, who had been murdered, and another time for a cousin who had been killed in a road accident in a car driven by another cousin who'd survived and gone on the run. Though Henry had nothing to do with these deaths, the family was quite happy to blame him.

And now, here he was, about to deliver another blow, and as much as Henry knew Rory was a wild, villainous boy – a chip off the old block – he felt extremely sorry for the family.

He and Billy were still standing, facing each other with hostility, on the living room carpet.

'Mr Costain,' he said softly, using calming hand gestures, 'Like I said, I need to speak to you and what I have to say is very important.'

'Do I need my brief?'

'No.' Henry shook his head, but avoided an impatient tut.

'Please. Mr Costain,' Keira O'Connell intercut with a soothing feminine voice, stepping between the men. 'Please take a seat, and if we may, could we sit too?'

Costain eyed Henry, then nodded begrudgingly and edged back into a leather armchair, slightly pacified by her words.

O'Connell looked at the couple hovering in the hallway, keen to be part of this scenario. 'We need a little privacy,' she said and tried to close the living room door. The nightie-clad girl said, 'Oi,' to her, then, 'Gramps?' to Costain.

'Bugger off,' he told her, 'both of you.'

O'Connell closed the door, the girl eyeing her malevolently as the gap closed, mouthing the word, 'Bitch.' O'Connell merely smiled and arched her eyebrows, then she sat next to Henry on the sofa.

'This better be good,' Costain said.

'Mr Costain, I'll just cut to the chase . . . the thing is, Professor O'Connell and myself have just come from the scene of a murder on the car park behind the chippy just off Preston New Road. You know where I mean?'

'Yuh.'

'A young lad has been shot . . .'

'Oh, aye, and you think one o' my lads had something to do

with it, don't you?' Costain concluded instantly, his blue touch-paper being lit. He leaned forwards. 'Well I can vouch for all of my family, you vindictive bastard.'

Henry simply stared at him, then said evenly, 'Mr Costain, I'm pretty sure the victim is Rory, your youngest lad.'

The words stopped Costain in his tracks.

'Say that again.'

'I'm genuinely sorry, but I think the dead boy is Rory.'

From the hallway came a scream of anguish and suddenly Old Man Billy Costain seemed to age ten years.

FIVE

As stunned as he was by Henry's revelation, Old Man Costain's mistrust of the police, ingrained and inflexible after fifty years of living on the wrong side of the law, made extracting any information from him a tortuous process. In spite of the reassurance that, for once, the forces of law and order were on his side, blood didn't come easily from the stone that was William Patrick Costain.

Eventually, Henry had had enough. Even getting Costain to tell him what clothes Rory had worn the previous evening had been hard work, but he was ninety-nine per cent certain now that the corpse of the car park was the aforementioned Rory. One hundred per cent would only come with a formal family identification, or a photographic and/or dental comparison, which Henry would have preferred. As much as Henry had 'issues' with the Costains, even he didn't want to have to put Billy through the trauma of having to identify Rory's body. The lad's head was a disfigured mess and not something he would have wanted any family to see.

But Costain insisted. 'He's my boy, I have a right.' And despite the less than subtle warning from Henry, Billy was going to have his way.

The ID took place at the public mortuary in Blackpool Victoria Hospital at six thirty that morning.

Costain drove to the hospital in his huge old Mercedes, accompanied by his wife of many years, the adorable Monica. She was quite a bit younger than him at fifty and had once been a real stunner, a raven-haired, green-eyed beauty. But the carriage and birth of seven children (plus two stillbirths), heavy drinking, smoking and the long exposure to the sunshine of the Costa del Sol, had ravaged her looks and body.

It had been a rush to get Rory's body in a fit state to be gazed upon, an undertaking that entailed cleaning up the face without compromising any evidence, and then wrapping his head in a muslin towel to hide the horrific wounds on both sides, the entry and exit. All that remained to be seen were his distorted features. The creepy mortuary technician, who Henry noticed had a lazy eye, making him even scarier, carried out this prep. A hump would have completed the tableau wonderfully. He did the job under the supervision of O'Connell. The rest of the body was covered with a sheet and was then wheeled on a trolley into the viewing room, and positioned underneath the curtained window on the other side of which was an anteroom for relatives to gather in.

Henry stepped into this room from the mortuary, O'Connell behind him. The Costains waited, muted and afraid.

Old man Costain rubbed his face continually, stretching his features. Monica stood there numb.

Henry took a deep breath. 'Look, you don't have to do this. I've got enough in terms of identification. The coroner will be happy with that.'

'We want to see him,' Costain said firmly.

'OK, OK, but I need to reiterate . . .'

'Reiterate nothing, Henry,' Costain cut in. 'We're ready, so just do it.'

Henry tapped on the glass and the mortuary technician drew back the curtain.

'I expect you're pleased.'

Henry was outside in the mortuary car park, standing next to Costain at the Mercedes. Mrs Costain was already in the passenger seat, still as shell-shocked as she'd been in the viewing room, the death of her son probably not yet having hit her properly. She was shrouded in grey cigarette smoke.

'I beg your pardon?'

'You'll be pleased, eh? Three Costains down . . .'

'No, I'm not,' Henry said.

'Less trouble for you and the rest of the cops, though.'

'Mr Costain, I'm truly sorry you've lost another son.'

'Hey – not to mention my niece from the car crash. I don't suppose you'll be putting much effort into this, will you?'

'I'll tell you what pleases me: catching killers. I'll put as much effort into this as I would any other murder – which means I'll work around the clock until I get a result – OK?'

Costain shrugged, disbelief written all over his face. 'You say he was with someone?'

'It looks that way . . . two lots of chips, looks like he was walking across the car park with a mate, yes. But like you said already, you don't know who he was out with. It's vital we find this person, y'know? It could even be his killer, who knows?'

'Have you been to the chippy? That might be a good start.'

'Yes we have, but the chip shop owners are new and they don't live over the shop like the last ones did, and they haven't seen fit to give their name and address to the police as yet, so we can't contact them.'

Costain considered the information, then said, 'I'll see what I can do – I honestly don't know who Rory was with, but I'll find out.' He climbed into the Merc and the big car rolled smoothly away. Henry watched it go wondering which poor soul would end up with the unenviable task of being the family liaison officer. The role would have to be given to a seasoned detective, one who had the bottle to brave things out with the Costains, if they would even allow an FLO into their lives. Henry guessed there would be a huge firewall of reluctance from the family at having a cop assigned to them full-time.

Henry walked back to the mortuary where he found O'Connell inspecting Rory's naked body. She was speaking into a hand-held tape recorder and stopped when she saw Henry.

'What d'you think?' she asked.

'I think we've got the preliminaries out of the way in terms of the bodies and we should schedule the post-mortems for this afternoon. That way we can both get a few hours sleep. On top of that, I need to get a pre-briefing meeting together at eleven this morning, followed by a full murder squad briefing at noon.'

'Not much sleep for you, then?'

'Doubt if I'll be going to bed at all.'

'I'm not remotely sleepy, myself, so I don't see bed as an option just yet . . . could you handle a coffee with me?'

Henry checked his watch, then looked at the dead boy. He was standing at his head at an angle of about forty-five degrees

and his eyes caught something on the scalp. His brow furrowed
and he stooped for a closer inspection.

'Have you seen this?' he asked. Without touching, he indicated what he was looking at. O'Connell came around to see.

'Admittedly. I haven't.'

They were looking at a recent cut on Rory's head, just on
the scalp line above his left eye, a thin red mark where it
looked like something had struck him, or his head had struck
something.

'Could he have done that when he fell after being shot?' Henry
asked.

She pulled a face. 'Not sure about that. Looks like he might've
caught his head on something, a door maybe, possibly the sort
of injury you get when you crack your head on a car bonnet, or
something. Know what I mean?'

Henry's mind stirred. 'Unconnected with the murder?'

'That's an assumption I won't make. I'll present you with the
facts as I see them after the PM.'

'Fair enough.' Henry said, unable to think it through, his mind
just a mush now. 'How about that coffee?'

'Sorry about that.' Henry slipped his mobile phone into his jacket
pocket after having dropped a text to Kate telling her he would
not be home for some hours yet, and could she sort out the last
bits 'n' bobs for the holiday. He added, 'SOZ', and put a whole
bunch of kiss crosses, hoping to appease her a little.

'Wife?' O'Connell said.

He nodded. 'Supposed to be off on a romantic break tomorrow.
I said I'd be a bit of a Teflon pan and pass all this on to someone
else, and I will,' he said, meaning it, 'but I'd like to get as much
done as possible before I hand anything over. And I only turned
out for one murder, not two.'

'You're just a man who can't say no, aren't you?'

He glanced at her, wondering just what he was doing here.
They'd driven across town in their own cars to the twenty-four-
hour McDonald's on Preston New Road, both collected a
McMuffin breakfast, hash brown and coffee at the drive-thru,
then headed down to the seafront at Blackpool south where the
prom meets Squires Gate Lane. They were on the car park adjacent to the go-kart track at Starr Gate, which was also the south-
ernmost terminal of the famous Blackpool tram system that plied
up and down the prom.

They'd eaten their breakfasts together in O'Connell's Mazda RX8.

He tried to tell himself this was just a business chat in an unusual location to discuss unusual business – murder. But he was only half convinced by that argument.

It seemed all too easy in the cops – if you wanted it to be.

Throughout his entire career, now spanning thirty years plus, Henry had been amazed at just how easy it was to get laid. The situations, often dealing with vulnerable people, or those who just could not turn down a man in uniform or a smooth detective – and the relationships with colleagues, working strange hours, being involved in stressful situations – brought you close to people in an extraordinary, often sexual way. And since his early days as a rookie, right up until very recently, he had been an avid follower of his penis, and that relatively small piece of equipment had dragged him into hot water on too many occasions. It had taken him to a divorce, an often penniless existence in grubby flats, and now that he had fairly recently remarried Kate he had sworn he would never go down the route of weak flesh again.

Yet here he was – and nobody but a fool would say there was any other reason for him to be there sitting in O'Connell's fancy sports car, other than to get his hands on her tits, which he had to admit were just about right.

'Oh, I can say no if I want to,' he said weakly, turning to her and going short of breath.

'I'm not sure I can.' She wound towards him and slid her right hand along his inner thigh, a movement that sent a shimmer up inside him, made him groan as a rush of blood left his head and coursed south. The hand moved further up, then even further and grabbed him through his jeans.

Henry pulled her to him and they kissed savagely, a moan escaping from O'Connell's throat as her hand tightened on him. Henry's left hand slid over her blouse. She fumbled for his zip. He could feel himself straining against his underwear, trapped at a wonky angle, desperate to be freed. As he heard the first unzipping noise, something came into his head that counteracted the testosterone, like oil on water.

He drew sharply away. 'Bloody hell,' he gasped.

'What is it?' she asked unsurely. 'Did I hurt you?'

'No – it's tight, but no . . . I've just thought of something.' He opened the car door and rolled out, remembering why he wasn't keen on sports cars. He wasn't built for them. 'Follow me back to the morgue,' he said, leaning inside briefly, then he walked over to his own car with a slight crab-walk motion and tried to adjust himself discreetly.

O'Connell watched him open-mouthed, blew out a long breath, readjusted herself and muttered, '*Follow me back to the morgue. Just what a woman wants to hear.*'

'Two things,' Henry said, opening the body-chiller and withdrawing the sliding tray on which the very dead Rory Costain lay, wrapped in white.

O'Connell watched impatiently, hands on hips. 'This better be hellish good.' Her foot tapped.

Henry shot her a glance, then turned his attention back to Rory and pointed to the injury he'd noticed earlier on the boy's head.

'And?' O'Connell said, her hands flipping out with impatience.

'Wait.' Henry gave her the double-handed gesture that meant, 'Stay right there.' He went to the far end of the room where the bank of steel property lockers was fixed up against the wall. He found the key he'd taken for the one containing the property belonging to the old man and opened it. He rooted out what he wanted and returned to Rory's body – brandishing the old man's walking stick. He showed her what he had seen on the cane shaft when he'd been recording the old man's belongings, pointed at it, rotating the stick carefully to reflect the artificial light.

'Hair and blood,' O'Connell said. Henry handed her the stick and she held it up for a close inspection. 'Hair and blood,' she confirmed.

Henry pointed to the injury on Rory's hairline. 'Could that have been caused by the cane?'

O'Connell held the cane a couple of inches above the wound, careful not to let it come into contact with the flesh. Immediately she said, 'Yes, and it'll be easily confirmed.'

Henry gave her a triumphant smirk. 'Two shootings on the same night in the same town . . . even for somewhere as lawless as Blackpool, that's some going.' His head began to spin a little, but he managed to level it as a wall of exhaustion rushed through him. Suddenly he was very tired, but he pointed at O'Connell and said, 'Something else, too.'

This time he went to the locker containing Rory's clothing

and pulled out a brown paper bag in which the boy's trainers had been placed. He broke the seal, knelt down on the floor and carefully extracted the footwear, looking at the soles of the trainers. O'Connell joined him, peering curiously over his shoulder. He tilted the left one.

'Excuse the lingo – but there might be dog shit on here.'

'Eh?'

'I can't quite see any, and it might have all come off in the rain, but deeply ingrained in the ridges, I'll bet some lucky scientist will find doggy-doo.' He sniffed gingerly.

'I'm perplexed.'

Henry explained. 'When I was at the scene of the old man's death, a bobby said there was some dog muck in the alley that had been stood in. He asked if he should protect it, just in case there was some sort of connection to the murder. I told him to do it. Let's hope he did – because even if there isn't any pooh left on the sole –' he shook the trainer – 'if there is an imprint of a shoe in the shit, we can make a match.'

'So Rory was at the scene of the old man's murder? Is that what you're saying?'

'I'm not leaping to conclusions yet – but if we get tie-ins to the cane and the head wound, and the footwear pattern in the dog muck, there's every chance he was there. And if he was, did he see it happen? And if he saw it happen, did he get killed because of that?' Henry shrugged. 'Just tossing stuff up in the air, here. It makes it vital to find out who was with him . . .' The detective and pathologist blinked at each other. 'I don't completely believe in coincidence . . . old man run over and shot, young lad shot . . . what I do believe in, as James Bond once said, is enemy action. I've got a little feeling in the pit of my guts that whatever remains of bullets we find will be the same in both heads. And if Rory did see the old man get killed, then got murdered himself, that other person needs tracking down, because if we don't get to him first, he's going to get a bullet in the skull just like Rory . . .'

'Sounds a bit melodramatic.'

'That's me, Mr Melodrama.'

'I wouldn't care if you were dealing with the Saint Valentine's Day Massacre . . . we go on holiday tomorrow, the taxi's booked, etcetera, etcetera . . . nuff said?'

'I have no intention of doing anything more than ensuring

the investigation is up and running properly.' Henry emerged
from the en-suite shower room, towelling his close-cropped
hair dry, into the bedroom and into the tiny walk-in dressing
room. He was completely naked and Kate watched him, her
eyes sparkling at the sight, even though she was laying down
the law with him.

'Besides which you must be completely exhausted.'

'I'll be OK,' Henry said, bending down to his sock and underwear drawer, revealing a view that Kate would rather not have
seen. She winced.

However, it did not stop her from standing up and sidling in
behind him, wrapping her arms around him and pushing her nose
into his back. 'You smell great,' she murmured, throatily, one
hand sliding across his stomach.

'The heady fragrance of pure soap,' he said.

Henry had dashed home for a revitalizing shower and a change
of clothing with a view to getting through the day. His head had
been thumping and he'd taken a couple of Nurofen to ward off
the worst effects of a tiredness headache. His intention had been
to be in and out of the house within a few minutes, but the stand-
up 'discussion' with Kate about the holiday had delayed him
somewhat.

She'd backed off a little and now Henry felt guilty on two
fronts. Firstly, today was actually a leave day – and he was
working. It was a day on which they'd planned to do all the last
minute holiday prep, a bit of shopping, a lingering coffee at
Starbucks, stuff like that. Kate had been looking forward to it.
He also felt terrible about the encounter he'd had with Keira
O'Connell and berated himself for being so weak in the flesh –
still. He had almost returned to his bad old ways. Could so easily
have done. He thought he was better now.

With those thoughts in mind, he turned into Kate, pushed
himself against her, kissed her face, lips and neck, and felt
himself harden, legally this time.

'If you're interested,' he said – as she squeezed his testicles
gently – 'I might have time for a quick one.'

One thing was certain, he thought, the old Henry knew how
to appease a woman. But even as he pushed Kate back on to
the bed and peeled off her tight jeans, he was thinking how
dearly he would love to run this double murder that had all the
hallmarks of a professional hit. So juicy.

* * *

The everyday sounds of the morning had not woken Mark
Carter. The estate coming to life. The whirring and clattering
of, possibly, one of the last milk floats in existence trundling by.
Cars passing, kids yelling, bin men shouting to each other as
they made their way by with their noisy truck.

None of that woke him.

The sound that jerked Mark Carter awake was that of footsteps creeping past the door, someone sneaking about.

He came to, suddenly and sickeningly, cursing himself for
having fallen asleep in the first place – into a slumber of shadows,
flashes, bangs and death.

And now, in real darkness, he was sure he had heard foot-
falls.

Although his heart was slamming against his chest wall, he
tried not to move, to remain immobile, hardly breathing, watching
the line of light around the ill-fitting door to see if anyone walked
past. Then he heard a knock on the door.

Mark shivered.

After having locked himself in his bedroom on arriving home,
there was no way he could get to sleep. He didn't even try, but
kept a vigil at the window, watching the avenue apprehensively.

Alone in the house he began to feel even more vulnerable.
So much so that just after two a.m., still wide awake, but
exhausted, he collected up his quilt and pillow and went downstairs, where he let himself out the back door and went to the
side of the house. Out here were two outbuildings with a lean-
to roof connected to the house, making a tight passageway up
the side. One of the buildings had once been a utility room and
even though there was still an old sink in it, it was no longer
used. Now it was basically a rubbish tip for things Mark's mother
couldn't be bothered to take to the dump. Adjoining that was
another 'room', a space where, in days gone by, coal was delivered to and stored. With the advent of gas central heating, this
was also somewhere no longer used and because it was still full
of coal dust, it wasn't even used as a dumping ground for rubbish.
It was into this 'coal-hole', as it was still referred to, that Mark
sneaked, thinking he would be safer here than in the house. He
wrapped himself in the quilt and fitted his pillow between his
head and shoulder.

The door, poorly fitting, rotting at the bottom, still had an
old mortise lock on it that worked and Mark was able to lock
himself in.

His reasoning was that if the killers somehow managed to identify him and discover where he lived, he'd be better able to escape from the coal-hole than his bedroom because they wouldn't be expecting him to be hiding there.

He made himself as comfortable as possible in the cold, brick-built, dusty space – then looked at the cordless phone he'd brought with him from inside the house, wondering if it still worked out here. There was a dial tone, so he entered 141 and then dialled treble nine and asked for the police. When the connection went through, he said, 'Have you found the body in the car park behind Preston Road shops?'

The operator seemed taken aback. 'I'm sorry, could you repeat that?'

'You heard – send a patrol to that car park.' Then he hung up. He stared at the phone a while longer, fully expecting a call back, believing they had the technology to trace any call, even if it was a withheld number. No call came.

He rested his head on the pillow and tried to stay awake.

Then he heard the footsteps and realized he'd been asleep for hours. Someone knocked on the front door of the house and he heard a voice shout through the letter box, 'Answer the door, Mark Carter, or you're fuckin' dead.'

'I've had a CSI do a quick comparison of the impression in the dog pooh with the sole of Rory's trainer and his assessment is that it's a match – but we'll need a footwear analyst to confirm it. Being sorted.'

Henry looked at Alex Bent, a man who'd had about the same amount of sleep as himself in the last thirty-six hours. None. 'I think we're on to a winner, then. So let's assume Rory was at the scene of the old man's murder.'

'And got whacked for what he saw?'

'It's a hypothesis,' Henry said, his mind churning. 'But it doesn't explain why the old man might have smacked Rory across the head with his cane – if that's what happened – and we won't actually make that connection scientifically until at least the end of business today, and only then if we're lucky.' The walking stick, samples of skin, hair and blood from Rory's head had already been sent by police motorcyclist to the forensic science laboratory.

The two detectives were in an office just off the major incident room at Blackpool police station from where the investigation

would be run. It was eight thirty a.m. Henry's quickie had been
unromantically but successfully executed to the satisfaction of both
parties, and now he and Bent were in the process of pulling things
together for later briefings, tasking and press releases. Henry wanted
a chance to review everything beforehand so the murder squad,
which was now being cobbled together, could hit the ground
running. Henry had a feeling this would be a fast running investigation.

Already the dry-wipe board was full of lines of enquiry and
several sheets of flip-chart paper were being filled up.

'How are we doing with the chip shop owner?'

'No joy yet, boss.'

Henry nodded, frustrated. He scanned the board, muttering
and murmuring to himself as he read through the scribble that
would later be translated into something more meaningful for
others to understand.

'Have we missed anything?' he asked Bent, who was also
checking the board.

'Don't think so.'

'Good – let's grab a brew, then head up to comms.'

'You scared the crap out of me, sneaking around like that.'

'What the hell are you doing in there?'

'Long story,' Mark said sheepishly. 'Anyway, what're you
after?'

'I was just taking the chance of asking if you were coming
to school today, for a change. You know, school? That place you
seem to be avoiding these days.'

'I'm probably going to give it a miss.'

His friend Bradley sighed despairingly. 'Mark, you're really
going to get yourself in deep crap.'

'You don't know the half of it.'

'And what're you so jumpy about?'

'Nothing – just get lost, will you, Brad?'

Instantly, Mark regretted his snappy words as an expression
of deep hurt came on to Bradley's face. He and Brad had been
mates since junior school, but they had seen less and less of
each other since Mark's sister had died of an overdose. At that
time Mark had been a half-decent student with plans to get
himself out of Blackpool and find a proper career. However, the
subsequent conviction of his older brother for numerous drug
trafficking offences, and the implication he could have supplied

the drugs cocktail that killed their sister, had knocked Mark off balance. Without a mother to guide him either – she was too wrapped up in her own life, work, drink and a succession of men, to be bothered about Mark – he had almost lost the will to live. He'd certainly lost the will to keep trying. Nothing seemed important to him any more, and after missing school on several occasions and suffering no consequences, he started to drift aimlessly. It wasn't long before he hooked up with known dead-leg Rory Costain.

It had been downhill from there.

Bradley hadn't let him go easily, but the lure of a lifestyle with no authority figures beckoned Mark with a seductive crooked finger. Mark's girlfriend, Katie, one of the brightest young lasses at school, also got to the end of her tether with him and cast him adrift, especially after spotting him in an amusement arcade snogging a well known slapper.

'Thanks, mate,' Bradley said indignantly. 'But you're not a mate any more, you're just a self-centred, uncaring, selfish git.'

Mark squared up to him.

'What're you gonna do, beat me up? You're getting a bit of a reputation as a hard nut, aren't you?'

'I will if you don't go,' Mark warned, tilting his face aggressively at Bradley.

The two lads stared at each other until Bradley finally shook his head sadly and said, 'You've got no real friends any more. You just shit on everybody. I'm still here, but not for much longer.'

Bradley spun away and stalked off without a backward glance.

'Have you found the body in the car park behind Preston Road shops?'

'I'm sorry, could you repeat that?'

'You heard – send a patrol to that car park.'

Henry, Alex Bent and the comms room inspector were listening, for the third time, to the recording of the telephone call alerting the police to Rory's murder. It had been downloaded on to a disc and they were in the inspector's office off the main communications room in the station. There was also a written transcript of the short call, including the time it was made and its duration.

Henry rubbed his eyes and the three officers listened again, all of them shaking their heads.

'I don't recognize the voice, but it's obviously that of a young lad, maybe the one who'd been with Rory,' Bent said.

Henry nodded. 'I feel like I know the voice, or I might just be kidding myself.' He sighed and looked at the comms inspector. 'Thanks for this,' he said, taking the CD from the player.

'No probs.'

Henry handed him a sheet of paper on which he'd scribbled out a basic circulation regarding the shootings, which was for the information of the force, other forces and other agencies that might be interested. It was headed, 'NOT FOR PRESS RELEASE.' All it contained was the basic details of the two murders and little else. No speculation that they might be linked, even though this was implicit by virtue of the fact that both were referred to in the same message. Even though he was sure there was a connection, he wasn't going to admit that just yet. SIO's had to keep open minds otherwise they screwed up. The message also contained a description of the old man, including a reference to the old bullet wound in his side and asked for suggestions as to identity, giving a number to call.

'Can you circulate that as normal?' he asked the inspector, then stood to leave but stopped in his tracks, took the message back. He thought for a moment, then scribbled something else on the sheet and then handed it back to the inspector adding, 'Can you also send this person a copy of the circulation by email – including a few actual photos of the dead man?'

'Sure, boss.'

Henry looked at Bent. 'Shall we go back and work the crime scenes?'

Scowling, Mark had jerked a middle finger up at Bradley's retreating back, then retrieved his filthy quilt and pillow from the coal-hole, which he rolled up and dumped in the kitchen.

He was famished but could not be bothered making anything for himself, and the thought of a fast food breakfast was very appealing. He hadn't eaten anything for over twelve hours – since his last burger, in fact – as his intended supper had been whacked into the face of last night's attacker. He had some money left over from his little crime spree and the McDonald's on Preston New Road was just about walkable.

He had a quick shower and shave – bum-fluff was sprouting

all over his top lip and chin these days and annoyed him intensely – got changed and headed out across the estate, taking all the back routes to keep out of sight.

It would have been easy to avoid Psycho Alley and the car park, but morbid curiosity drew him in that direction. He needed to know if it hadn't all been a sick dream, because that's what it felt like.

The fact that the alley was cordoned off with crime scene tape was Mark's first indication that it definitely wasn't his imagination. The barrier meant he had to come at the car park from a different direction, and he emerged on to it from the main road to see a huge amount of police activity and public gawping going on. Cops were crawling everywhere, literally in some cases, as a team of overall-clad officers did a fingertip search in a line across the car park. The whole area had been cordoned off. A huge tent had been erected over the exact spot Rory had been shot. Mark wondered if the body was still there, or had it been removed? People in white forensic suits entered and left the tent, clasping samples.

Mark's empty guts wound sickeningly. He closed his eyes momentarily and thought himself back to the town centre alley, seeing the old man get mown down, then seeing the face of the gunman as he turned to look at Mark and Rory, startled. It had been night-time and the face had only been illuminated by orange street lights, but Mark had seen him clearly with his young, sharp eyes and was certain that if he came face to face with him again, he would be able to ID him.

Good enough reason to do a runner, Mark thought. He spun away, almost stepping into the path of a car pulling up at the front of the shops.

'Stupid kid,' Alex Bent said, slamming on the brakes.

'Eh – what?' Henry glanced up from the paperwork he had been studying, only catching a fleeting glimpse of the back of the youth who'd nearly been flattened by Bent.

The moment was gone and forgotten as the two detectives got out of the battered 'Danny', the old slang term for a plain car used by detectives – in this case an ageing Ford Focus that looked as if it had never seen better days.

They walked to the front door of the chip shop and rattled the handle.

'Need to find the owners,' Henry said unnecessarily.

Next-but-one along was a newsagent owned by an Asian,

Mr Aziz. He was lounging at the door of his shop. Henry and Bent asked him a few pertinent questions but he didn't know anything about the incident or the chip shop owner, who was new. Aziz thought he lived somewhere in Preston.

Henry thanked him and went to the scene out back.

He intended to have half an hour here, then head across to the other murder scene in town and start to build up any connections between the two.

Suddenly, Mark was no longer hungry. Suddenly, he was as paranoid as hell as the thought hit him, the same one he'd had last night, that murderers always go back to the scenes of their wrongdoing. At least that's what they said in TV cop dramas. They liked to gloat, enjoyed the power and Mark realized he was stupid to go anywhere near the scene again. If the murderer was there, milling about with the onlookers, keeping his head down, Mark was a sitting duck.

Hence his thoughtless step in front of a car, almost resulting in him getting flattened.

And then the glimpse of the driver, who he did not recognize, and the even quicker look at the passenger who he did recognize and never wanted to see again.

The horrible feeling was that if Henry Christie was running this case, then it would only be a matter of time before he and Mark came face to face.

SIX

'You don't understand,' the man pleaded desperately. 'Firstly I cannot tell you anything because I know nothing.' He was using expressive hand gestures as he spoke. 'And even if I did, I could still say nothing because I would be dead within days, possibly hours, of speaking to you.' He snorted derisively. 'Don't think that because I will be held inside a Maltese prison that I am unreachable. They can get to me anywhere, so I say nothing, keep myself alive.'

Karl Donaldson tried to look sympathetically across the interview room table, but cared little for the man's predicament. He was on the trail of a killer and this individual was the best lead he'd had in three years of chasing shadows.

Donaldson shifted uncomfortably in the plastic chair, sweat dripping from his scalp, down his neck and all the way to his backside. The heat was oppressive, even here in what were literally dungeons below the streets of Valletta on the island of Malta. He glanced at the stern-looking Maltese cop standing rigidly by the heavy steel door, arms folded, face grim.

'Any air-con in here?' Donaldson asked.

The cop shook his head and allowed himself a wry smile. As if. Much of the police station above ground level had been modernized, but the money had not stretched as far as the underground cell complex. There was still a medieval feel to them, as though it was only days since the Knights of Malta might have incarcerated their Turkish prisoners before beheading them with their scimitars.

Which was an irony, albeit a small one, as the man sitting opposite Donaldson was a Turk, though he had left his homeland many years before and ditched Islam along the way. His name was Mustapha Fazil.

'I need a cigarette,' Fazil demanded.

Donaldson checked with the guard, who nodded, and Donaldson handed Fazil a pack of Camels and a lighter. Apparently, no smoking policies hadn't reached Malta just yet, which was good, Donaldson thought. Tobacco was always a useful interview tool.

Fazil lit up, inhaled deeply, then exhaled the acrid smoke with a shudder of pleasure. Donaldson tried not to cough. He was anti-smoking but did see its uses as Fazil visibly relaxed in front of him.

'In other words,' Fazil said, picking something from his tongue, 'I'm a dead man if I talk, so don't expect me to say anything.'

After a beat of silence, Donaldson leaned on to the table, his eyes searching the young man's face – the deep-set eyes, the hooked nose, the thick black moustache, the swarthy suntanned features – all mixed together to make up the stereotypical Turk. And also the face of a young man deeply embroiled in a life of organized crime that spanned international boundaries.

Donaldson vividly remembered the call-out three years earlier, the reason for him being here now, sweating in an ancient cell, desperately trying to extract information from a very unwilling source . . .

Midnight. Donaldson had been at work since seven a.m. that day, at the beginning of a manhunt to track down one of the world's most wanted terrorists, Mohammed Ibrahim Akbar, a man who had almost managed to assassinate the American State Secretary who had been on a visit to the north of England at the invitation of the British Foreign Secretary. The attempt had failed – just – but the terrorist had escaped. Donaldson had then been asked to become part of a multi-agency team dedicated to hunting down and apprehending, or neutralizing if necessary, the wanted man.

In the very early days of this manhunt, much of Donaldson's time had been spent with the other team members collecting, collating and sifting intelligence and information just to get a sniff of the whereabouts of their prey. Long days at the computer, on the telephone, and reading reports from agents across the globe, trying to pinpoint their guy and work out his next move. So they could be there, waiting for him.

On the day he got the call-out he'd been in his office for almost seventeen hours. His eyes were grit-tired and he knew he needed a shower, shave and about twelve hours sleep, the latter option being the most unlikely to happen.

He was in his cubbyhole of an office in the American embassy in Grosvenor Square, London, where he had worked for over ten years as a legal attaché for the FBI. It was one of the most prestigious jobs in that organization and something he did well.

Just before the witching hour, he closed his computer down, stretched, yawned and rubbed his eyes, when one of the other team members appeared by the door, leaning on the jamb. This was Jo Kerrigan, a CIA operative who was the only female to be drafted on to the team. Donaldson had struck up a good rapport with her. She was a six-foot blonde, a fantastic athlete who had once made the US cross country skiing team in the winter Olympics. In physical terms she was more than a match of Donaldson, who himself touched six-four, was broad-shouldered, fit and all-American handsome.

He knew that the relationship between him and Kerrigan could easily become intimate. But – and it was a very big 'but' for Donaldson – even though his marriage was going through a rocky phase, he would never allow himself to be unfaithful to his wife Karen, tempting though the prospect was.

'Long day,' she said.

'Yup – and getting nowhere fast.' He clicked shut the lid of his laptop.

'Going home?'

'Uh – naw – using one of the service apartments tonight. Need an early start.' This meant he would be staying within the confines of the embassy in one of the tiny en-suite rooms at the rear of the building. They were known colloquially as 'hell holes' and the team had been granted special permission to use them whenever necessary.

'Yeah, me too,' she said, smiling. 'How about a drink first? The night is young.'

Donaldson eyed her. 'Yeah, maybe,' he drawled.

'How about food? I bet you haven't eaten since that croissant this morning, have ya?'

In a reply that said it all, Donaldson's stomach growled loudly and they both chuckled.

'You're right,' he said patting his tummy. He was suddenly famished. He guessed it wouldn't do any harm to go get a bite to eat with Jo because he didn't intend it to go any further than food. Even though he'd had a very terse conversation with his wife earlier that evening when she'd castigated him for never coming home and being obsessed with work. The conversation had frozen after he'd announced his intention to bed down overnight at the embassy.

'There's a new Chinese on Curzon Street – opens late,' Jo suggested.

'Chinese sounds good,' he said but there was a touch of hesitation in his voice. 'Er . . . just need to make a couple of quick calls, actually,' he fibbed. 'Time zones, etcetera,' he explained. 'Won't take long . . . see you at the staff exit in five?'

'Yeah, no probs.' Her eyes shone brightly at him.

Donaldson waited for her to go before using his mobile phone to call Karen. He didn't call the home number, but her mobile instead (even though he still insisted on calling them cellphones). She did not answer. He left a faltering, apologetic message on the answering service and felt utterly guilty about going out for some late night nosh with the stunning Jo.

He rose reluctantly, resolving to enjoy the food and the company, and nothing else. He was, after all, starving. He jerked his jacket off the back of his chair and shrugged himself into it, checked the desk – computer closed down properly, drawers locked – and was about to head for the door when the desk phone rang shrilly.

Had he been less conscientious he would have ignored it.

He scooped it up. 'Karl Donaldson, Homeland Security.'

He squinted at the display but did not recognize the caller number.

Nor did he get to bed that night.

'Karl, this is Don Barber from the Madrid office.' From the tone of those few words he knew the news was bad, but he didn't have any idea what it would be. He knew Barber well. He was ex-special forces who had left the army after distinguished service in the Kuwait theatre, got himself a law degree and joined the FBI. They'd actually worked together for a short spell in the mid-nineties before their paths diverged. Barber had made a good career for himself and at that time headed up the FBI Madrid office. Instinctively, Donaldson checked the wall clock – midnight plus ten – one ten Spanish time.

'Don – wassup?'

'It's Shark,' he said, his voice jittering, spreading a horrible feeling of iciness through Donaldson.

'What about him?'

'I'm really sorry to have to tell you this, but he was shot to death a little earlier this evening in a place just outside Palma, Majorca.'

Donaldson sat down numbly. 'Tell me everything,' he said . . .

'Anyway, FBI man, why you so interested in three dead Italians?' Fazil wanted to know.

'I'm a law enforcement officer, that's all you need to know. This is simply an information-gathering interview.'

'I don't have to speak to you, then.' Fazil blew out several lazy rings of smoke, now completely relaxed since being allowed the cigarettes.

'That depends, my friend . . .'

'On what?'

Donaldson wiped a hand across his brow. It came away damp with sweat. 'The days of rules are well past. On the face of it I will obey the rules – of interview, of Human Rights, of fairness – but underneath I will be operating on a different level, like the feet of a duck.' Donaldson wiggled the first two fingers on his right hand to imitate a duck's feet. 'I will throw you to the wolves if you don't cooperate with me.'

Fazil eyed him cynically.

'I can be your friend or your enemy. Your choice.'

'Mr Donaldson.' Fazil smashed out the stub of his cigarette in the ashtray. 'I have killed a Maltese police officer in a firefight.

I will be found guilty of that and I will be incarcerated on this stinking island for many, many years. Even that thought will not make me talk to you.' His dark eyes looked down and his wide nostrils flared.

Donaldson caught the first BA flight from London Gatwick to Palma later that morning, three years before. Don Barber met him at the airport, hustled him through customs into a waiting car, which was driven for less than ten minutes to the beach front restaurant in Can Pastilla where the shooting had taken place the evening before.

The bodies had all been removed but otherwise the scene was as it had been, and the road in front of the hotel was cordoned off to through traffic. The local police scientific team was working the scene as professionally as anything Donaldson had ever witnessed.

He and Don Barber were allowed under the tape and Barber walked him through what had happened with the permission of the senior police officer present, who could only speculate as to why two FBI agents were here.

'Hell,' Donaldson said afterwards. 'Where are the bodies now?'

'Palma mortuary.'

'And do we have anything?'

'Only the names of all three victims.'

'What about evidence from the scene itself?'

'We could have something,' Barber said, consulting a flip over notepad he had with him. 'From the waiter, who despite being in shock, has given us a pretty good description of the shooter – which I'll come to later – it seems that another customer went to the restroom, which was then visited by the shooter. He then returned to the table, then opened fire. Bam!' Barber said bitterly. 'Paella everywhere. But don't get excited, we don't know if the shooter left any traces in the john or at the table. I reckon it's doubtful, but I've got our own crime scene guys on the way from Madrid and I've asked the locals to hold back a bit – not that I'm saying they aren't doing a good job. But obviously they are very interested as to why the FBI is sniffin' around, though.'

'As they would be.' The two men looked at each other know-ingly.

'Anyway, pal, back to basics,' Barber said. 'Just before our shooter visited the john, another customer went in a few minutes before him, then afterwards immediately left the joint.'

Donaldson blinked.

'I might be adding up to five here,' Barber said, 'but I'm guessing this could be the delivery man – and he was sitting right there.' Barber pointed dramatically to a table in the back corner of the restaurant. 'And his stuff hasn't been cleared away, which could be useful, scientifically.'

'That's supposing he was involved in some way.'

'If he isn't, fair enough . . . but we'll see what comes of it.'

Donaldson imagined the crime taking place, based on how it had been described to him. Suddenly he felt quite ill.

Shark wasn't his man, not directly, but he knew him, knew what his task was, but above all knew what it felt like to lose an undercover agent. He patted Barber on the shoulder and said, 'I'm real sorry, man.'

'Yeah,' Barber snorted, his eyes moist. Barber was Shark's controller. 'Fuck,' he added. Then, 'I want you to find the killer, Karl. I've cleared it with your boss. Hope you don't mind.'

'I can prove you were at the scene of a multiple homicide in a restaurant in Majorca three years ago – and I know you were the person who delivered the weapon to the man who carried out the murders.'

Fazil chuckled derisively.

Donaldson went on, 'You were sitting at a table in the same restaurant. You went to the toilet a few minutes before the killer. You secreted a weapon underneath the lid of the toilet cistern.'

Fazil shook his head.

'I can prove it,' Donaldson said again.

The lone, mystery diner had not been as careful as he should have been. The glass of wine and glass carafe on his table revealed an array of partial fingerprints, as did an examination of the porcelain cistern lid. These were run through the automatic finger-print recognition system and Fazil's details were eventually thrown up. He was positively identified from the lifts, but there was not enough detail to support an ID at court.

Fazil shrugged.

Donaldson did not speak, but regarded the man who could be the key to cracking the case he'd been working on solidly for eighteen months – as well as the rest.

Following his appearance at the scene of the shooting in Majorca, Donaldson had been diverted to other tasks through no fault of his own. One of these was the protracted manhunt for the terrorist Akbar that culminated many months later in a tiny square in Barcelona, where Donaldson had come face to face with him and took a bullet that almost cost him his life – though Akbar fared much worse. Donaldson had endured a long period of recuperation and eventually returned to work, picking up the threads of the investigation into the Majorcan murders.

By that time, Fazil had been identified from the traces he'd left at the scene and a full profile had been pulled together on him. He was a Turk involved in people smuggling and drug dealing across the eastern Med. At the time of the murders he was working freelance for a Camorra Mafia family from Naples and was suspected by the Italian police of being a man who collected, delivered and disposed of firearms used in the commission of crimes by that particular clan. Crimes that included murder – and in that part of the world he was kept constantly busy because murder was rife between warring factions.

But Fazil was an elusive man, always on the go, rarely in one place for any length of time. Although he was circulated by Interpol as wanted for questioning in connection with the Majorcan murders, he was never caught.

It was a frustrating time for Donaldson and the FBI, who had a vested interest in apprehending him because the man going by the codename Shark had been deep undercover for years and they wanted to nail the bastard who killed him, who it was believed had been hired by the head of a rival Mafia clan.

Other than occasional snippets of information about the assassin – a man who went by the moniker of 'The American' – Fazil was the best lead they had to the shootings, if only they could catch him.

'We have your fingerprints and' – here Donaldson stretched the truth a little – 'your DNA from the scene.'

Fazil shook his head.

'We can protect you if you speak to us,' Donaldson assured him, hoping his body language didn't say anything different. 'If you admit your part, tell us who you worked for and who pulled the trigger, who set up the hit – everything – we will protect you.'

'I don't speak to the law.'

It had taken almost three years for Fazil to surface and that had been only by pure chance and bad luck on his part. He had been involved in running a rigid inflatable boat, an RIB, full of contraband from the southern tip of Italy to Malta and back, and a low-level snitch blabbed to the police in Valletta. He told them that a night run was due to take place to drop off drugs on St Paul's Bay on the island's north coast.

Fazil was accompanied by three other men, all Turks.

The police were waiting in ambush. Unfortunately, what should have been a well-planned and executed reception turned into a bloodbath. Fazil and his heavily armed colleagues opened fire on the police in a desperate attempt to evade their clutches and get back out to sea. The only miracle was that Fazil was left standing after the broadside, as his three mates were riddled with bullets and one cop felled by Fazil's MP5 and almost beheaded by the stream of bullets.

It was the second time in Maltese history that Turkish blood had been spilled in St Paul's Bay, the last time being in 1565 when hundreds of Turkish soldiers were slaughtered as they lay siege to the island. Their blood made the waters run red.

It was much less dramatic this time in terms of its scale, as three dead smugglers lay at the water's edge, twitching and bleeding in the surf.

'And anyway,' Fazil sneered at Donaldson, 'you still haven't told me why you Americans are so interested in feuding Italians.' Then, suddenly, he had a thought, churning the question through his brain again. 'Unless . . .?' He shook his head and grinned, and he realized he might just have the answer.

Donaldson was relieved to get out of the miserable heat of the dungeons and into the equally hot, but breezy streets of the Maltese capital, Valletta. He slung his light jacket over his shoulder and sauntered through the high, narrow thoroughfares, jam-packed with people and cars. He mulled over what Fazil had quite correctly surmised, although Donaldson had not let on that the prisoner was right, had kept his face as impassive as a professional poker player.

'One of them was an undercover cop, wasn't he?' Fazil had gushed. 'One of yours.'

Donaldson had sighed and shook his head, then quickly taken his leave, saying he would return later. He left Fazil with his cellphone number just in case.

Outside, he wended across to Upper Barracca Gardens for the splendid view over Grand Harbour, where he thought about Malta's strategic position in the Mediterranean. That, coupled with the superb harbour, meant this barren little rock had had a torrid history over the centuries, No doubt, he thought, the same would apply for centuries to come.

He sat on a bench savouring the late afternoon sun on his face, his mind once more turning to Fazil, the man who had delivered the weapon used to murder three Italian Mafia men.

Except . . . one of the men, codenamed Shark, whilst being of Italian origin, had actually been a deep cover FBI agent. And that was why the Americans wanted to catch the killer, because he was one of theirs. A brave, resourceful man who had spent five years undercover, gaining trust, gathering information secretly, before ultimately betraying them. At least that had been the plan.

And Shark was one of the best. Real name Giuseppe Cardini, an FBI agent to the core, who had found himself actually advising members of the Marini Camorra clan on matters of business. And they had met a man who had promised them an entry into the vast US clothing and footwear markets, but he had turned out to be a killer.

An elaborate set up. Lured to Majorca, then murdered.

Donaldson scrunched up his fists in frustration, cursing silently. He was annoyed he hadn't been able to devote as much time as he would have liked to Shark's death, but that was often the nature of FBI work. Nor did it help that Akbar's bullet had shredded his insides, the kind of setback that tends to mess up any plans. When he did return to full duty, there had then been distracting personal issues, like a wife who wanted out, and other sidetracks, so that when he eventually managed to devote some quality time to it, the trail was well and truly chilly. The 'American' was still at large and no one had been punished for the crime.

Punished legally, that is.

Donaldson knew that the three killings in Majorca had kicked off a spate of tit for tat murders in Naples and surrounding districts, as several Camorra clans went head to head in a brutal struggle for dominance. More than twelve people had been killed in reprisal and counter reprisal, probably more. It was a very ugly, prolonged war that seemed to have no end.

He fished out his cellphone and speed-dialled a number.

'Don – it's me, Karl Donaldson.'

'Hey, pal,' Don Barber answered. 'How's it going?' Barber, who was now Donaldson's line manager at the London embassy following a promotion from the Madrid office, knew exactly where Donaldson was and what he was doing.

'I've spoken to the guy – and so far it's a no-no. At the moment he's stewing, literally and metaphorically, in a cell.'

'What's your gut feeling on the outcome?'

'In the air at present. He's too frightened to talk just yet.'

'But he is the right man, yeah?' Barber probed. 'The man who delivered?'

'I'm sure he is.'

'Keep me posted.'

Barber hung up and Donaldson slid his phone away. He watched a pretty girl walk past. She glanced sideways and smiled seductively. Then she was gone with a swish of her hips. He forced himself up from the bench and sauntered back into the city. He stopped for an iced coffee at the Bridge Bar on St Ursula Street before making his way back to his hotel, the Excelsior on Grand Siege Road. He let himself into his air-conditioned room, stripped down to his Uncle Sam boxers and splayed out on the bed, revelling in the cool wafts of chilled air.

An hour later he awoke, shivering. He rose stiffly from the bed and, as was often the case when he came upright from a prone position, a searing pain creased though his abdomen following the exact trail of the bullet he'd taken from Akbar. A line that corkscrewed up through his chest like a cord of steel cable had been inserted into him.

He sat back on the edge of the bed allowing the agony to subside before padding to the bathroom. On returning, he checked his phone – no messages or missed calls – then sat down at the tiny desk, opened his laptop and logged on to check his messages. The process seemed to take forever, so whilst the little egg timer showed, Donaldson went on to the balcony to enjoy the view of Marsamxett harbour and Manoel Island. Some of the heat had gone out of the day, but it was still warm, a sultry breeze listlessly touching him.

He placed his hands on his hips and inhaled the lemony scented air, expanding his chest. Then he turned back into his room, catching a glimpse of the lady on the adjoining balcony. He hadn't noticed her initially, but she had certainly spotted him from the comfort of her lounger. She had lowered her sunglasses to get a view of the extremely fit-looking man clad only in tight fitting boxers that left hardly anything to her imagination.

Embarrassed, Donaldson scuttled back inside and settled at the laptop, now successfully logged on.

The number of new emails he had received appalled him. Most, he guessed, were rubbish. He went to the inbox and scanned the unopened messages to see if any caught his eye. He didn't want to make the mistake of opening any that might require any sort of action or response, unless it suited him. If he opened one that needed him to do something, there was no way he could say he hadn't opened it because of the way emails were tracked. Senders always knew if they'd been opened or not.

'Ugh,' he moaned, wishing for the pre-Internet days. He easily understood why spies – and terrorists – had reverted to more basic ways of communicating with each other, such as clandestine meetings, landline phone calls and dead letter drops. With every electronic contact leaving a trace, it was the sensible thing to do. On the minus side, it meant that people who hunted down baddies were finding it harder to track the more intelligent ones.

But one email did make him sit up, only because he recognized the organization that had sent it to him: Lancashire Constabulary. It was entitled, 'MURDER OF UNIDENTIFIED MALE'. It was the only message he bothered opening.

He read it quickly, noting that it began by saying that the message had been sent to him at the request of one Detective Superintendent Christie. It told the story of the old man being hit by a car, then getting his brains blown out. A very nasty killing. He read the description of the man, including a mention of an old bullet wound in the dead man's side. A further shooting was then outlined, that of a young boy. Neither meant anything to Donaldson at that stage because his mind was still mulling over Fazil and the way forward with him. Part of the problem could have been that no one outside the FBI knew they were searching for a hit man called the American. Nor did anyone know that one of the three men killed by this man was an FBI undercover agent. It had been decided to keep both facts from general circulation, hopefully so that the investigation would be easier.

So far that theory hadn't got anywhere, a thought that gave Donaldson an idea. If the FBI came clean, admitted one of their operatives had been murdered, declared they were launching a full scale manhunt and went completely public about the whole thing, it might put the cat amongst the pigeons and cause a bit of panic in some quarters. Panic often led to mistakes; mistakes usually led to arrests.

Maybe something to discuss with Don Barber as it was his show.

Donaldson read through the message from Lancashire police again, then clicked on the attached file accompanying it, hoping to hell it wasn't carrying a virus.

Millimetre by painful millimetre, photographs unfolded on screen, Donaldson watching impatiently. A series of post-mortem shots of the dead man. Horrific and gruesome.

'Thanks for this, Henry,' Donaldson mumbled.

At first Donaldson scanned them fleetingly, but then with growing interest.

'Well, would ya—' he began to say, but his exclamation was cut short by a knock on the hotel door. Annoyed, he rose, peering through the spyhole before opening, even though whoever was there had their back to the door. It was his next door neighbour, the lady on the adjoining balcony who had spotted him in his underwear admiring the view. She swirled around as the door opened, dressed in a flimsy, see-through wrap fastened at the neck, opening outwards in an inverted V-shape, over a skimpy bikini.

In her left hand was a bottle of champagne, in her right two fluted glasses.

'Uh, hi,' Donaldson said, keeping most of himself out of sight behind the door, as he was still only dressed in his boxers.

She was mid-thirties, tanned, beyond attractive with ample breasts and slim hips. 'I hope you don't mind my impudence,' she said in a vaguely Scandinavian accent, 'but I thought perhaps we could perhaps . . . you know.' With a swish of gossamer she came through before he could mouth any protest.

'I . . .' he stammered feebly, but she was already in the main section of the room before he could stop her.

She spun. 'I'm Vanessa, and I'm *all alone*.' Her eyes slithered across Donaldson's broad chest, down across his stomach, then widened at his crotch. Her lips parted wetly.

'Look, I'm sorry,' he said, flustered.

'We can have some fun – no strings,' she promised wickedly.

Donaldson made a chopping gesture with the side of his hand. 'Look, sorry, I'm rather busy . . .'

She spotted the laptop. 'We can watch porn together, if you like? Is that what you're doing now?'

'No,' he almost screamed.

But he wasn't quick enough to stop her stepping to one side

and seeing the image on screen. Her face dropped in horror and slowly turned to Donaldson, the colour having drained from it. 'My God, what are you into? You sick bastard.'

Donaldson's shoulders sagged. 'Time to go,' he said and wafted his hands towards the still open door.

'It certainly is.' She gathered her slip around her as best she could and flounced out of the door, champagne and glasses and all. Donaldson followed and closed it softly behind her, exhaling gratefully when she'd gone, but still reeling a little from the encounter.

'Jeepers,' he said.

He had some urgent phone calls to make.

SEVEN

'Henry Christie,' came the tired voice.

'Henry Christie, you old son of a . . . something.'

'Well, well, well, Karl Donaldson, FBI agent *extraordinaire*, how the hell are you?' Henry's voice perked up.

Donaldson was back out on the balcony, dressed this time in Chinos and a polo shirt. The next balcony along was noticeable for its emptiness. Obviously Donaldson's fetish for post-mortem pornography had terrified his sexy, forward neighbour into locking herself behind closed doors. Donaldson had his mobile phone clamped to his ear. 'I'm good, pal – and you?'

The two men exchanged personal pleasantries for a while. Now old friends, they had first encountered each other over a dozen years earlier when Donaldson, then an FBI field agent, had been investigating American mob activity in the north-west of England. Since that meeting when their friendship had blossomed, their professional paths had also crossed on several occasions over the years. Also, Donaldson had met a Lancashire policewoman way back then, had wooed and married her, had two children with her, so his connections through her to Lancashire were very strong, even though the marriage was going through a rocky patch that had lasted way too long.

'Got your email,' Donaldson said.

'What email would that be?' Henry asked. From his tone, Donaldson guessed he was harassed and irritable, as usual, and was only giving the time of day through politeness.

'The dead guy email.'

'Oh yeah,' Henry said, remembering asking for a copy of the circulation to be sent to Donaldson, plus photos.

'Have you identified the guy yet?'

'Nope.'

'Anywhere near identifying him?'

'Who can tell?'

'Any suspects?'

'Not as yet.'

'Witnesses?'

'I think we have one dead witness and maybe another who's not over keen to show his face . . . still working on it.'

'What the hell does that mean?'

'There's the possibility that someone saw the murder and was killed for it, and maybe another witness saw the same thing but is still out there . . . would you like me to spell it out for you?'

'Ooh, mister touchy . . . but the dead guy is still unknown?'

'At the moment, yes – why?' he demanded.

'Now don't get shirty with me, but would it help you at all if I knew who the victim was?'

Donaldson's next call was to Don Barber, his boss. 'Don – Karl. Can you speak?'

'Go on, pal.'

'I'm assuming you've got an email from Lancashire Constabulary?'

Barber hesitated. 'It's one of many I haven't opened – and at the moment I'm nowhere near a computer. Why, Karl?'

Donaldson briefly outlined the nature of the message. Barber listened without comment.

'Sounds horrific,' Barber said when he'd finished talking. 'What's the issue?'

'I'm pretty sure the dead guy is Rosario Petrone.'

There was a gap of silence. 'You are joking. Jesus.'

'No, Rosario, Don, not the messiah, but the guy who ordered the hit in Majorca? The guy who went to ground when the bullets started flying afterwards. The guy you've been searching for, for the last three years, almost. The guy, who even though he didn't pull the trigger, is ultimately responsible for Shark's murder.'

'Petrone?' Barber said incredulously. 'In freakin' Blackpool, England – *that* Blackpool?'

'Yep, I'm pretty sure it is. Get to a computer, check the circulation.'

'It'll be sometime before I can, but if you say it is, Karl, then I believe you. You're great with faces.'

'It might be worth my while getting up to Lancashire,' Donaldson suggested. 'I'm on good terms with the cops up there. I think we need someone on site to see what the score is . . . and they think they have a witness. What d'you think?'

'A witness?'

'Yep.'

The line went silent. Then Barber said, 'OK Karl, get up there as soon as you can, see what's happening, see if we need to be involved.'

'Something I need to do here first, though.'

'What's that?'

'Check with Fazil. If he comes across, I think we need to deal with him. He could be the key to the American.'

'You're certain he's the one who delivered the weapon?'

'As I can be.'

'But he doesn't want to deal?'

'Not at this stage.'

'In that case, let him rot a while. You can come back to him later.'

'I don't want to miss the chance of a lead to the killer, Don.'

'I'll bet he's a nothing guy. Let him rot.'

Donaldson groaned and said OK. But he hadn't come all the way to Malta not to get a result of some sort, and even though he promised Barber he would not revisit Fazil, he intended to give the guy one last opportunity.

He clicked his phone shut, pondering. He needed Fazil to talk and maybe the brutal death of an old man on the streets of Blackpool, thousands of miles away, would be the lever he needed to do just that.

Donaldson was unable to book a flight back to the UK until the following morning anyway, an Air Malta flight to Manchester, so he had time to kill. He decided firstly to get into one of the hotel's restaurants for an early evening meal, then he would visit Fazil, who had been cooking so long in the heat of those cells that, surely, he was now all casseroled and ready to fall apart.

He was in the restaurant at seven and out by seven thirty, passing his very available neighbour entering as he left. There was an expression of horror on her face at being in such close proximity to such a monster. He gave her a crooked leer and left the hotel, calling his wife on the mobile as he walked out into a Maltese evening that was hot and dry.

Whilst the marriage might still be rocky, it was still afloat, and they had an amiable conversation that did go slightly chilly when he told her he would be flying back to Manchester not to London next day. She did cheer up considerably when he suggested that she might head north herself with the kids and meet up at her mother's, who lived in Lancashire. A date was made.

They finished the call on a loving note. And Donaldson heaved a sigh of relief, but wondered where the relationship was headed. He folded his phone away, but then had another thought and called Henry Christie to make arrangements to be picked up at Manchester airport.

Then he strolled through Valletta, back to the police station.

The heat had not left the dungeons. It was stifling and within minutes Donaldson was sweating heavily again, dark patches under his arms.

Once more he was face to face with Fazil.

'You know, the more I come to talk to you, the more it will look as though you are talking to me . . . word gets out about that sort of thing.'

'You are trying to scare me, FBI man.'

Donaldson nodded. 'To be honest, you've been pretty lucky, haven't you?'

'How?'

'Let's see . . . what happened in the aftermath of that shooting in Majorca?'

Fazil shrugged, a gesture he had honed to perfection.

'I'll answer that for you: many people died, many people.'

'People die all the time.'

'Not always in a hail of bullets.'

'In this world, dying in a hail of bullets is commonplace.'

'What would you prefer? Bullets or old age?'

'You're still trying to frighten me. It's not working.'

'Or how about old age after years of rotting in prison? That could very well be arranged,' Donaldson said. 'America and Malta are on excellent terms behind the scenes.'

'Fuck you,' Fazil sneered.

Donaldson sighed and changed tack. 'The killings in Majorca

were the opening salvo of a gang war, as I'm sure you know.
And I'll tell you what I know. Rosario Petrone, the head of a
Camorra Mafia clan in Naples, ordered the killings, and you
were working for him. Three men were lured to their deaths and
you provided the weapon that killed them. No, don't deny it,
because I can prove it, Fazil,' Donaldson said harshly. 'Those
three murders opened up the floodgates. More killings, more
reprisals, one clan against another . . . no winners. Somehow, you
didn't get your head blown off . . . yet.'

Fazil moved uncomfortably. 'I got out,' he admitted.

Donaldson noted the slight crack. 'You may have got out, but
you haven't got away,' he said cruelly. 'No one gets away, not
ever, especially people like you – you know that.'

Fazil rubbed his sweaty unshaven face.

'I have some news for you,' Donaldson announced. Fazil's
eyes rose shiftily. 'I won't insult your intelligence, so I'll tell it
to you straight. I know you were working for Petrone. Don't
insult me by denying this.' Fazil's mouth clamped shut. 'Petrone
went to ground some time after the gang warfare started, didn't
he? Hasn't been seen for, what, one, two years? The fighting
has continued in his absence, though, with him still directing
operations by all accounts. The general not on the field of battle
. . . a real hero,' Donaldson said sarcastically.

'Wouldn't know,' Fazil said, reverting to his original standpoint. 'Don't even know who you're talking about.'

The FBI man shook his head sadly. 'Let me just clarify here,
Fazil. You can help yourself by helping me. All you have to do
is tell me about the American.'

The prisoner chuckled sardonically, said nothing else.

'The way I see it is this: As it stands, you will either rot in
a Maltese jail or somehow you will be murdered in it. Even if
you get through your sentence here, as soon as you're released
you will be handed over to the Spanish authorities. Then you'll
be convicted of supplying a weapon used to kill three men, as
well as murder, because even though you might not have pulled
the trigger, you killed 'em just as much as the assassin, pal. You
will then rot in a Spanish jail or you will be murdered in it.
Speak to me and—'

'I'll be murdered anyway,' Fazil interjected.

'Not necessarily. Speak to me, Fazil,' Donaldson continued
patiently, 'and I'll ensure your safety, a new identity, money, a
life in the US, protected by the authorities.'

Fazil considered him. 'You are full of shit, FBI man . . . you said you had some news for me . . . where is it? I haven't heard it yet.'

'Where is Petrone?'

'Who?' Fazil answered stubbornly. Donaldson had a flash to cop dramas and movie thrillers where the villains always seem to crack, even when faced with little or no evidence, just the authority and overwhelming aura of the hero and a load of hearsay. Real life sucked, he thought. No one ever admits a damn thing, even when faced with a cut and dry case.

'I'll tell you where he is,' he said. 'Dead – that's where he is. He went to ground when the going got too tough, but they still caught up with him.'

'Who are "they"?' Fazil asked.

'Doesn't really matter, but the fact remains he could not hide forever and now he's dead. The head of a major Camorra family – found and murdered.'

'Like I said, you're full of shit. A liar.'

Donaldson unfolded the sheet of A4 paper he'd been keeping under his hands, then revealed its contents to Fazil. 'If you want, I can stop this happening to you.' He showed him the photographs he'd printed off of a very dead Rosario Petrone.

Actually, Karl Donaldson did not know for certain if Fazil would be a serious target in the ongoing reprisals that were still happening in the world of the Camorra. Fazil was a bit player, nothing more than a gofer, and it would not have surprised Donaldson if he'd been forgotten in the grand scheme of tit-for-tat killings, especially as he'd seen sense and kept his head down after the shootings in Majorca.

But that didn't stop Donaldson from scaring the living crap out of him and manipulating him to come across.

The other truth was that Fazil probably knew little about the assassin, known as 'The American'. Fazil would have been employed solely to source and drop a weapon for the American's use. But this had put him in a position in which he would have seen the killer, would have had chance to scrutinize him and therefore be able to give the most detailed description yet, something the FBI was woefully missing, despite what the nervous waiter had seen. Wringing Fazil dry would be very useful, if only Donaldson could get under his skin. He wasn't completely hopeful of success. Fazil would be more afraid of Camorra repercussions than anything Donaldson could lob at him. But the FBI man was reluctant to let him go.

Fazil *had* been at the scene of the murders. He had seen the American, he was part of the set up, and that was more than anything Donaldson had so far. Fazil was also a useful source of intelligence about organized crime in Europe, so Donaldson wasn't about to let that go either.

It was a very complex situation, and as Donaldson ambled back up the cell corridor to the prisoner reception area, his mind somersaulted with it all. He walked alongside a gaoler who had just put Fazil back in a new cell in the otherwise empty female wing of the complex. He was told that this was because murder charges were going to be put to Fazil and all suspected killers were kept isolated from other inmates if possible. Fazil would be put before a magistrate in the morning and then, once he was in the judicial system proper, there was little Donaldson could do, or promise, after that.

Once enmeshed therein, Donaldson had much less clout.

He nodded at the gaoler, then walked past the desk sergeant who watched him leave with shifty eyes. Donaldson stepped through a security door into the public foyer of the police station and paused in deep thought, trying to work out the angles. He had to offer something to Fazil that would tip him over the edge. But what?

His brain hurt. He was tired. He wanted to go home. He wanted a drink. He wanted to go to sleep. Not necessarily in that order. A devilish part of him also wanted to knock on the door of the next hotel room and get laid whilst watching porn and drinking champagne, but that was one thing that would not happen. Certainly not to the ultra conservative and very faithful hound dog that was Karl Donaldson, no matter what the state of his marriage was.

Maybe, he thought, bunching up his fists, maybe just one last stab at Fazil. Put his cards on the table. Admit that one of the dead men was an undercover FBI agent. Let Fazil gloat over that. Admit he was desperate to catch the killer. Then offer him a good package in return for good information. Promise him immunity from prosecution, both from the Maltese and Spanish authorities. Then offer good money and relocation. And then tell the Turkish bastard that if he didn't come across, he would definitely see to it that word got out that Fazil was an informer, even if he wasn't. Then see how long he lived.

Sounded like a plan. Or the last refuge of a scoundrel.

Donaldson looked across at the enquiry desk. It was choc-a-bloc with members of the public. Normally, the constable on duty behind it would have buzzed him back through, but he was harassed, so Donaldson turned back to the door and tapped in the entry code himself. Any self-respecting FBI agent always sneaked a look and remembered keypad codes if at all possible whilst being escorted through buildings. The officer who had first shown him into this police station hadn't been particularly security conscious, and Donaldson had seen and easily digested the four digit entry code – just in case.

It opened, he stepped back in, made his way along the corridor and trotted down the steps leading to the underground cell complex, then through another secure door (keypad entry code remembered) into the prisoner reception area. There was a door leading to an outer yard off an underground car park that prisoners were brought in from. Then there was another door to the cells behind the charge office desk and two other doors, one into an office and another to a set of stairs leading to another part of the building.

Donaldson smelled cordite as soon as he entered the prisoner reception area. He came alert, because of all the odours in such areas, that was one that should not be present. There was no one at the custody desk. Donaldson approached it and peered over, also noting that the barred gate to the cells was open. Usually it was kept locked. Maybe the sergeant was making his rounds. Donaldson knew there were about four other prisoners in custody besides Fazil. They were listed on the big whiteboard on the wall behind the desk. None were in for anything as serious as Fazil. He also noticed that Fazil's name had been transferred from his original cell into the one on the female wing, which consisted of only two cells separated from the rest of the otherwise male dominated complex. Putting a male into a female cell was usually only done as a last resort, generally when cells were full to overflowing, although a man and a woman never shared a cell under any circumstances. Looking at the board, Donaldson was a little confused, though. He understood that it may be policy to keep murderers apart from other prisoners, but there was actually plenty of room on the male side and Fazil could easily have been separated from the others without shoving him into a female cell.

Donaldson stepped behind the reception desk, which was a

chest-high counter at which prisoners were presented on arrival at the station.

He almost tripped over the man's protruding legs.

The body of the station sergeant was jammed up against the bottom edge of the counter, which explained why Donaldson hadn't seen anything when he'd looked over a few seconds earlier.

It also explained the whiff of cordite.

'Shit.' Donaldson twisted down to his haunches and saw that the man, who not many minutes earlier had given him a suspicious look, was now dead, two bullets having torn off the upper left quadrant of his skull. A puddle of bright blood was growing under the poor man's head and shoulders.

Following his next expletive, Donaldson rose quickly to his full height as everything slotted into place. He stepped through the barred gate into the cell corridor, his right hand automatically going to his left armpit to touch the gun that wasn't there. He hadn't carried a firearm as a matter of course for over ten years, but still missed it dreadfully. Especially when he needed it.

Straight ahead was the male cell corridor. Through a door to the left was the female cell corridor. Donaldson pushed open this door, which was unlocked – and should not have been. Even though there were only two cells down here, it was still a long, dank passageway, angling downwards, poorly lit by flickering fluorescent tubes. The cracked concrete floor sloped unevenly away. The two cells faced each other at the far end.

Both cell doors appeared to be open from what he could see.

He swallowed. His throat dried up as a pulse of adrenaline gushed into his system. His heart thumped and the track of the bullet that had nearly killed him in Barcelona burned. He took four quick steps, tensing. He heard something from one the cell on the right – Fazil's cell. A scuffling noise. A gasp. A thud. A groan.

He flattened himself against the wall and edged down the corridor silently.

There was a scraping noise.

He was perhaps ten feet from the door now, teeth gritted, trying to keep his courage, wondering if the face-to-face confrontation he'd had with an armed terrorist had sapped him of it.

Then a man appeared at the cell door, turning cautiously into the corridor, wearing a full face mask, a pistol fitted with a bulbous silencer in his hands, holding it up in front of his masked face.

Donaldson forgot all doubts about courage. He reacted as he'd been taught to.

In spite of the man's caution, he clearly hadn't expected anyone to be in the corridor and Donaldson's presence jarred him, but only briefly. However, that nanosecond of hesitation was the opportunity Donaldson needed. He launched himself low and hard into the man's torso, driving him back with the force of an American footballer. He forced all the breath out of the guy as the two men smashed against the wall. Donaldson reared up and knocked the gun out of the man's hand with his right forearm. It skittered across the floor.

But whilst he might well have knocked the wind out of him, the gunman was not beaten that easily. He came at Donaldson with a raging ferocity and the contest became a primal fight for survival. He hit hard, accurately; Donaldson responded, instantly aware the man was hard, dangerous and knew how to fight.

They rolled around the tight corridor.

The man landed a vicious punch on the side of Donaldson's head, sending a shockwave through his brain. He went blank and staggered away, but his senses returned almost immediately and he came back at the man with a growl of anger.

There was nothing heroic or beautiful about this contest.

Donaldson felt his nose go. Blood splashed. His fist connected with the man's cheekbone. It crunched and broke.

Then they were wrestling, rolling through the open cell door, chest to chest. Donaldson could smell the man's hot garlic breath, felt the man's knee jerking up, trying to connect with his balls and crush them. And suddenly the man was on top, straddling Donaldson's chest. His powerful gloved hands took a vice-like grip around his neck and squeezed as Donaldson squirmed desperately under him. His eyes bulged, his windpipe was being crushed.

Instead of trying to wrench his fingers free, Donaldson made a V-shape with his own arms and shot the point up between the man's arms, broke the grip, then chopped down on the man's neck with the hard sides of both hands. It was a powerful, double-edged karate-style chop that knocked the man to one side, giving Donaldson the chance to roll sideways – straight up against Fazil's dead body that lay along the cell floor behind the door. Like the desk sergeant, he'd been killed by a double-tap to the head and for an instant his and Donaldson's faces were inches apart, almost nose to nose, but the FBI agent didn't have time to be shocked.

The attacker was off him. Now he had to somehow regain the advantage by getting to his feet. He did this in a fluid, well-practised motion, rising before the other man could regain his senses.

He kicked him hard in the side of his head, knocking his face out of shape.

It was going to be over now.

Donaldson towered over him, a position from which he had never lost a fight.

Unless someone came up behind him and crashed a baton across the back of his head, sending him into brain-spin land. A searing pain shot across his head, fired down his spine, his legs went weak, he staggered, attempted to turn, but another blow to the head came from his new attacker. He slumped stupidly against the wall, trying to hold himself up, but he slithered down to on to his backside. His head lolled and his fuzzy vision looked at Fazil's dead eyes. Then his own eyes rolled upwards in their sockets and everything went black.

EIGHT

Henry had been in Blackpool public mortuary when he got the call from Karl Donaldson that afternoon.

'Who was that?'

He folded away his mobile phone, a thoughtful expression on his face, hidden when he replaced the surgical mask that covered his nose and mouth. He positioned himself behind the figure of Keira O'Connell who was standing by the body of the old man on the mortuary slab. The delayed PM had begun, the incision from neck to groin made and the body cavity opened out, the skin having been pared delicately away from the crushed ribcage.

The pathologist looked over her shoulder at Henry.

'A guy I know in the FBI, works down in London,' Henry said.

'Ooh, very sexy.'

'Mm, he really is a good-looking so and so.'

'From what I overheard, he was calling about this chap . . . does he think he knows who he is?'

'Yeah, I sent him a circulation and some dead body photos
. . . he does think he knows who he is,' Henry said tantalizingly.

'Don't keep me in suspense.'

'Could be a Mafia godfather.'

O'Connell had an electric saw with an oscillating safety blade
in her hand, the type used for cutting through bone.

'In Lancashire?'

'In the backwoods, you mean, where the natives have lazy
eyes and play the banjo really well?'

'Exactly.' She flicked the switch on the saw and the blade
vibrated.

'Not as ridiculous as you might think,' Henry said.

He didn't expand on the remark there and then, but it wasn't
so long ago that two men with strong Mafia connections and
suspected of murders had been arrested in Lancashire on behalf
of the police in Naples. He'd had no involvement in the arrests,
but knew that the Constabulary had some concerns about Mafia
linked individuals lying low in this corner of the world.

Henry had mixed feelings about Donaldson's call, though. If
the ID was correct, it meant, as Henry suspected anyway, this
was a professional execution and would be a far reaching investigation. That was an exciting prospect and he'd already had his
customary bum-twitch.

The flip side of the coin was that the chances of a successful
resolution in terms of arrests and prosecution would be more
difficult. Professional killers didn't usually hang around to get
caught, although this lot had hung around long enough to kill a
potential witness . . . so maybe they were still around, especially
if they thought there was another witness out there who remained
a threat. And if that was the case, Henry could not allow anything
to slow down the flow of the inquiry.

He stood back to allow a CSI videographer to get into a better
position to record the post-mortem as O'Connell busied herself
with the complexity of removing the old man's crushed ribcage.
It was a bit like removing pieces from a Roman mosaic.

Henry checked his watch: three p.m. Would that make it five
in Malta? he thought fleetingly, wondering what his old mate
Donaldson was up to in the Med. *Concentrate.* It was more than
likely he would be tied up in the mortuary for about the next five
or six hours, because it was planned to do Rory Costain's examination immediately after the old man and both would be fairly
long drawn-out tasks. As lead SIO, Henry had a responsibility

to be present, even if it tied him up for a considerable period of time. Had the case been less complex he might have delegated the job over to a deputy, but he realized he needed to know absolutely everything about these deaths. So while it went against his natural instinct – he would have preferred to be out and about – it was something that had to be done.

He settled down for a bit of a marathon, but that didn't mean he was unable to direct ops from the mortuary. He fished out his phone again and dialled directly to a number in the Intelligence Unit at HQ.

'Ullo,' came the sullen voice at the other end of the phone.

'Jerry, it's Henry Christie.'

'I know,' the detective constable replied. He could obviously see Henry's number on his phone display.

'Aren't you happy to hear from me?'

'Ecstatic.'

Henry chuckled, allowing Jerry Tope his moodiness, even though he was a mere DC and wasn't showing Henry any respect. He let him get away with it because Tope was a whizz at his job of intelligence analysis – and, unbeknown to many, also a super-duper computer hacker. The latter was a skill that had almost got him into hot water a few times, but it was something Henry was happy to use for the benefit of law and order.

'What can I do for you?'

'Firstly, as of this moment, you have been co-opted on to my murder squad. I want you to run the intelligence cell . . . I assume you know what I'm on about?'

'Yep.' Jerry knew all about the double murder in Blackpool. He was expecting a call from Henry and was only surprised it had taken him so long.

'First job . . . I want to give you a name and I want you to do some research on it. Then I'd like you to get across to Blackpool for seven tonight, ready to debrief the squad at eight thirty with what you've got.'

'Unph . . . fire away then.'

That done, Henry then called Alex Bent for any updates. Henry had appointed the DS as the Major Incident Room Manager so that nothing happened without Bent knowing. Henry had briefed the quickly assembled murder team at one that afternoon, and all the deployments of staff – controlled by Bent – had been based on the fast track actions that needed to be taken within the first twenty-four hours of an investigation. There was a wide range of headings for these enquiries, such as – identify suspects, exploit intelligence, scene forensics, witness search, victim enquiries, possible motives and others. Each had a pair of detectives working on them.

'Anything new?'

'Not as yet. How's the PM going?'

'Only just begun . . . but I have had an interesting phone call . . .' Henry related Karl Donaldson's news to him and he could hear the scratch of Bent's pen as he jotted down the details, then added that Jerry Tope was now doing some background. 'If this is the guy,' Henry said, 'we're probably looking for a basic flat somewhere near to where he was hit. What do they call it when Mafia members go to ground? Going to the blanket, or something? Can you get more uniforms into that area, if possible?'

'Will do.'

'Anything further on the missing witness?'

'No. I spoke to Billy Costain again, but he hasn't got anywhere as yet.'

'Right.' Henry sighed. 'Forensic links? Footwear? Dog shit? Hair and blood?'

'Nothing back yet . . . but if the information about the ID is correct, that gives us a tremendous boost, doesn't it? Will you just repeat the name again, so I've got it right?'

Henry did. 'Rosario Petrone. Got that?'

Mark Carter spent the day being chased by shadows. Everywhere he went he was followed. Suspicious, accusing eyes tracked his every move. No one was who they seemed. Everyone was a killer. Car drivers only stopped at zebras to watch him cross, so they could mow him down. Anyone with a collar turned up was a gun-toting assassin.

He moved through his usual haunts in the resort. The huge, impersonal amusement arcades, the cheap cafes, shops where he'd shoplifted on many occasions. He never stopped anywhere long, afraid if he did, they would move in on him.

He had never been more afraid in his life, at least for his own safety. It had been a different kind of terror when he'd found his sister dead from a drug OD on the kitchen floor. A different kind of horror when his brother came home bleeding after being shot by rival drug dealers.

He did not know what to do. Part of him wanted to go to the police. It was an option he spat out vehemently. The past had taught him to steer clear of the manipulative, self-serving bastards who cared only for arrests and fuck everyone else. They use you, they discard you and there is no way they can protect you.

He had to look after himself.

It took a full day of mulling over, but in the end he decided he would simply drop off the end and disappear. In Blackpool that would be easy enough. Thousands did it every year. He'd just be another statistic.

'I want to talk to you.'

Mark was in a cafe, sipping strong, sweet tea, making his mind up. And he'd committed the first cardinal sin of a fugitive. He'd lost focus, been consumed by his own thoughts and forgotten that he was a target. He looked up slowly at the young man in jeans and a sweatshirt.

Mark made to move, but the guy gripped his shoulder and sat him back down with firmness. Mark stared at the face. Was this the killer he'd seen? It wasn't. That man's face was imprinted on the hard drive of his mind, never to be erased.

But who was this?

'Who, me?' Mark sneered.

'Yeah.' The man flicked open an ID card quickly. There was a passport-sized photo on it and it all looked official. There could have been a Lancashire County Council logo on it. 'Truant patrol . . . I want your name, age, date of birth and name of school – and I want to know why you're not there, sonny.'

'I'm off sick.'

'You don't look ill to me . . . you need to come with me. My car's out back.'

Mark rose cautiously. Maybe the guy was who he said he was, maybe he was the killer's wheelman, the one who drove the Volvo that ran the old man down and had also tried to flatten Mark in the foot chase after Rory had been killed. Or maybe he was just a pervert preying on vulnerable kids. God knew there were loads in this town – pervs and kids.

As he stood, his fingers were still wrapped around his mug of tea. Without hesitation, Mark flung the tea into his face, almost a mugful of burning hot liquid that Mark had been tentatively sipping and blowing on. It went into the guy's face with a searing splash.

Mark did not even wait to see the result.

The man screamed, reeled back. Mark ducked and launched himself to one side. And ran.

* * *

It took four hours to complete the first post-mortem and even
then the paperwork wasn't done. It had been a gruelling job and
nothing was overlooked. Every little detail was systematically
recorded and commented on, but even so the result told Henry
no more than he already knew – just in greater detail.

Two bullets to the head causing massive brain trauma was put
down as the cause of death.

Massive internal trauma to the body consistent with having
been struck and then run over twice by a car was also recorded.
Injuries that would have been fatal without the coup de grace
of the bullets.

Henry looked at the old man's brain on the dissecting board.
It had been a horrible, grey, blood-mushed mess when O'Connell
had removed what was left of it from the shattered cranium,
the bullets having torn it to shreds. Now it was even worse after
she had sliced her way through it and managed to recover some
minute shards of the bullets.

'The internal injuries would have killed him, but he was alive
– just – when he was shot in the head,' O'Connell said. She
exhaled tiredly, eyed Henry. 'I want to leave Rory's PM until
the morning, now. I want to do him justice and I don't feel as
though that's possible at the moment.'

'Not a problem,' Henry said. He knew how she felt. Being
up all night, then working through the day with hardly any
sleep had drained them both. His mobile phone rang – as it
had been doing all afternoon. He answered it. Jerry Tope was
on the line saying he'd done Henry's bidding and was ready
with a PowerPoint presentation at Blackpool nick. Where was
Henry?

Henry checked his watch, not realizing the time – having had
so much fun, of course. He promised Jerry he would be at the
station soon. There was to be a murder squad debrief at eight
thirty and he didn't want to piss a lot of people off by being
late. Another call came through as soon as he ended the one to
Jerry. He glanced at O'Connell, who was watching him patiently.
He opened his mouth to say something, thought better of it and
answered the phone.

'Just for your information,' Alex Bent said. 'Two items.
Number one – there is a match between the hair and blood on
the old man's walking stick and Rory's hair and blood; secondly
the shoe print in the shit is also a match, so Rory was definitely
at the murder scene.'

'Rory is definitely tied to the old man,' Henry confirmed out loud for O'Connell's benefit, raising his eyebrows.

'Affirmative,' Bent said.

Henry thanked him and hung up. 'Now all we need to do is find out who was with Rory, then we could be on to a winner.'

'I'll get everything typed up, well, as much as I can within the next half hour, then I'll email it to you,' O'Connell promised.

'That would be good. Thanks for this afternoon and everything else.'

'Will you get chance for a drink later?' O'Connell asked.

He wavered. 'Er, probably. Have to see how the debrief goes and what all this new information throws up.'

'I'll be at home. Waiting.'

Henry turned to leave. His phone started to ring again. The caller display revealed it to be his wife, Kate.

On the short journey back to the police station, Henry assembled his thoughts as to how he would address the team of officers – detectives, uniformed, specialists and support staff – who had been brought into the enquiry. He hoped he wouldn't forget anything. On his arrival at the nick he abandoned his car in the underground car park, effectively blocking in two other cars, because he couldn't find anywhere else to park.

As he entered through the caged door that led through to the custody complex, two uniformed PCs were manhandling a reluctant prisoner in between them. He wasn't being violent, just uncooperative and obnoxious.

Henry held the gate for them and they nodded a thanks as they heaved the unwilling man between them.

'I tell you, I was not going to do anything,' the prisoner said haughtily, yanking his arm out one officer's grasp. 'We were simply going for a little walk, that's all. I wasn't going to hurt the little guy.'

Much to their credit, neither officer responded to this as, even from the short exchange Henry had picked up, it sounded as though this man was possibly a child molester caught in the act.

Having said that, one of the officers did propel him hard through the next door into the custody suite.

Henry caught a glimpse of the side of the prisoner's face. It looked red raw all the way across his cheek and chin, and extremely painful, as though he'd been scalded.

Then, they were gone, and in a few minutes the prisoner would be in the sausage machine that was Blackpool's custody system, just one of over twelve thousand prisoners passing through each year.

Henry clamped the door shut and made his way along the tight corridor and smacked the palm of his hand on the lift-call button.

'Oh yes, Fazil's definitely dead . . . hell, these Malts wouldn't know security if it jumped up and bit their asses.'

Karl Donaldson sat on one of the sunloungers on his hotel room balcony. With his left hand he held a bag of crushed ice, wrapped in a towel, on to the back of his head. In his right, the mobile phone was to his ear. He alternated holding the ice pack with picking up the triple measure of whisky he'd assembled from three miniatures in the hotel room minibar. Two Black Label and one Jack Daniel's. An unusual but effective mixture.

'I can't believe it. I'd only been gone a matter of minutes before I decided to turn around and speak to him again.' His head pounded from the blow he'd received, arcs of pain pumping out like circles in a pond. Fortunately, his nose hadn't been broken and the bleeding had been easily stemmed, although the two cotton wool balls jammed up his nostrils did make him look ridiculous.

'You're damned lucky you didn't buy it, too,' Don Barber said.

'Don't tell me.' He made a puzzled face, wondering why he hadn't 'bought it' as Barber succinctly termed it. 'Guess something musta spooked 'em and they were happy enough with Fazil.'

'How in hell did they get into the freakin' cop shop anyway?' Barber demanded yet again.

'Like I said, they're way behind with security over here – and that's where the accomplice came in – one of the gaolers. The desk sergeant obviously saw what was happening and got killed for his troubles.'

'How did they escape?'

'When they hit me, they went out through an emergency exit that's usually chained up, but wasn't in this case – they took the keys from the sergeant's key ring. Bastards.'

'Damn . . . and no video evidence?'

'None . . . the gaoler must've fixed that too, tampered with the recording equipment.'

'What a mess,' Barber said.

'Means we're running outta witnesses,' Donaldson said.

'Yeah . . . you're certain Fazil was the gun-dropper?'

'As can be.'

'Then he got what was coming to him . . . I know it ain't the perfect scenario, but there's some justice in it. And he wasn't coming across to you, was he?'

'But I'm still way behind the American,' Donaldson moaned.

'Fazil was a helluva good lead.'

'You'll get to him,' Barber reassured him. 'That's why I put you on him, because I know you'll nail him sooner or later.'

'Whatever . . .'

'Hey, don't sound so despairing. A bad man's bit the dust, let's not mourn,' Barber tried to sound upbeat. 'And you're still alive.'

'OK, OK, I get the message . . . ahh!' A jolt of pain crackled through his head. He took the ice pack off his head and took a mouthful of the whisky mix. There wasn't much left in the glass.

'What can you tell us about the killer?' Barber asked.

'Not much. Biggish guy, mask on, gloves on, overalls, I think, didn't even make the weapon, which seriously annoys me, other than it was revolver with a silencer, probably a .38, so no ejected shells. And he's probably got one sore face, because I managed to land a good one on him.' Donaldson thought he heard Barber sigh at the other end of the line. 'Sorry, Don?'

'Nothing, pal. You sure you're OK?'

'Positive. Heck of a sore head, that's all. And pissed off. I should've realized the danger, though, but I'm still trying to work out why Fazil was important enough to take such a risk to nail him. Real heavy stuff.'

'Shit like that happens. We deal with desperate people, Karl.'

'Oh God, do we!'

'What are your plans?'

'Ugh . . . tidy up here, make peace with the locals who are running around like headless chickens. Finish my statement for them, then I want to get back to Lancashire . . . see where, or if, Petrone's death fits into all this.'

'I can deploy someone else to that if you like?'

'No. I know them up there, especially the guy in charge of the investigation. We go way back and he always needs my help.'

'Only if you're up to it, but don't overdo it, OK? If it's eyeties versus eyeties, let's not get too involved, eh?'

'I hear ya.'

Their conversation ended. Donaldson groaned as he stood up, unsure whether it was injury or old age – or possibly a combination of both – and a lifetime of law enforcement. He stood by the balcony railings overlooking the harbour and noticed, peeking over the frosted glass panel separating his balcony from the next one, that the sliding doors into the room were open. Gentle jazz music filtered out. He edged along until he could see on to the balcony, also empty, although there were signs of recent activity on the lounger and table. An empty glass, a half-full bottle of wine, a paperback book, cigarettes and a lighter. Donaldson's eyes honed in on the cigarettes and something moved inside his chest. A yearning. He'd been a light smoker in his teens, but hadn't had a cigarette for many years and was very much against them – usually. But there and then, with a bad head, in a horrible situation, he found he had an irrational need for a cancer stick.

A movement caught his eye. He glanced up, moving his head a little too sharply, causing him to emit a muted howl.

Still clad in her bikini, the forward Scandinavian lady stepped out through her net curtains on to her balcony. There was a wry smile on her face.

'Spying on me now?' she admonished him. Then she saw he was holding the ice pack to his head. 'My, what happened to you?'

'Long story, ma'am,' he replied, quickly pulling the blood-soaked cotton wool out of his nostrils and dropping them on the floor. 'But I wonder if I could trouble you.' She regarded him with deep misgiving. 'I know, I know.' He held up a hand to reassure her he wasn't the sick pervert she thought he was after seeing the photographs on his laptop. 'I'd really love a cigarette. Been a bad day.'

'O-K,' she said unsurely, but took the pack, shuffled one out for him and one for her. They were Superkings and as he inhaled the smoke spread into his lungs with a deeply pleasurable sensation.

He exhaled deliciously. 'First one in twenty-five years.' He held the cigarette between his first and second fingers and pointed it at her. 'I'm not going off the wagon, though, even though this is absolutely wonderful and I thank you kindly, ma'am.'

She too was smoking and regarded him through a cloud of her own.

He took another deep draw and as he exhaled this time it was

with a growl of pleasure. Then he looked at his neighbour. 'Sorry
for freakin' y'all out earlier,' he said in his best Yankee drawl.

'Yes, I was freaked.'

'OK, understood. My name is Karl Donaldson and I'm an
FBI agent,' he said, not even beginning to understand why he
was telling her this, because he did not need to, nor should he
have done really. 'The photos you saw were of a dead guy, obviously, and I was asked if I could identify him.'

'You're an FBI agent,' she asked in disbelief.

'Really, I am.' He didn't wish to explain exactly what he did
in the Bureau because that made things complicated. Everyone
sort of understood the concept of an agent.

'What are you doing in Malta?'

'Interviewing a witness . . . that's where the bad day came in.'
He showed her the ice-packed towel, then tilted his head. 'Hit
on head . . . long story. See it, touch it.'

She reached across the partition and felt his scalp and the
quail egg-sized lump on it. Her fingers withdrew quickly.

'Ooh, the witness did not like you?'

'Something like that.' He took another drag, enjoyed it, then
said, 'I think that did the trick. And you are?' He knew she had
introduced herself at their previous encounter, but that hadn't
gone too well and he couldn't quite recall the name. Then it
clicked. 'Vanessa.'

'Vanessa Langstrum.'

'What are you doing in Malta?' he asked. The combination
of alcohol and cigarette smoke was having an effect on his social
skills. Normally, he was pretty shy and reticent with women, but
for some reason he wanted to talk to this one.

'I'm a photographer on assignment for a Scandinavian
woman's magazine.'

'Nice,' Donaldson said. He swayed slightly. Despite his bulk,
he wasn't too good at holding his drink. 'Care to step around
and maybe we could restart our relationship?' He gave her a
very childish smile.

The MIR was silent. The lights were lowered, the hush respectful
as DC Jerry Tope took centre stage at the front of the room. He
set up his laptop, wirelessly connected to the ceiling-hung data
projector. For a few seconds it looked as though technology was
going to let him down as the screen turned blue and the words
'NO INPUT DETECTED' came up.

He pressed a couple of buttons and the screen came to life
with the photograph of a man – short, grey-haired, sitting at
a street cafe, leaning across the table pointing at someone
who was out of shot. The man looked angry. In front of him
was a large cup of coffee and in his left hand was a walking
stick.

Tope positioned himself so that he could see his laptop screen
without having to crane his neck to look at the projector screen
behind him and the audience in front.

'Let me present our victim: Rosario Petrone,' he said. The
eyes of all the assembled officers flitted between the screen and
him. 'Although we have yet to have a formal ID, information
suggests that this is the man who was murdered last night in
Charnley Road. Comparison between the photographs of the
dead man and photographs I have acquired are pretty conclusive – plus, this.'

He pressed the enter button and the next slide came up.

'The photo you've just seen is one of a series of surveillance
shots taken by an anti-Mafia task force in Naples – and this is
a blow up of one section of that photo.'

And indeed it was. It showed, in quite good detail, Rosario's
left hand, his fingers gripping the walking stick. 'The head of
the walking stick in this shot is the same as the walking stick
found at the scene of the murder . . . so I have no doubt that
Petrone is our victim.'

He picked up the remote mouse and right-clicked. The next
slide came up – showing the first slide again of Petrone at the
cafe table. Tope held up the walking stick that had been found
at the scene, which, back from forensic analysis, was in a long,
thin plastic cover, just to emphasize his point.

'So, who is Rosario Petrone and why did he die?' he posed
the question dramatically. 'Why,' he went on, 'did the head of
one of the most ruthless Mafia families in Naples, otherwise
known as the Camorra Mafia, end up dead on a Blackpool street?'

Everyone sat and listened earnestly.

'But I'll come to that later,' Tope said, easing the tension in
the room, rather like the evil quizmaster with everyone in the
palm of his hand. 'First off, I think it might be useful to give
some background on the Camorra, so it'll give you an idea of
what we might be dealing with . . .'

The next slide was simply entitled 'Camorra' and had a series
of bullet points under it, which came in with the special audio

effect of gunfire, a simple device that seemed to please Tope no end. He spoke over the prompts.

'The Camorra is like the Mafia and is based in and around Naples in Italy. Its activities include drugs, protection rackets, smuggling people and goods and the production of high quality fake goods in factories in the area previously mentioned. Murder levels are horrendously high in the areas it operates in and to put that boast into perspective, the Camorra have been blamed for . . .' With a flourish he jerked the remote mouse at the screen and a figure '4' appeared thereon, accompanied by a gun shot, then three zeros – '0', '0', '0' – each with their own sound effect. 'Four thousand deaths in the last thirty years, mostly in that geographical region.' The next slide, mercifully appearing silently, showed a map of Italy with the Campania region highlighted.

'Da-da-daah!' one of the detectives in the audience said dramatically, causing a ripple of laughter.

Tope shot the offender a look of stern disapproval. 'Hm,' he muttered, not impressed. This was his show. 'Anyway, the Camorra have probably been in existence since the 1700s and they've always operated in a decentralized way, meaning their structure has always been flatter than the hierarchical structure of the main Mafia clans. Because of this, the Camorra clans are always at each other's throats, but they are more resilient when their top men are arrested, or go into hiding.

'The 1980s saw the number of clans increasing and today, if Wikipedia is to be believed, with over a hundred clans and over six thousand members, they outnumber the Sicilian Mafia. Rosario Petrone is – was – the head of one of the most ruthless clans of them all. No prizes for guessing its name . . . the Petrone clan.

'This lot produce fake luxury goods in their factories in Naples, they traffic thousands of people across the world each year, they control unions in Naples – particularly in public service facilities. They deal drugs, prostitution, money laundering and kidnapping. They are huge and are reckoned to turn over about a billion Euros each year . . .'

'Did you say a billion?' someone asked.

'Yeah, you heard right, a billion and, depending on the exchange rate, about eight to nine hundred million pounds – ish – every year. They are phenomenally rich and well organized.'

'So what was Petrone doing in Blackpool?'

'He was in hiding following a particularly brutal fallout

between clans, as a result of which it's believed about thirty people have been murdered in the last three years. Certainly a dozen have, and the figure may be as high as fifty. Lots of people just disappear and are often never found. Some have fled, like Petrone, others are encased in concrete or rotting on rubbish dumps . . . whatever.'

Henry Christie, watching and listening to all this at the back of the MIR, felt his arse twitch with excitement again. He loved it. Loved being in murder room briefings, loved setting off on the hunt for a killer. He knew it was the sort of thing he did well and the thought of having to hand it over to someone just because he was going on a short break made him sweat with frustration. Damn the holiday, he cursed inwardly.

'Let me take you back about three years,' Jerry Tope was saying at the front of the room. 'To a tale of jealousy, revenge and murder . . . and garbage.'

'I should apologize for my earlier forwardness,' she said. 'I was a little tipsy and a little annoyed, I suppose.'

'Annoyed?' Donaldson said. He and his neighbour were out on his balcony, sitting alongside each other on loungers. He was sipping a small beer from the minibar and she had a gin and tonic from the same source. Donaldson's supplies were sparse now.

'My boyfriend. He was supposed to be joining me but,' she shrugged, 'pressure of work, or so he says.'

'Where is he now?'

'In Sweden . . . probably being laid by the twenty-year-old tramp I caught him texting last week,' Vanessa said fiercely. She took a long drink of the G&T. 'So I was annoyed and I made a bit of a fool of myself because of my rocky relationship.'

'Ah, rocky. I know that.' Donaldson raised his glass to salute that intangible phrase.

'So I am sorry.'

'Apology accepted.'

'But.' She turned to him and despite his best intentions he could not keep his eyes off her cleavage. 'I would still like to fuck you . . . you know, now that we have ironed out our misunderstandings. I know you are an FBI agent, not a pervert. You know I was a bit mad, but I've had some sleep since then and my head is clear.'

Donaldson averted his eyes and squinted across the harbour.

Even in the extended trough that his relationship with his wife was foundering, he had never been unfaithful to her. He'd had the opportunity. Women at work. A very sexy female Cypriot detective he'd met – and that had been a very close run thing – but he'd always held back, hoping things would improve with Karen. A forlorn hope. Even though both had tried, it was a struggle.

His head turned.

Seconds later they had dragged each other through to the bedroom, wrestled each other out of what little clothing they wore and passionately attacked each other. But as Donaldson finally clambered above her, the fingernails of her left hand digging hard into his muscled backside, the fingers of her right curled around his hard cock, easing back the foreskin, and he was about to commit adultery, there was a loud, incessant knocking on the door.

'Jesus, not now,' she hissed.

The knocking persisted. A woman called his name.

'Shit,' he said, rolling off the bed and grabbing a hand towel that he could have hung on his full-to-bursting penis, holding it in front of him. He padded to the door and peered through the spyhole. The fisheye lens distorted the view, but he could still work out that two people were in the corridor, a man and a woman, in the uniform of the Maltese cops.

'Yes?' he shouted through the door.

'Mr Donaldson.' The woman leaned to the door. 'Could you open up?'

He sighed impatiently and opened it on the security latch. 'What is it?'

'Please could you accompany us?'

'Why, am I under arrest?'

'No, nothing like that . . . we . . . we've found the body of our colleague. He's been murdered.'

'That was good.' Henry congratulated Jerry Tope on his presentation. Tope nodded.

'I did my best. Is that everything?'

'For now, thanks, Jerry.' Henry was in one of the tiny offices off the MIR, leafing through a paper copy of Tope's PowerPoint. Tope gave Henry a nod and left.

Henry's eyes went to the slides giving some background to Rosario Petrone, head of the Petrone clan. Born in Naples in

1934, making him seventy-five years old, he had spent his entire
life in the gangs of the Camorra. His early years were mainly
running protection rackets and drug dealing, even in those days.
But as times moved on, people trafficking became profitable, as
did running factories making fake designer goods and taking a
stranglehold on the garbage disposal service in Naples. This latter
business didn't actually give a shit about how rubbish was
disposed of. Often lethal chemicals were simply dumped by road-
sides or burned, or tipped into streams causing dangerous water
and land pollution. But the Camorra-run businesses did it cheaply
and legitimate businesses were more than happy to use their
services. Petrone's empire flourished.

But there was always inter-clan rivalry. Shootings were
common. Ruthless scare tactics were regular – such as cutting
off victims' genitals and stuffing them into their mouths, from
which their tongues had already been cut. Petrone was believed
to have either killed or ordered the assassination of forty rivals.
Some were found with their heads blown off, others were burned
with the garbage, others were never found. There were times
when he was on the run from rival factions or the police or both,
although he was never successfully prosecuted for any of the
murders he was suspected of. The disappearance of vital witnesses
was usually the reason for his acquittals. About six years ago,
he was involved in a shooting incident in Naples when he took
a bullet in his side and survived. He was sixty-nine at the time
and the people believed to have winged him were found later,
dunked in a vat of hydrochloric acid one of his companies was
supposed to have disposed of.

About three years ago a very powerful rival clan, the Marinis,
decided to move in on Petrone's businesses. After a series of
unsuccessful negotiations, followed by brutal beatings on either
side, a Mafia war kicked off when Petrone, it was alleged, ordered
the murder of a Marini clan leader in Majorca. He brought in
an outside hit man to carry out the killing that also eliminated
two other Marini members. Collateral damage.

That was the beginning of a terrible campaign.

Ten more people were dead within three months.

Henry shook his head. And he thought Blackpool had its problems.

Things got too hot for old man Petrone, who certainly could
not realistically expect to survive another shooting, and he went
to ground and, according to Tope's research, had not been seen

in Naples for over a year. Until he turned up dead on my patch, Henry thought, and a silly lad got caught in the crossfire.

So Petrone got what he deserved, probably. Murdered on the orders of the head of a rival gang, Henry guessed. But Rory Costain did not deserve to die in such a way. This was not the streets of Naples. A seething anger spread through Henry at the thought. His mouth dried up. How dare that old man bring his violence to Lancashire? Henry knew it was his job to fight for the dead and there and then he realized that this murder enquiry was about seeking justice for Rory Costain, not Rosario Petrone who would probably have died by the bullet anyway. Rory Costain was who Henry would be fighting for and he resolved to bring the killers to justice, not least because he owed the Costain family something, as bad as they were.

'Hey.'

Henry looked up from the notes. 'Hey,' he said back to the individual who'd appeared at the office door. For a moment it felt like an exchange in an American sitcom where characters always seemed to greet each other with a cheery, 'Hey.'

It was Detective Inspector Rik Dean, Henry's old friend and prospective brother-in-law now that Rik and Henry's will o' the wisp sister Lisa were 'an item'. Lisa had turned up like a prodigal a short while ago when their mother had been taken ill. She had ended up in bed with Rik, the serial seducer whose motto was, 'Vulnerable is good'. At the time Lisa had been vulnerable to Rik's undoubted charms, but the two seemed to have weathered that storm and were now firmly in love with each other. Wedding bells were possibly in the offing. But, Henry thought cynically, that step would be one giant leap for mankind.

Henry knew that Rik, who was a DI at Blackpool, had been away on holiday with Lisa.

'How was Lanzarote?'

'Nice. Warm. Sunny,' Rik said entering the room.

'I quite like its barrenness for some reason,' Henry said. 'When did you get back?'

'Yesterday afternoon. Just landed back at work this evening.'

'Uh-huh.'

'Only just got the chance to come and see what was going on up here. Been going through all the crap, seeing what I have to do, etcetera.'

'Yup,' Henry said, wanting to get his head back round to Petrone.

'Been doing some paperwork – dealing with a few street robberies from last night that need following up. Had a bit of a chat with the victims on the phone.'

'Right, good,' Henry said, failing miserably in his attempt to feign interest. Rik was a good detective and he was angling to get him transferred on to FMIT, but it wasn't as easy as clicking fingers, even if you were a superintendent. Only the Chief Constable could do that, bless him.

'Quite interesting, actually,' Rik said mysteriously. 'I've also been down as second jockey on a preliminary interview with a guy who tried to abduct a young lad earlier today. He was posing as a school truant officer, fake ID, the business, then luring kids away for naughties.'

'I think I saw him being locked up.' Henry shuffled his papers, hoping that the great detective in front of him picked up on the bit of a clue to get lost.

'Two things,' Rik went on, grinning slyly, seeing Henry's growing impatience.

Henry regarded him stonily.

'Even earlier, the paedo-guy got a face full of hot tea from one of the teenagers he tried to bullshit into going with him for a wanking session. The description of that lad fits the description of one of the offenders from last night's two robberies. One took place in town, one just outside the nick on Bonny Street.'

'Rik, as interesting as this is, I'm kind of bogged down with a double murder.'

Rik grinned even wider and said, 'Connections, Henry. You're always bleating on about connections.'

'What is your fucking point?' Henry said.

'My point, sir,' he said mockingly, 'is that when Lisa and I got back from Lanza-grotty, we were still technically on holiday. So we decided to go out for a quick jar across at the Pump and Truncheon.'

'You really know how to treat a lady.'

'I do, actually . . . but the point is we only had an hour in there and we had a bit of a barney, and we were knackered from flying, so we left about nine-ish, and who should I spot strolling past the pub down Bonny Street as we came out arguing with each other?'

The hairs on Henry's nape moved. 'Go on.'

'None other than Rory Costain.'

Henry didn't speak. Just waited for Rik to come good.

'Obviously, I didn't really think about it then, but he must have gone down the road and literally bumped into his robbery victim . . .'

'A teenage girl,' Henry stated.

'And if I'm not mistaken, you had some dealings with her in the front office yesterday evening.'

'And another – a Goth.'

'Yup – two robbery victims, both attacked by the same lads I would say, from the offender descriptions, that is.'

Henry's mind flipped it all over. 'You said the description the paedo-guy gave you fitted the description of one of the offenders from last night? When did he get tea chucked at him?'

'This afternoon.'

'And you said you saw two lads walking past the Pump?'

'Yep.'

'Rik, very soon I'm going to pull rank and whup your sorry arse if you don't tell me everything, like now.'

'I saw Rory Costain.'

'And who else, dammit?'

'Your mate – Mark Carter.'

Henry was already rising to his feet. In his mind he heard the recording of the call made to alert the police to the body behind the shops. He thought he recognized it and now he could put a name to the voice. 'Grab your coat,' he said to Rik.

The body had been discovered by a strolling holiday maker, rolling to and fro in the gentle surf of Mellieha Bay, Malta's longest stretch of beach. Since the discovery some well-meaning civilians had dragged it from the water's edge before the police arrived.

Donaldson ducked under the cordon tape and went along the plastic walkway that had been unrolled to the body to ensure that everybody who had to, went on the same route there and back.

Lighting had been erected and the body was now hidden from view by windbreaks pushed into the sand. He was relatively impressed by the scene protection, but he doubted much would come from it.

He was allowed to view the body and recognized the corpse as the gaoler from the police station cells in Valletta. The one who had accompanied him on his visits to Fazil and who had now paid the price of corruption and collaboration. He had been shot to death, two to the head, two to the chest.

Donaldson did not need to spend long looking. He came quickly to his own conclusions about motive. Obviously, this simple man had colluded, had his palms crossed with silver, and then paid the price.

Witnesses were always better off dead.

He turned and walked slowly back to the police car that had brought him, glad as hell he hadn't had sex with a woman he didn't even know. It had seemed a good idea at the time, as most hare-brained things usually do, but he was relieved he hadn't gone all the way. Integrity intact – almost, he thought. He would sneak silently back to his room so as not to disturb her. He knew for certain the only woman for him was Karen, the only woman he wanted to make love to. He pulled out his mobile phone and as he sat in the back of the police car, he called her just to tell her how much he loved her.

Unfortunately, the call went straight through to answerphone.

NINE

Henry and Rik helped themselves to a set of keys for one of the CID cars and hurried down to the garage. Henry's Mondeo was still causing a potential obstruction so, ever the gent, he moved it somewhere less obstructive, then jumped into the battered Focus Rik was waiting in, revving an engine that pumped out clouds of unhealthy-looking blue smoke. Henry's intended jump into the passenger seat was interrupted by the necessity to scoop the scrunched up chip papers and an empty coke can into the footwell, before sitting down gingerly on stained upholstery that he hoped was drier than it appeared.

Despite the best intentions of everyone concerned, it was an impossible task to keep the interior of runabout cop cars clean. Their lifestyle just did not allow for it. Henry didn't comment, but his face showed displeasure.

Rik drove out of the car park on to the wild streets of the resort and Henry's excitement was not diminished despite the car's grotty interior. This was a major breakthrough in the investigation. A crucial witness.

He thought about Mark Carter, who he knew pretty well since being the detective who'd investigated the death of Mark's sister from an OD. A concoction of drugs traced back to the dealer – Mark's older brother, Jack. It had been a messy investigation and Henry had used Mark as a snout, an informant, along the way. The poor lad had ended up witnessing the murder of another young lad on the same piece of no-man's-land between the back of the shops and Song Thrush Way, aka Psycho Alley. A case of history repeating itself, Henry mused.

Henry knew Mark was a good lad, someone with dreams and ambitions and the intelligence to make something of his life, which then begged the question – what the hell was he doing hanging around with Rory Costain? And did he commit two quite violent robberies with him? And did he witness the old man's death and then Rory's?

'You sure it was Mark Carter?' Henry asked Rik, who threw the danny around a corner causing a plastic Fanta bottle to roll off the dashboard.

'I am.'

'And you think Mark and Rory committed two robberies?'

'Description fits with what I saw and what the victims say. Another thing might help prove it. The Goth had an imprint of a shoe on his face, y'know, in his make-up? I know you've got Rory's footwear, so it might be worth comparing the soles with the CSI photos of the Goth's face. From what the lad says, it's the one who fits Rory's description that stomped on him, even though the other one gave him a good whacking, too.'

Henry sighed. He looked out through the grubby window, smeared by hand prints, and watched the town whizz by. 'I expected better from Mark Carter.'

'I expected nothing else,' Rik said pragmatically. 'His mum's a drunk and a slapper, his brother's banged up for drug trafficking and his sister's a junkie corpse. Who can blame the little shit?'

Henry went hollow at Rik's words of reality. It was such a shame a lad of Mark's potential should hit the skids like this. And if he was witness to another two murders, the future looked very bleak psychologically for him, too. Henry could not even begin to imagine what the lad was going through. As well as the horror of reliving the events, he could be terrified he was next on the list.

'Why the hell hasn't he come forwards?' Henry demanded.

Rik sniggered. 'Because they don't. People like that don't. He might be shit scared, his shed might well have collapsed, but we're still the enemy. He won't trust us lot one iota.'

'No,' Henry said sullenly. And he, Henry Christie, had given Mark no reason to trust the cops. He'd used, then abandoned him after making some promises that were never kept. It was no wonder Mark would think twice about coming to the police. He'd been let down badly by them once. Henry went silent, his eyes defocusing as his mind turned inwards. He remained in that semi-catatonic state until Rik pulled on to Shoreside.

It was a decent enough night, no rain like the previous one and quite a few kids were milling about on the streets. A gang of six watched them drive past, immediately making the Focus as a plain cop car. Two stuck middle digits up at the detectives. Mouths opened and obscenities were shouted.

'Shits,' Rik observed.

'Abandoned kids,' Henry countered.

'Bollocks. Shite parents. No control.'

'No jobs, shit housing, no one cares,' Henry said bitterly.

'Jeez,' Rik said, staring at Henry's profile. 'You going soft in your old age?'

'And preyed on by people like the Costains,' Henry ranted.

'Shits,' Rik said again, closing the conversation.

They were glared at by more street hanging kids, but got by without incident. Police cars were often stoned on this estate. Then they were outside the Carter household on the edge of the estate. Lights were on, someone was at home.

'You want to take the back, just in case he does a runner?'

'Sure,' Rik said.

The detectives climbed out of the car, walked up the path and Rik peeled off between the side of the house and the outbuildings, positioning himself by the back door.

Henry gave him a few seconds to get settled, then knocked. From inside he could hear a TV blasting out. Curtains were drawn across the front window, so he couldn't see inside. He rapped more loudly and peered through the frosted glass of the UPVC front door, a replacement for the one shot up by an armed gang that had chased Mark's brother to ground here a couple of years earlier.

The lounge door opened, a figure approached the front door.

Mandy Carter, Mark's wayward mother opened the door.

'Hi, Mandy, remember me?'

'How could I forget?' She was in her early forties now, Henry guessed. She had close-cropped blonde hair, old watery eyes and a harsh, alcohol affected complexion that looked as though all her capillary vessels had burst just under the surface of her skin. This was a shame because she had been a pretty woman but the ravages of her lifestyle had taken an early toll on her. She was dressed in the bib of a local superstore and had obviously just returned from work. Henry knew she worked long hours, then played even longer. She pursed her lips. 'What's the little shit done now?' she pre-empted his question.

'I know you love him really.' Henry smirked. 'Is he in?'

She shrugged non-committally. 'Dunno, just landed home meself.' She cricked her neck and shouted, 'Mark', harshly. There was no response, so she upped the volume and yelled again. Still nothing. 'Guess not,' she said to Henry.

'Can I come in and check?'

She gave him a withering look. 'Got a warrant?'

Henry mirrored her expression until she dropped her defiant eyes and her shoulders slumped. She took a step back and angled herself to allow him inside. 'What the hell,' she moaned, 'you're coming in anyway.'

'Thanks Mandy.' He sidled past and stuck his head around the kitchen and living room doors. No Mark. Then he went upstairs into the bedroom he knew belonged to Mark. Not there, either, but he took a few extra moments to case the room. He noted Mark's brand new Xbox 360, the huge array of games for it, all very expensive. There was also a new laptop and a big, flat screen TV, as well as lots of clothes scattered around. Henry picked up a snazzy tee shirt and saw that the label was from an expensive high street store. Last time Henry had been in here all the equipment Mark owned was first generation PlayStation stuff, a knackered TV and certainly no computer. Mark had been immensely proud of his gear, all brought together by hard graft and saving money earned from his newspaper rounds. The stuff Henry was now looking at hadn't come from the few quid he got from stuffing papers into doors. There was at least two grand's worth of equipment here. Henry's mouth turned down disdainfully. Mark had gone up in the world.

He had a quick peek in the other two bedrooms, Mandy's and the one that had belonged to Mark's dead sister, Beth. Both were empty. Beth's was stripped and bare. He trotted back down to where Mandy was leaning against the front door jamb, blowing smoke out into the atmosphere.

'Didn't think he was in,' she said.

'Where will I find him?'

'No idea. He comes, he goes.'

'What's he up to, these days? Who's he knocking around with?'

She considered Henry with amusement. 'Why the hell are you asking me?'

'You're his mum,' Henry said, the inflexion rising in his voice. 'Mum's usually know things about their kids.'

'Not this one.' She exhaled a lungful of smoke that hung lazily around Henry's head. He guessed she wished she was blowing it up his ring piece.

'I need to speak to him urgently, Mandy. Have you got a mobile number for him?' He asked only in vague hope because he remembered that Mark had been one of the few kids who didn't have one of the evil devices. That situation could well have changed. Judging from the gear in his bedroom, Mark was probably now kitted out with a stolen one to match.

'Far as I know, he hasn't got one,' she said unhelpfully, 'but I'm not sure.' She sounded totally unconcerned about her son. Henry wanted to give her a slap. 'You going now?' she prompted him. 'I've got a busy evening.'

'I'll bet,' Henry said. 'When you see him, tell him to call me.' He flicked her one of his business cards. 'He knows my number, but here's a reminder.'

She picked it from between his fingers and made to close the door, almost shoving him out. Henry hesitated on the top step, then went to the side of the house and beckoned for Rik to join him.

As they drove away, Mark Carter emerged from the coal-hole and walked cautiously to the front corner of the house and watched the Focus disappear, proving that even the most experienced cops can overlook the obvious.

Mark jerked a middle finger at them.

'Frustrating, but he won't be far way,' Henry said to Rik, pulling his mobile phone out and answering it. It was Alex Bent.

'Boss, interesting new twist.'

'Fire away.'

'We've had the manager of a clothing and footwear shop on from the town centre, a shop called Lucio's, just a bit further up Church Street than the Winter Gardens, opposite side of the road.'

'I know it.' His daughters had bought stuff there.

'Well, the guy's the manager, not the owner, and he says that the owner comes in everyday and is always there at the end of the day when staff leave. Apparently, he stays on and leaves later.'

'Only he didn't turn up today,' Henry guessed.

'Spot on – and his description fits that of our dead man.'

'Would that also explain one or two of the keys in his possession?'

'It would.'

'Where is this manager guy now?'

'Still at the shop, stayed on himself for a stocktake.'

'OK, we're just leaving Shoreside . . . can you get hold of the keys from the old man's property and one of the photos of him from Jerry Tope's presentation and meet us at the shop. We'll be there in about five minutes.' Henry ended the call and turned to Rik. 'I love developments.' He rubbed his hands together exaggeratedly.

Karl Donaldson was dropped off outside the hotel, pausing at the entrance to inhale the night air. Walking through the foyer he decided against using the elevator and trotted up the stairs instead because he wanted to get silently to his room. He didn't want to advertise his return to his neighbour, wanted to get in quietly and get some sleep before tomorrow's early flight to Manchester.

This motive for a quiet approach was the only thing that saved his life.

He came up the stairs and paused on the penultimate step before turning into the corridor leading to his room. He checked the corridor before stepping into it and saw it was silent and empty.

Not realizing he was holding his breath, he exhaled with relief, and started to approach his room, four doors down on his left. He found himself tiptoeing like a cartoon character. He was pretty sure he could get in without disturbing her. After all, he'd been trained in silent approach tactics, and he saw it as a transference of skills to get into his hotel room avoiding a sexy woman as opposed to a terrorist or master criminal. He had his pass card ready, aware that slotting it into the reader would unlock the door with a loud click.

He reached the door, leaned back and looked slyly at Vanessa's door, and inserted his card when he heard the door behind him on the opposite side of the corridor being opened.

Nothing unusual in that.

The pass card turned on the green light with a click and a whirr.

Simple curiosity made him turn slightly to look at the guest emerging from the room opposite. He was about to smile at whoever came out. The door opened – and Donaldson once again came face to face with a masked man, the guy's face obliterated by a balaclava. There was a revolver in his hand – silenced as before. The same man he'd faced in the cell.

Donaldson computed that the man wasn't expecting to see him. There was that awful moment of dawning recognition. Just a fraction of a second. Almost nothing, but for Donaldson it was the moment that saved his life and exactly the moment his neighbour's door opened. Another distraction.

The guy's gun was down at his side and he was still partly obscured because he was still half behind the room door that he'd opened inwards with his left hand, which meant he was encumbered.

Then he started to react, to bring up the gun.

Donaldson spun one-eighty in that moment of hesitation and distraction and hurled himself across the corridor, a distance of maybe three metres.

The man realized his position, not the best from which to kill a man.

As the gun came up, Donaldson saw that although it would be a rushed shot it would probably hit him somewhere in the groin region, maybe taking out a testicle or two, or even a penis.

He ducked to his right and the man tried to follow him with the muzzle, but was still hampered by the door.

Vanessa screamed, the sound filling the corridor with horror.

The man had to take a step back to open the door and free himself from his disadvantageous position. At the same time, Donaldson realized that if the man were to get out, then he would be unable to defend himself, so he had to take the fight to him. All this went through Donaldson's mind as he ducked right, so he immediately weaved left and threw himself at the door with the intention of trapping the man behind it. He put all his weight into the manoeuvre and it worked, pinning him in the 'V' between door and wall, but ensuring that the man's hand was still free. That became Donaldson's target and he grabbed the man's right forearm with both hands and pounded it against the wall.

The gun discharged, the bullet driving into the ceiling right

above the two men. Then it went off again, but this time
Donaldson had managed to wrestle the man's arm down parallel
with the floor, and the bullet smashed into the patio doors at the
far end of the room, disintegrating them spectacularly.

Donaldson had the man's arm tight up against the wall.

The man fought back, heaving his weight against the door,
his whole body tensing with muscle as he forced the door back
against Donaldson.

Both of the FBI agent's hands went for the gun, trying to tear
it out of the man's grip, but the reaction to this took him by
surprise. The man simply opened his fingers and let the gun drop
to the floor, kicked it away into the room, and with a supreme
effort, tore his arm free of Donaldson's fingers, then put all his
power behind the door, keeping it there as a barrier between
them. He got himself into a better position like a man trying to
push a tractor and Donaldson, despite his undoubted strength,
felt himself being pushed backwards as the man, inch by inch,
managed to close and lock the door against Donaldson, who
roared with anger and pounded it with frustration.

Then he had a sudden thought and reeled away from the door
just as two bullets came through the wood at chest height. Had
he stayed where he was, beating a closed door, he would have
taken both in the heart.

Then another two shots ripped through at head height.

And the neighbour screamed again.

And in a parallel mind-thought, Donaldson was glad that
Vanessa had witnessed this. There was no way now she'd want
to have sex with him.

Having worked in Blackpool on and off for many years, Henry
was used to dealing with gay men. He hoped he always treated
them with courtesy, consideration and fairness. Most of the ones
he'd encountered were generally well balanced blokes with a
slightly effeminate touch, very unaffected and straightforward.
There were those, however, who were completely off the counter,
at the far end of the stereotypical scale and would have been
booed off stages.

'Well,' the manager of the clothing store known as Lucio's
said, clasping his hands together, 'the thing is this,' He spoke
with a slight lisp and a wave of the hand. 'I wasn't worried when
he didn't show up this morning, because he doesn't keep regular
hours, but when he didn't show up this afternoon I got a bit

concerned.' He pursed his lips, gave Henry a once up and down, did the same with Rik and liked what he saw, his eyes bulging at the sight. Rik reddened and tugged his collar. Henry smirked. The manager's lips pursed more tightly and could have even been a kiss. He tore his eyes from the younger of the two detectives and brought his attention back to Henry, who he clearly did not find attractive. Henry could see it in his eyes. Maybe he was just too rugged. 'Then I heard on the radio about the murder and even though there was no name mentioned, I got to thinking. The description sounded a bit like Mr Casarsa.' He shook his head. 'I mean, I've no reason to think it was Mr Casarsa,' – he pronounced the name as 'Cathartha' – 'but I was worried by his non-appearance so I called in, just in case.' He clasped his hands together again. 'I hope I haven't inconvenienced you.'

'No, Mr Gooden, you haven't,' Henry assured him.

They were in Lucio's. It had closed for business and they were on the shop floor, near the till by the front door. Henry glanced at the stock, the displays of footwear, clothing and jewellery. Most of it had names he recognized and it all looked good quality stuff. But Henry wondered . . .

Alex Bent hadn't arrived, but was expected soon.

Henry said, 'We haven't formally identified the dead man as yet, and I don't want to jump to any conclusions, but from the description you've given me it sounds like he could be the victim, this Mr Casarsa.'

Gooden looked deeply shocked and saddened. 'I'm mortified. Who could possibly want to kill him? He was such a nice, gentle man and so proud of this business. And I think he has more shops, too.'

Alex Bent's car drew up outside.

'Are the goods you sell genuine?' Henry asked out of the blue, fingering a ladies jacket on a rack. It had a very well known designer label.

'I have no reason to think otherwise.'

Henry nodded, but held back from asking any more questions. There were many that had to be posed.

Alex Bent came in.

'Oooh,' Gooden gasped and almost fainted, his legs buckling. He held himself up from falling over by gripping the counter. Neither Henry nor Rik dashed to his assistance. 'Oh my.' He held a hand on his forehead.

'What's the matter?' Henry asked.

'That . . . that . . .' He pointed weakly at one of the items Bent was holding in his hand.

'What?'

'The cane . . . the walking stick . . . it belongs to Mr Casarsa. I recognize it. Oh, poor, poor Mr Casarsa.'

Or, thought Henry, poor, poor Rosario Petrone, as he was better known to the police.

TEN

Henry treated the store manager to his nicest smile and said, 'This officer will look after all your needs.' He stressed the word 'all' and patted Rik Dean's shoulder. The DI's eyes drove daggers into Henry's heart and Henry gave him a wink. Mr Gooden adjusted himself primly on the interview room chair and smiled seductively at Rik, who squirmed. Henry then left the both of them in the interview room so they could get on with the task of getting a statement down from Gooden, who seemed only too pleased to be assisting the police with their enquiries. Henry started to make his way back up to the MIR up on the sixth floor.

Time had dragged. It was almost ten thirty p.m. Henry still had a lot to do before calling it a day and leaving the investigation in a suitable state for someone else to take over.

At the moment it all seemed very bitty and incoherent.

Two murders, both connected, one witness out there to both killings – probably.

One of the bodies, that of a Camorra Mafia chief who had been lying low in Blackpool; the other, an innocent boy, a rascal, maybe, who had seen too much. Henry churned it over, shuffling his thoughts into order with a view to then getting them down in the murder policy book, the record he was obliged to keep – supposedly contemporaneously – of the investigation as it unfolded. Then he had to call the detective superintendent who was going to take over the reins tomorrow and give him a heads up. Henry had been told who this would be and had no doubt that the man, one of his FMIT colleagues, would do a stand up job.

He stepped into the lift. As the doors closed his mobile rang, but as the steel plates came together and sealed him in, they sliced off the signal and Henry was unable to take the call from the Chief Constable.

Henry shrugged. The little fat bully would have to wait.

The lift clanked upwards and the doors reopened on the sixth floor. As he came out, his mobile chirped annoyingly. In the short space of time he'd been in the lift rising up through the building, he'd had two more missed calls, one from Kate, one from a number he didn't recognize.

He called Kate first, fearing her ire way above that of the Chief.

'Hi, babe,' he cooed, hoping he could soothe her savage bosom. It seemed such a long time since they'd had that morning quickie.

'Don't you 'hi, babe' me. Why the hell haven't you called me? We go away tomorrow in case you've forgotten.'

He held the phone away from his ear, cringed and resisted the temptation to get back in the lift. 'I haven't forgotten,' he simpered.

'Have you handed it all over to someone else, like you said you would?'

'Hon, I was just about to do that, honest.'

'I've packed for us both. Everything's ready. Money, passports, tickets.'

'Hey, you're a good gal,' he said. 'I should be home in an hour.'

'I won't hold my breath.' She hung up.

Henry screwed his face up at his phone. Carrying it in his hand with an almost crushing grip, he walked into the MIR in which Alex Bent was hard at work in an otherwise deserted room. The DS acknowledged the superintendent with a nod and a 'Boss', and Henry wandered into the office he'd claimed, seething at himself after Kate's call.

His desk was an array of sticky notes, reminders and 'call-me's', including one from Keira O'Connell, the Home Office pathologist, giving a landline and mobile number. He inspected it and muttered, 'Professor Baines, wherefore art thou?' wistfully. It was so much easier working with a male pathologist who had stuck out ears and who he didn't fancy the pants off. The time noted on the sticky was since he'd last seen O'Connell. For a moment Henry wondered if he could juggle getting the paperwork done, brief the superintendent who was taking over from him by phone, race over to O'Connell's house near Kirkham, fuck her, and get home before midnight. Then go on holiday tomorrow with Kate.

It was a serious consideration but then he laughed. Days, times, like that, were long gone. He screwed up the note and tossed it in the bin.

He opened the murder book and held his pen aloft.

His phone rang again: the Chief Constable.

As Henry thumbed the answer button, Alex Bent appeared at the office door, pulling on a jacket, eager to tell Henry something. Henry shushed him with a finger across his lips.

'Hello, sir.'

The Chief Constable, Robert Fanshaw-Bayley, known as FB to friends and enemies alike, had known Henry over twenty-five years. For some reason Henry had started calling him 'Bobby Big-nuts'. He couldn't explain why, but he'd said it once and it just seemed to fit. He would never say it to his face, of course, not if he wanted to live. Their relationship had begun when Henry was a mere PC working the crime car in Rossendale and FB was a lording-it-over-everyone DI back in the days when detective inspectors were ferocious Gods. Since those early days, FB had used Henry ruthlessly to achieve his own aims, then discarded him coldly when it suited. That said, Henry would not be in the position or rank he was if it wasn't for his involvement with FB, so the hate-hate relationship continued to this day.

'Do you never answer your phone?' the increasingly portly Chief whinged to his subordinate.

'I got cut off in the lift.'

'What's that a euphemism for?' FB asked, no amusement in his voice.

'Just losing the signal.'

'Anyway, you should've called me back immediately. I shouldn't be the one chasing you up, Henry. I'm the friggin' Chief Constable, after all.'

'Point well made, sir.' Henry watched Bent jigging excitedly at the door. He gave him a hang fire gesture.

'How is the murder inquiry going?' FB asked.

'Good. Things happening all the time.'

'I'm glad to hear that. You can give me a full update in the morning.'

'I'm handing over to Dave Cottam,' Henry said. 'He'll be i/c tomorrow.'

'Well, there's a thing,' FB said. Henry's heart sank. 'I take it

you haven't heard about the murder-suicide over in Burnley?'
FB said.

'No,' Henry replied cautiously, drawing out the single syllable.
His eyes narrowed.

'It's Dave Cottam's territory,' FB said, a fact Henry knew well.
There were four detective superintendents on FMIT and each had
a geographical area of responsibility. Henry's was the Fylde coast
and the northern part of the county. Cottam covered the east, the
other two central and south, but these divisions were often blurred.
No detective superintendent would refuse to cover a job just
because it happened off his allocated patch, because each of them
loved dealing with murders and other serious crimes. And they
always covered for each other in cases of leave, sickness and
other unavoidable commitments. However, Henry knew what
was coming: Dave Cottam was just as snowed under as he was
and to expect him to take on Henry's complicated double murder
and a murder-suicide would be a very big ask. 'I'm going on
holiday tomorrow,' Henry said firmly.

'Leave's for wussies,' FB said. 'There's no way you can go
away at this moment in time.'

'Boss, I'm going.' He stood his ground bravely.

'Cancel it – it's just a mini-break, as I understand.' FB's voice
was as cold as stone.

'And lose almost a grand? Don't think so.'

Silence came on the line.

'Boss?' Henry said. 'Let's put a chief inspector in – at least
until Dave Cottam can get free.'

'You need to think about what you're saying here, Henry,'
FB warned him. 'You're a superintendent now, and I put you
there.' The line clicked dead.

'Hell,' Henry uttered, looking at Alex Bent. 'I've just seriously pissed off the Chief.' He blew out his cheeks. 'What is it,
Alex?'

'Mark Carter . . . up on Shoreside.'

Before Alex could finish, Henry's phone rang again. He
answered it without thinking.

'Mr Christie, it's Billy Costain . . . I phoned you a few minutes
ago, you didn't answer, so I phoned your incident room and
spoke to that Bent guy.'

'What is it, Billy?' Henry rose from his desk, and closed the
murder book and put his pen away.

'You said you wanted me to find out who Rory was with?'

'Yep,' Henry said, not letting on that he now knew this fact.

'It's that little shit, Mark Carter – and I've got the little twat here in my hands . . .' In the background Henry heard scuffling sounds. 'You'd better hurry up, he's struggling to get away. I might have to punch his lights out.'

'Don't do that. Where are you?'

'Shoreside Drive, near the old shops on the square.'

'On my way.' Henry ended the call and didn't add, 'Oh, you mean the shops your family vandalized and destroyed?' He looked at Bent. 'What are we waiting for?' Henry picked up his personal radio and called into Blackpool comms, telling them to get patrols up on to Shoreside urgently.

Having watched the coppers leave his house after annoying his mother, Mark retreated back into the coal-hole where he'd stashed crisps, chocolate, some packed sandwiches and a bottle of Coke from an easy shoplifting venture earlier. He settled back into the blackness, which was warm and comforting, to wait until his mother left the house, as he knew she would. She was seeing a guy who owned a pub out on Preston New Road, and as soon as she'd showered and changed, she would be out on the razz.

It didn't take her long. The lure of booze and sex made her hurry. She didn't spend a lot of time getting tarted up, and she was teetering down the front path on her high heels within half an hour, as spruced up as she would ever be.

Mark sneaked into the house by the back door. He did not turn on any lights and moved furtively through the house and upstairs, where he had a hot shower in the dark and changed his clothes. Then he went into his mother's bedroom and helped himself to ten pounds from her secret stash tucked away at the back of one of her drawers. He let himself out of the house and moved through several adjoining back gardens before emerging on to one of the avenues.

He was famished, despite his food supply. It was intention to head to the KFC on Preston New Road for a boneless chicken feast.

Like most teenagers, he didn't really have any plans beyond the immediate, although he did try to think through his predicament. But it muzzed his brain, and he decided to leave those thoughts until he was in the restaurant and the southern fried chicken was making him feel a bit better.

He made it to KFC without a hitch, bought food and drink

and tucked himself behind a corner table from which he had a view over the restaurant and passing traffic on the road.

As unhealthy as it might have been, the hot, tasty chicken made him feel good again. He wolfed his meal down, then went back for a chicken burger that he munched at a less frantic rate, and tried to get a grip.

Fact – he'd witnessed two murders. The old man and Rory Costain. The images from both tumbled around his mind.

Fact – he'd got a damned good look at the old man's killer – and Rory had also managed to get off some shots of the guy on the stolen mobile phone that he'd then dropped as they legged it from the scene.

The killer had assumed the boys could identify him and that was why Rory had been killed and he, Mark, had narrowly escaped with his life thanks to a bag of hot chips and a meat pie.

At first, Mark had thought no one would know who he was, but that had been a mistake. The cops obviously knew – and if they knew, there was every chance the killer would if he had anything about him.

Suddenly he stopped eating the burger and placed it down on its wrapping. The horrific realization had taken away his appetite and he wasn't hungry any more. He now felt nauseous. His hand shook, he started to sweat and he was certain the whole world was staring at him, knowing his secret.

God, if only he could speak to Jack, his brother. But Jack was in jail for ten years, so that wasn't an option.

Then Mark knew what he had to do – and it certainly didn't involve the cops and being a witness.

Appetite returned, he finished the meal, drank his cola and left the restaurant. Hunched down in his hoodie, he flitted his way back to the estate, using short cuts and routes only kids would know, ending up back at his house. This time, in his mother's bedroom, he wasn't content to take a tenner, but took the whole amount of her hidden cash, just short of fifteen hundred pounds. He pocketed it, then in his bedroom he filled a rucksack with clothing and a spare pair of trainers, before going to the kitchen for a couple of packets of biscuits, crisps and some cheese from the fridge. He also found a rolled-up sleeping bag under the stairs.

He was in the house less than five minutes, going out the back again and making his way through the nooks and crannies of the estate, keeping low in the shadows, to Bradley's. He didn't dare knock on the front door of his friend's house, but sidled around to the back, scaring the life out of Bradley's mum who was working away in the kitchen, oblivious.

Still hooded, Mark tapped on the condensation streaked kitchen window. She looked up and Mark immediately saw her eyes widen with shock at the figure at the window. He quickly yanked off the hood to show his face. Her shoulders slumped with relief and she opened the back door, shaking her head.

'You scared me.'

'Sorry. Is Brad in?'

She regarded him suspiciously. 'Why? I thought you two weren't friends any more.' She knew of Mark's decline and wasn't best pleased to have him on the doorstep. Bradley was a good, honest, hard-working lad, as Mark had once been, but now she didn't want her son associating with him, even though deep down she quite liked him. She peered more closely at him. 'You don't look well.'

'I'm OK.'

'Right,' she said cynically, making the assumption his pallid complexion was a result of drug taking.

'So, is he in?'

She sighed, relented, allowed him inside. The aroma of her cooking almost knocked him out. It smelled wonderful. He knew she made a meat and potato pie to die for, and although he had just eaten Mark suddenly had a craving for it. Bradley's mum went to the kitchen door and called upstairs. 'Bradley, someone here to see you.' There was a muffled response, then a door closed and footsteps came downstairs.

When Bradley appeared, he was stunned to see Mark.

'What d'you want?'

'Just a chat. That all right?'

'What about? We're just going to have tea.'

Bradley's mother was back at the oven.

'Bit late, innit?' Mark commented.

'My mum and dad work late, and we always have tea together. You know that.'

Mark's nostrils flared at the thought of a family eating together. Neither concept, the family or eating together, was a part of Mark's life and he felt a surge of jealousy at Bradley's normal existence. 'I just want a few minutes,' Mark said, trying to keep a pleading tone out of his voice.

'Mum, how long before tea?'

'Ten minutes, love.'

Mark swallowed. His mother had never called him love. Bradley twitched his head and turned upstairs. Mark followed.

Bradley's room was cosy and decorated nicely, done by his dad. He had all mod cons, including the obligatory TV, Xbox and laptop, all bought and paid for. There was a small desk and office chair on which Brad sat, swivelled and motioned Mark to perch on the bed. He swung his rucksack and sleeping bag on to it, then sat.

'You off somewhere?' Brad sniggered.

'That's what I've come to tell you,' Mark said. He sat squarely on the bed, clasped his hands between his thighs. 'I know we've not been proper mates for a while, and I know it's all my fault. But I need to tell someone . . .'

Brad's eyebrows knitted together. 'Tell someone what?'

'I'm going, I'm leaving,' Mark blurted. He angled his face to Bradley's and said, 'I've witnessed two murders and I think I'm the next victim.'

'Shit,' Bradley said, stunned by Mark's story. At first he hadn't believed a word of it, thought it was just some fantasy playing out in Mark's increasingly convoluted mind. But as he spoke and Bradley linked it to what he'd heard on the news and at school, his bottom lip sagged even further and further. He snapped his mouth shut. 'You need to go to the cops, Mark.'

'No, effin' way.'

'They'll protect you.'

He shook his head derisively. 'They can't even protect old people from yobbos; how are they going to protect me from a killer?'

'We need to talk this through.' Bradley leapt from his chair. 'You fancy some food?'

'Eh?'

'I'll see if mum'll plate up a couple of dinners for us – meat and potato pie, peas, red cabbage. You know you love it.'

In spite of his earlier KFC, Mark almost salivated. He said yes please. Brad dashed out of the room and returned bearing two dinner plates crammed with steaming, heavenly smelling food. 'She always makes too much,' he said, putting the plates and cutlery from his pocket on the desk. He disappeared again, returning with brown sauce, salt and pepper, and two cans of Coke.

'Thanks, mate,' Mark said. He edged along the bed and wolfed the food down. It tasted superb. Simple but exquisite.

'What exactly are your plans?'

'Dunno exactly, but I couldn't tell you even if I knew. The fewer people who know, the better, if you get my drift?'

'Jesus, man,' Bradley uttered.

'But probably London. I can make a do there. Just disappear, y'know?'

Bradley shook his head.

'I can get a job. I'm a grafter, you know I am.'

'You were,' Bradley corrected him doubtfully. The two boys eyed each other. 'Despite everything in your life, you were.'

'I got a crap deal,' Mark whinged. 'Beth dying, Jack getting sent down . . . Mum . . .'

'I know.'

'How are you going on with Katie?'

Bradley screwed up his face. 'OK – ish. On the whole she'd rather be with you, I reckon,' he admitted wistfully. They were talking about Mark's ex-girlfriend who had ditched him unceremoniously when he'd started hanging around with Rory Costain and started going out with Bradley. It was a situation Brad obviously wasn't completely comfortable with. 'You lost a good 'un there,' Bradley said.

'Whatever . . . look, I need to be making tracks, mate. You are my pal and I know I've been a complete cock and I'm probably getting what I deserve, but I thought I'd just try and make it up to you a bit before I did a runner.'

Bradley's right hand shot out. Mark eyed it, confused. 'Shake, you tosser.'

The boys shook hands.

'Hey, look, this might help a bit.' Bradley stood up and took an old biscuit tin down from his bookshelf and prized it open. He pulled out a couple of ten-pound notes and offered them to Mark.

'What?'

'Take them. You'll need some dosh.'

'No, no, it's right. I've got some. I'll be OK.'

'Every bit helps. There's like three days' food here if you're careful . . . and you are my mate, Mark.'

Fighting back a tear, Mark took the money. 'I'll pay you back, honestly.'

'Yeah, you bloody will.'

Mark stood up and embraced Bradley, then Bradley said, 'Hey, if you're not in a rush, how about a game on the Xbox – *Call of Duty* or something? We haven't played for ages.'

'Uh, yeah, OK,' Mark said lugubriously.

Later, after an embarrassed thank you to Bradley's mother for the food, he was back out on the streets of the estate, planning to head to the railway station. He was going to jump a train to Preston, the nearest mainline station, and from there get on the first train through, north or south, Glasgow or London. He wasn't that bothered.

He jumped over a couple of backyard fences and emerged on to Shoreside Drive, aiming to cross that and go via the back streets into the town centre.

That was when the arm went around his throat.

'Got yu, yu little bugger.'

For a moment Mark expected to feel the muzzle of a gun at his head, to have his brains blown out, to die in the middle of the streets, never having achieved a damn thing in his life.

Instead, beer-loaded breath wafted into his face from Billy Costain's mouth.

'Cops're after you – an' so am I,' Costain growled. 'You were with my Rory when he got murdered, weren't you?'

Mark gagged. The crook of Costain's arm crushed his windpipe and he could not have answered if he'd wanted to. Costain bent Mark double in a chokehold and it was as if his head was trapped in one of those seaside exhibits where punters poked their faces out through some cartoon character or other. He gurgled. Costain held tight as Mark attempted to prise his head free – without success. Billy was a big, strong guy and he'd battled and held bigger brutes than Mark.

Without much of a problem, Costain fished out his mobile with his left hand and made the first of three calls to the police. The first was to Henry Christie, which the detective didn't get because he was in the lift. Costain had pre-programmed Henry's number and that of the MIR phone line into his mobile.

Mark continued to struggle valiantly, gouging and kicking, but old man Costain was impervious to his assaults and clung easily to the lad.

After he'd spoken to Alex Bent in the MIR, then to Henry, Mark had sagged with the effort of trying to escape. His energy drained out of him and he hung in the crook of Costain's arm like a bonfire night Guy.

*   *   *

Henry tutted at his PR, but held his tongue. Comms had told him there were no patrols available to make to Shoreside, all were busy. Sorry. There wasn't much Henry could say to that. If the town was lucky, there might be about four patrols out there firefighting, and Blackpool was a busy place for cops.

Bent screwed the CID Ford Focus through the gears and streets, and only a few minutes after leaving the cop shop he was turning on to Shoreside, then on to Shoreside Drive which was the main spine running through the estate.

Henry spotted Costain and the figure of Mark Carter about fifty metres ahead. Bent drew the CID car in alongside them. Both detectives climbed out, Henry with a triumphant grin on his face. He shone the beam of his penlight torch into Mark's face as he looked up from the headlock.

'It were only a matter of time before I caught him,' Costain said.

Henry put his hands on his knees and looked at Mark. 'Now then, young fella me lad, I'm going to ask Mr Costain to let you go free, OK? And if you even think of doing a runner, I'll flatten you. Got that?'

'Get this ugly git off me,' Mark growled.

'Only if you say you won't run.'

'I won't bloomin' run, OK.'

Henry raised his head to Costain and out of the corner of his eye he spotted a car cruising down the road towards them, but did not give it much credence. He gave Alex Bent a 'Grab him' gesture and the DS took hold of Mark's right arm. Costain slowly released his grip when he was certain that Bent had got hold of the lad.

'I found out who Rory was hanging about with,' Costain said, sticking a roll-up into his mouth and lighting up. 'Then it were just a matter of nabbin' him.' He chuckled. 'Make a good cop, me.' He inhaled then brew out acrid smoke.

'What d'you want me for?' Mark protested, still squirming in Bent's grasp. 'I've done nothing. This is not fair.'

Henry sighed. 'Fair? Fair is a place where you go to ride on rides, eat cotton candy and step in monkey shit, and, as corny as it sounds, Mark, you can do this the hard way or the easy way. Whichever you choose, you'll be coming with us.'

'Oh yeah?' Mark responded impertinently.

'Don't give me a hard time.' Henry wagged at finger at him. 'I need to talk to you about some serious crimes, don't I? Not least of which are two street robberies.' Henry gave him a pointed look.

'Don't know what you're talking about.'

'And the fact you've witnessed two murders, one being that of your mate, Rory.'

'Crap. Still don't know what you mean.'

The car that had been crawling along accelerated. Everyone's head jerked in its direction as the engine screamed.

It was a Volvo. With the passenger side nearest to the kerb.

Henry ingested it all in a split second.

The big car hurtling towards them. Two dark figures in the front seats, both bulky, definitely male, their features unrecognizable because of the main beam of the headlights putting them in shadow. And the man in the front passenger seat leaning out of the fully open window with the evil black shape of a Skorpion machine pistol in his hands, aimed at the foursome.

Henry, Mark, Bent and Costain were on the footpath, maybe ten metres ahead of where the CID car had been parked. Immediately behind them was a pair of semi-detached houses, both unoccupied and boarded-up.

Even then, a simultaneous thought in Henry's head said, 'Thank God for that. At least no residents will be caught in the shooting. No innocent person sat watching TV will get shot by accident.'

Henry knew they were about to be the victims of a drive-by shooting.

The car was closer now. It was a big, heavy estate, but no slouch. It was moving fast, now almost level with the CID car.

Henry twisted to Mark and Bent. With a yell, 'Get down, get down,' he powered into Mark, tearing him from Bent's grip and drove him over the edge of the low wall that formed the boundary of one of the boarded-up houses. He heard the rake of gunfire, saw the flicker of flame from the muzzle of the Skorpion as the two of them went head first over the wall.

He saw Bent drop like a stone where he was. In another thought he hoped his colleague hadn't been shot. But the same could not be said for old man Costain. He hadn't reacted, other than to jerk his head from side to side, wondering what the hell was happening, his roll-up still between his lips.

There was a second burst of fire, a quick 'Drrrrh' sound and a line of four bullets sliced across Costain's chest, flicking him like a demented puppet, driving him backwards.

Then a third burst. Henry kept Mark pinned down. The bullets ripped into the low wall that protected them and just above their heads. Henry felt them go by, their slipstream almost parting his thin hair. He knew that if the car stopped and the shooter got out, they would all be dead.

But the Volvo accelerated past and was gone.

Henry raised his head cautiously. He saw Alex Bent kneeling over Billy Costain. Henry crawled over the wall to them. Bent's face rose, terrified.

'He's dead,' the DS said, a wobble in his voice.

Henry bounced down on to his haunches. Costain had been wearing a white tee shirt, now soaked in blood. Amazingly, the cigarette was still wedged at the corner of his mouth, bent double but still lit, smoke rising from it. Henry removed it.

'Are you all right?' he asked Bent, who nodded.

Then Henry stood up and looked over the garden wall for Mark.

But the teenager wasn't there.

ELEVEN

'Yeah, yeah, I'm OK, Don.' Karl Donaldson paced the hotel balcony, his phone to his ear as he spoke to Don Barber, his boss. 'We musta surprised each other. I don't think he was expecting me and I got lucky and managed to trap him behind the hotel room door . . . yeah, an empty room opposite . . . no problem for a professional to get into . . . hmm, he's been a busy guy, first Fazil, then the cop, then me. I just got lucky, as I said.' Donaldson paused and listened. 'Yeah, the locals have got cops crawling everywhere, but I doubt if we'll see him again. No, I didn't get a look and no he didn't utter a word . . .' He looked out across the harbour, breathed in the warm night air. 'There's two cops outside in the corridor now, so I'll be fine . . . Yeah, still returning to the UK tomorrow, at least that's my plan . . . No, I'll do it, don't send anyone else. I'll liaise with the SIO up there . . . Yeah, the witness to Petrone's murder intrigues me. I've no doubt there'll be some connection with what's going on here . . . OK, Don, see ya pal.' He ended the call, breathed out, massaged his temples and mentally worked thorough his injuries. His head still had a lump on it the size of an egg and it throbbed, but the skin wasn't cut. His nose had stopped bleeding and wasn't broken, thank God. Other than that, just minor cuts and grazes. It could have been far worse. He'd left sports fields with nastier injuries.

'I need some of that.' He spun quickly. A very pale and shaken neighbour was standing unsteadily on the adjacent balcony. 'Something to ease the pressure.' She rubbed her own temples. 'You know what I mean?'

He gave a short laugh and realized that the incident had had quite the opposite effect on the woman than Donaldson had anticipated. Instead of wanting to get away from him, she needed comforting, to feel protected, to be wrapped up in someone's arms.

Donaldson had been about to phone Karen, but decided he needed something more immediate than the voice of his wife a time zone away, as harsh as that might seem.

He nodded. 'There's a helluva big bath in my room,' he said, 'and I don't know about you, but I need a long, hot soak, maybe accompanied by a glass of whisky. Maybe accompanied by you, too.'

Her eyes came alive.

He moved across and helped her to negotiate the frosted glass panel that divided the two balconies. She fell into his arms with a little squeak and a gasp as he caught her and pulled her to his chest. Her chin rested on his wide body and her eyes danced at him. She hugged him tight and his senses responded instantly with a surge of blood. She moaned as he bent to kiss her, then picked her up. She was light, easy to carry. He took her through to the bedroom and laid her gently on the unmade bed.

The soak, he thought, would have to wait. He tore off his tee shirt, and she unbuckled his belt skilfully and released him.

And in that different time zone, two hours behind Maltese time, Henry Christie, Senior Investigating Officer, was coordinating a third murder investigation with the help of the Force helicopter, Armed Response Vehicles, uniformed patrols, and trying to placate an irate wife.

'Look, honey, I'm really, really, really sorry . . .' The line went dead. He almost chucked the phone against the wall and he made a strangling motion with his hands, tightening on something.

'Henry,' came a commanding voice. At that moment Henry was facing the back wall of the office in the MIR. He spun to see the somewhat bedraggled figure of Lancashire Constabulary's chief constable filling the door widthways. Bobby Big-nuts, no less.

Grim faced, Henry greeted him. 'Boss.'

'You lost the witness,' FB accused him. His opening gambits were often confrontational and without preamble.

Henry could not stop himself glaring. 'At least he's still alive, and if he's still alive we have a good chance of bottoming this mess.'

'Mess being the operative word.'

Henry continued to glare.

'It looks like time we brought in New Scotland Yard,' FB teased him. The myth of bringing in 'the Yard' to help solve cases was just that. A myth perpetuated by second rate forties and fifties B-movies, but it cut like a dagger into Henry. 'Maybe this thing's beyond you,' FB went on nastily.

'Not long ago you were telling me I had to miss my holiday,' Henry started to fume, the Scotland Yard jibe really annoying him.

'That was before you got some poor bastard killed, even though the guy is no great loss to humanity.'

Henry ground his teeth. He was feeling just a little bit delicate. He could feel his head starting to shake as he spoke. 'Let me tell you what we're dealing with here, Bob. A hit man, or men, have taken out a Mafia godfather who was lying low on our patch. These killers have then murdered someone who witnessed their crime, and now they've tried to do the same to a second witness and in the crossfire have killed an innocent man, great loss to humanity or not. At the same time they almost killed me, one of my officers and the second witness. I – we – are lucky to be alive.' Henry's whole being churned at the words. He shook as he spoke. 'These are ruthless killers who will stop at nothing to remain free because they are frightened of being identified.'

'You still want to go on holiday?'

'Actually going on holiday sounds like a damned good option at this moment. And until some bastard took a pot shot at me, I would have gone away, believe me, Bob, I would've, whatever you said. But not now. Now it's stepped up a notch . . . and if you'll just excuse me.' He stood up and barged past the astonished chief, rushed into the corridor and headed to the nearest gents, where the combination of fear and anger bubbled up and made him throw up into a washbasin.

'Oh hell's teeth,' he said, looking at himself in the mirror over the washbasin after he'd emptied his guts. He washed away the vomit, then splashed his drained, exhausted face, and tried to get a measure of control over himself. He leaned on the basin with both hands and stared at his reflection, not liking what he saw. The harsh light in the gents made him look old and haggard. And afraid. He swore again.

The door opened behind him. Alex Bent stepped in.

'Alex,' Henry said.

'Boss?'

'You OK?'

'I just did that in the ladies, couldn't make it this far.' The DS looked as pale and sickly as Henry. It was one thing to be dispatched to a murder scene, something else completely to be part of one, and both men were emotionally screwed by their near brush with death. They regarded each other wordlessly and blew out their cheeks, and then it was done. There was work to do, killers to catch, and to get into any touchy-feely navel-gazing would only be counterproductive at that moment.

'Let's get a coffee, have a chat,' Henry said, 'and do a bit of hypothesizing – if there's such a word.'

'Coffee's filtering as we speak.'

They left the toilets and bumped into Rik Dean in the corridor, last seen taking a statement from the clothing store manager.

'Guys,' Rik said. He looked concerned. 'How you doing?'

'The bullets missed us, so we're OK,' Henry said bravely. 'Billy Costain wasn't so lucky.'

'I'm only glad I didn't go out with you,' Rik said. 'I'd no doubt be on a mortuary slab now. I take my life in my hands every time I go out on a job with you,' he said to Henry. This referred to the unlucky run he'd had in the past when he'd been stabbed once and shot twice, whilst Henry remained more or less unscathed.

'We're heading for a coffee. Join us?' Alex asked.

Rik waggled the sheets of paper he was holding. 'Yeah, and I'll go through the salient points of the shop manager's statement if you like.'

The coffee was good, dark, rich. Henry had it black, no sugar, and it hit the spot. He settled himself down in a chair opposite

Alex Bent's desk in the main CID office and rotated his neck to ease the massive tension in his muscles. He felt like a block of steel and desperately needed to wind down, but doubted if that luxury was something he'd get to enjoy.

Alex was behind the desk and Rik had pulled up another chair alongside Henry. The rest of the office was deserted.

From inside his jacket pocket, Henry's mobile vibrated as a text landed.

'One sec,' he said. Checking the phone he found the message was from Keira O'Connell. It read: 'IM STILL UP. COMPANY?' Henry's eyes narrowed, lips pursed thoughtfully as he speculated whether or not the pathologist was a rabbit-killer. The prospect of 'popping' around to see her was still very appealing, especially after the argument he'd just had with Kate, but he would only want O'Connell for one thing and wondered if that would be enough for her. If it wasn't, then he'd find himself with problems, not least having shagged a woman who knew how to dissect a human body with precision. He would also have to explain why she hadn't been turned out for Billy Costain's death. Henry had requested another pathologist be called instead. He deleted the message. 'OK, Rik, just run through what you've got first.'

'To be honest, not much. The shop was opened about twelve months ago, staff were taken on through a jobs agency and Mario Casarsa, as they knew him, was in charge. He did all the whole-sale buying, telling staff it was all genuine stuff at knock down prices because he claimed he had "contacts".' Rik emphasized the last word. 'No one questioned him, they did a good trade and he paid them slightly above the going rates. He was a good boss – apparently – but according to the manager, no one got close to him. And no one knew where he lived. His habit, usually, was to arrive mid morning and leave late. On the day he died, he did that and was still there when the staff left. The manager said he usually left around the nine o'clock mark, from what he knew. When he didn't show the morning after he wasn't too concerned, until he heard the radio later in the day and guessed it could have been Casarsa . . . Petrone.'

Henry scratched his head as he listened to Rik's exposition. 'So, it looks like he locked up and started to make his way home on foot. Two lads who wanted to rob him then accosted him?' Henry looked from one detective to the other. 'Yeah? Possibly? Which could account for Rory's hair on the walking stick.

Y'know, get back you little rascals, or I'll whack you, and then he did? And then he got run over and shot in front of them.'

'What I don't get,' Alex said, 'is why these guys are so intent on plugging witnesses.'

'Fear of identification,' Rik said,

'OK, I kind of get that, but even if Rory and Mark actually saw the killers, it was night-time, street lighting was pretty crap, there could have been obstructions, lots of movement, bad weather. Even the best witnesses would struggle in court, R. v. Turnbull and all that,' Alex said, referring to a stated case regarding the identification of suspects. 'Any good defence barrister would tear that evidence apart, and, *and*,' he went on excitedly, 'if the killers are Camorra hit men, surely all they need to do is disappear back to Naples and the chances are we'll never find them.'

Silence. All three detectives considered this.

'But supposing Rory and Mark got something better than just a view?' Alex suggested. 'Mobile phone? Digital camera?'

'Yeah, maybe they got photos or even a video of the murder,' Henry said. 'But no phone or camera was found on Rory, nor at the scene of his death, and Mark Carter, unless he's changed, which he may have done, was the only kid I know who didn't have a mobile.'

'But the two people who were robbed both had mobile phones stolen, so the lads could have used one or both of them,' Rik said.

'And that's why they're after the remaining witness,' Alex declared. 'Must be.'

Henry rubbed his very tired, unshaven face. His stubble felt like sandpaper. 'They want the phone and the witness.'

'And so do we,' Alex said.

'Something else bothers me,' Henry said. 'How did they know we'd be up on Shoreside, going to pick up Mark Carter? *How* did they know? They couldn't have just been cruising on the off-chance and got lucky, surely.'

'Channel scanning?' Alex suggested. 'There was a lot of stuff over the PR's about it. Comms not having anyone to send. What the job was. There was nothing guarded about our transmissions.'

'And why should they have been? These radios –' Henry picked up his PR and waggled it – 'are newfangled, state of the art, and we are assured that people can't listen in like they used to. I could listen to police transmissions on my dad's radio, once over. Now everything's supposed to be encrypted. The technology side of this worries me a bit.'

'What are you getting at, Henry?' Rik asked.

'I'm not sure,' he admitted, 'but if Petrone got whacked by a rival gang, are they organized and resourced enough to have scanners capable of listening to police radios in the UK?' He looked at his colleagues' fatigued faces. Neither man had any response to give, their brains now severely addled. 'Just something to think about, or maybe they did just get lucky.' He shrugged and wiped his eyes, pinched the bridge of his nose. 'Best thing we can do now is get some sleep. I think we've got most things covered for the moment, haven't we?' He looked expectantly at Alex Bent.

'Yeah – I've arranged for uniform to hit Mark Carter's house at four; British Transport Police have been contacted to keep an eye out for him at Blackpool railway station. All patrols have his details. The crime scene's been covered and secured. CSI and scientific support will be back at daybreak. Motorway patrols in the north-west are pulling every Volvo estate they spot. I have a couple of DCs coming on at six to kick things off. Think that's about it.'

'Right, let's get some sleep.' He checked his watch. 'And be back for a briefing at nine thirty, by which time we should have a team firing on all cylinders. Thanks for your effort, guys.'

Henry drove through the streets of the resort. They were litter strewn and a stiff breeze whipped around the alleyways, blowing torn newspapers and discarded burger packaging out into the main thoroughfares. He stopped at a junction, no others cars on the roads as yet, and looked at his mobile phone. He wished he hadn't deleted O'Connell's text now. Idiot, he chided himself for even thinking that he should have kept it. How could he possibly want to sleep with a pathologist? The thought of where her hands had been and what they'd done should have made him shiver with revulsion. But it did not. He turned left.

Eight o'clock next morning, Henry was at Manchester Airport to be the one who greeted Karl Donaldson. He sipped a strong Americano from a polystyrene cup and waited underneath the meeting-point board at terminal two, whilst keeping an eye on the flight arrivals monitor. The scrolling information told him the flight from Malta had landed and that passengers were now collecting their luggage. They began to filter out through the exit, suntanned individuals and couples. Eventually, the big Yank he proudly called his friend, even though he was totally envious of his looks, emerged with just hand luggage and a beaming smile, drawing secret looks from each and every woman in the vicinity.

Good-looking bastard, Henry thought uncharitably, standing his ground and allowing Donaldson's eyes to find him, which they did almost instantly. He approached Henry with a crooked smile, which Henry was certain was a rip-off of his own boyish grin, designed to weaken all female barriers. Not that Donaldson needed such ammunition. His all-American good looks, stature and general aura of naivety around woman were enough to lower the knickers off nuns. Only thing was, he didn't know he had it, that magical sex-factor.

'Henry, you son of a gun,' he smiled. 'I thought I was getting the monkey, not the organ grinder.'

'You have got the monkey – Bobby Big-nuts couldn't make it,' Henry joshed and the two men embraced in a manly way, of course. 'Let me take that.' Henry took Donaldson's hand luggage from him and the weight almost dislocated Henry's shoulder. 'Hell, what you got in here?'

'Just man stuff – and a laptop.'

Henry frowned at him as he noticed the American's battered appearance. 'You been in the wars?'

'Sort of . . . tell you later.'

They walked out of the airport side by side. Henry was a reasonably big man, six-two with the poundage to match, but Donaldson was at least two inches taller, wider at the shoulders, narrowing to a slim waist. Henry felt like the weedy younger brother and couldn't wait to get him into the car.

Henry had parked on the short-stay car park opposite the terminal, and after getting out and negotiating the increasingly complex series of roundabouts at the airport, he hit the motorway and relaxed a little.

He glanced at his friend who had now developed a frown that brought his eyebrows together.

'Something up, mate?'

'Mm.' Donaldson's mouth twisted.

'What?'

He was on the verge of saying something, but held back and shook his head. 'Nah, nothing.'

'I've fixed up for you to use Jenny's room,' Henry said, referring to the bedroom once inhabited by his eldest daughter. It
was now a guest room with a double bed and new furniture.
'Karen's coming up, I gather.'

Donaldson gulped. 'Yeah, thanks, matey,' he said, affecting
an English accent for the last word and trying to sound jolly.
Henry could see something behind the eyes.

'You two still going through a rocky patch?'

'Something like that.'

'Not serious, though?' Henry probed. He'd known Karl and
Karen for many years. Mostly their marriage had been solid,
happy. Two point four kids. Nice house within commuting
distance of London. Good jobs, probably the best part of two
hundred grand coming in. But the cracks had started to show
when Donaldson became obsessed with hunting down the terrorist
who almost killed him and Karen began to doubt his commitment to the family. Ultimatums had been made. On the face of
it, they seemed to have got their act together, but Henry knew
they weren't completely OK.

'Thing is,' Donaldson blurted. 'I've cheated on Karen.'

Henry almost collided with the central reservation.

Coffee again, this time from Costa situated inside the motorway
services at Charnock Richard on the M6. Two medium
Americanos carried carefully by Henry out to Donaldson, who
sat on the litter-strewn terrace overlooking the car park. Henry
had pulled in because he thought it was important to show a bit
of empathy to his friend. And, using the power of rank, he'd
called Alex Bent and told him to delay the morning briefing, get
everyone a brew and a bacon butty, then get them out on the
road, knocking on doors.

Donaldson eased the lid off the coffee and emptied two mini-
milk cartons into it, stirring with the wooden stick.

'Strangers in the fucking night,' he said, whirring the coffee
around and around. 'Fucking a stranger in the night,' he amended
the song title.

Henry sat down opposite.

'You know me, Henry,' Donaldson said plaintively. 'I'm a one-
girl guy. I'm loyal, like a freakin' puppy. I don't do infidelity.'

Henry muttered encouragingly. 'Mnhuh.'

'But I just couldn't help myself. Things are not exactly hunky-
dory at home. I don't think we've had sex for over a month

now . . .' Henry squirmed at the revelation and was about to interrupt, but Donaldson held up a hand. 'That's a hell of a long time, believe me. We're a once a night couple, me and Karen, seven nights a week, at it like hot knives.' Henry squirmed even more and winced at the image of his friends doing it. 'So when we don't do it, something's wrong. Problem is,' Donaldson concluded, 'I loved it doing it with a hot Scandinavian babe.'

'First things first, eh? See what you think.'

They'd reached Blackpool after a longish heart to heart about cheating, wives, lovers, relationships and adultery, both men finding it hard to express their feelings and were relieved to get back on the road.

At Henry's suggestion, the first task on the agenda was for Donaldson to have a look at a dead body on a slab, which meant going directly to the mortuary at Blackpool Victoria Hospital.

On entering, Henry spotted Keira O'Connell in the office. She saw him and rose from the desk, a confrontational look on her face.

Donaldson picked up on this and hissed, 'Not you too?'

'You know me so well. But no, not this time. I resisted temptation.'

'And that's what she's fuming at?'

'Probably.'

The two men approached her. Henry introduced Donaldson to her and they shook hands perfunctorily. 'He's come to have a look at Petrone's body.'

'Fine . . . Henry, can I see you? Inside? Alone? It's important.'

Henry followed her meekly into the office. She turned to him, arms folded under her bosom.

'Two things,' she began frostily. 'First off – another murder? You didn't call me out and yet it's more than likely to be connected to the other two. Why not? What about the chain of evidence? One pathologist carrying out all the related post-mortems would surely make evidential sense.'

'I thought it better to let you get some rest. I was just thinking of you. You're going to do Rory's PM today and I wanted you to be firing on all cylinders. The pathologist who turned out was more than capable.'

'As I said, I'm talking continuity of evidence here – and I think I should be the judge of whether or not I'm fit enough to do my job, don't you?'

'Point taken,' Henry conceded. 'I would like you to do the PM on Billy Costain, though.'

'And secondly,' she said as though she hadn't heard him, 'I sent you a text. I expected you to come around on a personal basis.' She arched her finely plucked eyebrows.

'I'm sorry. I'm very flattered. Old bloke like me, and all that, but I'm happily married, so it's not going to happen.' He pointed at her, then himself to make his point and shook his head. 'Sorry.'

She nodded begrudgingly.

Henry slid out the drawer on which the old man's body was lying, post-mortem. Donaldson inspected the face, then the old bullet wound. 'That's him – Rosario Petrone, one of Italy's most murderous Mafia dons.' He gazed over the body at Henry.

'You know, one thing's for certain pal,' Henry said. 'If Karen ever finds out you've been unfaithful to her, you can wave goodbye to your bollocks. She must never find out.' He waved an admonishing finger at his friend and said, 'No, no, no, no, no. No.'

Henry, Donaldson, Rik Dean and Alex Bent had commandeered the TV lounge adjacent to the top floor dining room at Blackpool police station. Out of the meagre FMIT budget (FMIT being one of those departments that expected divisions to fund their expenditure wherever possible) Henry had ordered more coffee, bacon sandwiches and toast, and the three English detectives gathered around to listen to what Donaldson had to say.

'We had an undercover agent, deep undercover, in the Marini clan of the Camorra Mafia who was basically killed on orders from Petrone at the beginning of a very violent dispute between two clans . . .' The door opened and a tray bearing wonderful smelling food and drink was wheeled in by one of the canteen staff. The detectives descended on the free food like hyenas on a dead wildebeest. 'The short story is that I was assigned to the task of trying to track down the hit man Petrone brought in for the kill, someone we know only as the American. Unfortunately . . .' Donaldson bit into a toasted sandwich and made a pleasurable grunt, 'I got shot doing something else, which kinda blocked my enquiries . . . however, I got better, but discovered no one else had got anywhere with tracking this guy down, so I got back on the case little by little. In the meantime, Petrone went to ground, no one knew where, but there was a lot of killing going on. Next,

I got information about the arrest of the guy suspected of providing the weapon for the American, a guy called Fazil. I went to Malta to interview him but before I could persuade him to come across, he got blown away in his cell, as did a Maltese sergeant and a constable. At the same time I heard Petrone had been found here – a bit unwell.'

'What are your conclusions, Karl?' Henry asked him.

He shrugged. 'That a rival gang has a hit squad operating and that they've taken out Fazil and Petrone and your witness. These guys don't give a shit about human life, they'll kill you as soon as look at you.'

Henry took a sip of even more coffee. 'How do you think they found out about Fazil being in custody and were able to operate so quickly?'

'That I don't know. We, the FBI, found out pretty quickly via Interpol, and I was there talking to Fazil within hours of the arrest.'

'They must have good communication and intelligence channels,' Alex volunteered.

Henry considered what Donaldson had said, feeling a great disquiet about it all. 'Just how good are those channels?' he posed.

'I'm not sure what you're getting at.' Donaldson said.

'Well,' he pursed his lips. 'Somehow they get to know about Fazil almost as quickly as you, which suggests their strategic comms must be of the highest order. Secondly, the more I think about it the less I'm convinced it was a coincidence that they turned up at the exact spot where one of my witnesses had been found. That means their tactical comms are also of the highest order. Does that sound like the Mafia to you?'

'They are very sophisticated,' Donaldson said. 'But I see where you're coming from.'

'I don't,' Alex said.

'Nor do I,' Rik seconded.

'What I'm saying is this: supposing we're not dealing with the Mafia, at least where Petrone and Fazil are concerned. Suppose we're dealing with an entirely different animal.'

'Such as?' Donaldson asked.

Henry gazed levelly at him. 'Long shot,' he admitted, 'but the baddies out there are pretty desperate to wipe out witnesses. I know the Mafia are too . . . but maybe we're actually dealing with someone, some people, some . . . body, who have a great deal to lose if they're identified.' Henry suddenly thought he sounded very lame and unconvincing. 'I don't know, but I aim to make sure we keep a very open mind on this. If we get tunnel vision and only look on Petrone's death as a gangland murder, then we could end up showing our arses.'

It was Donaldson's turn to regard Henry thoughtfully as they munched their bacon sandwiches.

'But our operational priority this morning is to find Mark Carter and that will be the thrust of the day,' Henry said. 'He could be the key to this and I don't want to lose him again. He must be found.'

Then, Henry became very tired. He checked his watch and thought back a few hours to the decision he'd made in the early hours as he drove through the streets of Blackpool – to go home instead of seeking solace and wallowing in self-pity between the breasts of a woman who wasn't his wife. It had been a very close run thing and he almost found himself banging down Keira O'Connell's front door. Instead he'd driven home and sneaked into the house. He'd needed to get a few hours' sleep for the day ahead and had hoped to use one of his daughters' rooms.

But Kate had heard him and, clad in a silky dressing gown, was waiting for him at the top of the stairs. Henry half expected to see curlers, a hair net and a rolling pin in her hand.

But as he looked up he saw the beautiful, understanding woman he'd been with for most of his adult life. She was slightly younger than him, but the gap could easily have been ten years. She still had a small frame, no excess fat on her, boobs he had often died and gone to heaven for. The landing light backlit her and Henry could make out her shapely outline through the thin material of her gown. He caught something in his throat as she came downstairs, the big, fluffy slippers making her look slightly comical. She stayed on the bottom step and almost came up to his height.

'I'm sorry,' she said.

'Me too.' He took her in his arms and they embraced warmly. Henry could smell her soap and scent, could feel the outline of her body against his, soft yet firm, making him realize how musty he reeked. He pushed her slightly away and looked into her eyes. 'Look, I know it's crap, but someone took a pot shot at me tonight, nearly killed two others and did kill the guy I'd been standing next to.' Kate nodded as he spoke, her eyes rimmed with moisture. 'I need to catch these guys and I don't want to have to hand it over to anyone else. I promise . . .'

His uttering was cut short by the placement of Kate's index finger on his lips. 'Shush.'

'And I need to be at Manchester airport at eight to pick up Karl.'

'I know. Karen rang. She's going to try and make it later.'

'I will make it up to you. Prom—'

Once again, the finger. 'You need a quick shower, then some sleep.' She took his hand and led him upstairs, her bottom coming level with his face on the way up. He couldn't resist – never could – placing his hands on her arse. 'And just to help you sleep, I'll fuck your brains out first, if that's OK?'

Her faced angled coquettishly towards him.

'It's the only way I will get some sleep.'

He grinned stupidly at the memory, his mind returning to the present.

The internal telephone next to the TV rang. Alex Bent picked it up impatiently. He listened, said a few yes's and his face began to go pale. He hung up slowly. All eyes were on him. 'That was comms. Patrols are at Mark Carter's home address . . .'

TWELVE

There was nothing subtle about the way in which Mandy Carter had died. She had been gaffer-taped to a dining chair in the middle of the kitchen floor, over the exact spot, Henry noticed, where her daughter Beth had died of a drugs overdose. Her ankles had been strapped to the front chair legs, her wrists to the back legs.

Then she had been tortured and beaten to death.

Henry stood at the kitchen door and surveyed the scene. She had been stripped down to her panties, but there was nothing sexual about this assault. Her head lolled pathetically on her chest, blood and liquid dribbling from her mouth, at such an angle that Henry wondered if her neck had been broken. The final, killing act.

Dressed in a crime scene suit, Henry stepped carefully into the room using the path decided on by the first officer at the scene, one that every person must now take. He walked around Mandy, carefully avoiding the blood splatters, and when he was in front of her, he eased himself slowly on to his haunches and gazed at her pulped face.

He looked at it for a long, long time.

It was an awful mess, her features beyond recognition.

He looked at her feet. They had been smashed flat. Then her shins, which had been broken probably by the force of a sledge-hammer, then her knees, pounded to nothing.

The fingers on both her hands had been snapped backwards. And her face destroyed. Henry's eyes took it all in. Then he stood up and left the room.

He ripped off the paper suit and boots, signed it back in, and the constable in charge of the comings and goings from the scene re-bagged it and dumped it in a container.

Rik Dean, Alex Bent and Karl Donaldson were outside the house and Henry approached them. They broke off the conversation they'd been having and waited with anticipation for the detective superintendent.

'I thought this place was being given a visit at four a.m?' he demanded of Bent. 'To try and catch Mark?'

'I checked, it was, but there was no reply.'

Henry emitted a muted grunt. 'Right – Rik, scene manager, please. The pathologist will be here soon. It's Keira O'Connell by the way. Alex, you continue as office manager and general dogsbody, please. Get a DC up here ASAP with some uniforms and get them knocking house-to-house. Somebody must have seen something.'

'We're pretty stretched,' Alex said. 'The scene's still being worked where Costain was shot and we've still got people at the scene of Rory's and Petrone's death. We're running out of monkeys.'

Henry nodded. 'I'll sort out the staff . . . but let's get things moving here, now, quickly.' He took a deep breath. 'Karl, let's go and hunt down a teenager.'

'What do you know about this kid?' Donaldson asked as he settled in the passenger seat of Henry's Mondeo. 'Is he a hoodie?'

Henry chuckled. 'Decent lad, crap upbringing, a wonder he hasn't taken the left-hand road before now. And none of this is helping keep him on the straight and narrow. But every cloud has a silver lining . . . at least because he and his mother didn't communicate, she couldn't tell anyone where he was.'

'And you think that' – Donaldson jerked his thumb – 'is why she was murdered?'

'I don't need anyone to tell me she was tortured, do you? And that's a rhetorical question.'

'OK, where are we going now, buddy?'

'They always go to their mates and girlfriends, don't they?'

'Is that rhetorical, too?'

Bradley wasn't at home, no one was, so Henry's next stop was Shoreside High School where Henry demanded an audience with the head teacher, a man called Stirzaker who Henry knew vaguely and who was only too willing to have a chat. A cop at Shoreside High was always welcome. He was a modern type of head, flashy suit, stubble, but very child orientated. He let Henry and Donaldson into his office where Henry explained the situation leaving out the gory bits.

'Let me see.' Stirzaker sat behind his desk and tapped the keyboard on his computer, checking the attendance register. 'No, Mark's not in. Not been in for four days now, so he's a cause for concern – educationally, that is. Computer's flagged him up for further attention today, actually.'

'Have you done anything about him so far?'

'Two phone contacts with mum – no help. Next up was a home visit from Mark's head of year. That'll probably be tomorrow, now.'

'Is Bradley Hamilton in?'

Stirzaker looked questioningly at Henry.

'He's Mark's best mate, isn't he?'

'You know a lot about Mark.'

'I dealt with his sister's death.'

'Ahh . . . that had a big effect on the lad. Let's see.' He checked the computer. 'Bradley's in.'

'We need to speak to him.'

'I'm not sure . . .' Stirzaker's voice tailed off.

'I'll come clean, Mr Stirzaker, Mark's mum isn't just dead, she's been murdered.'

'Do you suspect . . . ?'

'Mark? No. But we urgently need to find him, as you'll understand.'

'Poor, poor lad. I'll get Bradley.'

'We need to speak to him alone.'

Stirzaker looked uncertain, but Henry's stern face made the decision for him. 'And while you're at it, bring in Kate Bretherton, too. Mark's girlfriend, as I recall.'

Stirzaker checked the register again. 'That's odd, she's not in. Very unusual. Just one second.' He picked up the phone on his desk and dabbed in a number. 'Yes, it's me . . . Katie Bretherton? Not in today. Any idea why? Any phone call from the parents? Nothing. How odd. Thanks.' He hung up and said, 'Reception – all absences should be reported to there, but nothing in Katie's case. Very odd. She's one of our star pupils, a real achiever, never sick.'

'OK, wheel in Bradley, then, please,' Henry said.

'Now then Bradley,' said Henry after introducing himself and Donaldson, though the fact that Karl was an FBI employee seemed to fly over the lad's head. He had been seated in one of the comfy chairs in Strizaker's office, whilst Henry perched the cheek of his bum on the corner of the desk and Donaldson lounged by the door.

The young lad's eyes darted from one man to the other, clearly frightened and intimidated – just as Henry liked 'em.

He smiled ingratiatingly and said, 'I know we haven't met before, but I do know you're Mark Carter's best friend.'

'Was,' Bradley corrected him.

'Whatever . . . fact is, you know Mark well, don't you?'

'Look, am I in the shit, or something?' Bradley reared. 'Cos if I am you need to arrest me and caution me, and I need an appropriate adult present. I know my rights. I do Citizenship, you know.'

'Let's just forget that little outburst, shall we? Hm?' Henry jiggled his eyebrows. 'Mark came to see you last night, didn't he?'

'No,' Bradley sneered.

'I'll go and ask your mum the same question, shall I?'

'No,' Bradley blurted. 'Yeah, he came – so what?'

'Bradley, you seem like a decent lad, so let's drop the attitude, OK?' Henry knew he sounded patronizing, but he was past caring. 'What did he want? What did he say? And where can I find him?'

'So I'm not in trouble?'

'No, but Mark is, and not from the cops.'

'He told me what had happened, the old man and Rory, and that somebody'd tried to run him down, too.'

Henry hadn't heard about that, but he let it go for the moment.

'He said whoever'd killed the old guy was after him, too, and he wasn't safe in town, so he was going to run, go to London, he said. Then he went.'

'Did you hear about last night's shooting?'

'On the estate, yeah, course. Kids doing a drive-by. Not really news any more.'

'Wrong . . . men attempting to kill Mark and killing an innocent person instead.'

Bradley faded to ashen. 'Is Mark OK?'

'He did a runner, but Billy Costain is dead.'

'Oh my God.'

'I need to find Mark, I need to protect him.'

'He said you couldn't. He doesn't trust you.'

'That doesn't change anything. There's no way on earth he can protect himself. Has he got a mobile phone yet?'

'Nah, he just doesn't like them.'

'You've been no great help.'

'Well what do you expect? All I did was give him something to eat, a bit of cash, and then he went. Last I saw of him. I went to bed, y'know?'

There was a knock on the door. Donaldson opened it to find the head teacher, Stirzaker, there, hopping about worriedly. 'I thought you should know. It's about Katie Bretherton. I've just spoken to her mum. Apparently, she did set off for school this morning as usual.'

Mark had landed hard under Henry Christie's body as the detective shoved him over the garden wall just a second before the bullets started flying. Mark had seen the car approaching, like some terrible bug in a sci-fi movie, and he'd recognized its outline immediately – because he'd seen it before when it had tried to flatten him just after Rory had been murdered.

The breath went out of him under the detective's crushing weight and everything became a visual blur.

He heard the dull firing of the automatic weapon, then saw the slow-motion dance of Billy Costain under the street lights as the slugs ripped into him and tore open his chest.

Then Christie's weight came off as Henry peered over the wall, at which point Mark took his chance. Scooping up his sleeping bag, he rolled away, up on to his feet, running hard down the side of the unoccupied house without a backward glance. He realized that distance was the most important thing for him at that moment in time.

So he ran. Vaulted fences, stumbled blindly through gardens. Powered across roads without looking until he was on the complete opposite side of the estate, where he stopped, then walked casually up someone's footpath, down the side of the house and into darkness where he slumped down exhausted and tried to control his breathing.

Eventually, his heart rate subsided and he found he was sitting by the side of a garden shed in someone's back garden. He crept to check the back of the house. Lights were still on and a TV blared loudly in the living room at the front. He sneaked back to the shed and tried the door. Locked. He tugged at it and it rattled in its frame. Not very secure, but Mark was no burglar, knowing nothing about locks. He could ease the tips of his fingers inside the door, which he pulled back. He paused, took a look around, then braced himself and pulled hard. The hasp and lock came away from its mounting, the tiny screws ripping out of the wood.

He went rigid, expecting the householder to appear with a machete. Thirty seconds passed. All he could hear were the sounds of the night and police and ambulance sirens in the distance.

He stepped into the shed and pulled the door closed, hoping it would not sag open. It stayed closed.

It was a fairly big shed with all the usual gardening equipment. Mark made out a set of four folded-up patio chairs stacked next to an old mountain bike. He took one and eased it open. There was just enough floor space in the shed for him to place it down and sit on it.

He leaned forwards, hands clasped between his knees, then started to cry.

He'd folded the chair away, unrolled his sleeping bag and curled up inside it in the space on the shed floor where the chair had been. It was warm and almost pleasant, smelling of wood and humus, and he'd slept well for a few hours before waking up desperate for the toilet. At first he did not want to move. The floor was hard but he was comfortable and it felt safe. But he had to. Dawn was approaching and he could see light around the edges of the door. He had to be gone before the household came to life.

His bones creaked as he moved, having been in the same foetal position all night. He rolled up the sleeping bag tightly, then took a careful look through the crack in the door at the house, now in darkness. As silently as he could he opened the door and manoeuvred the old, heavy mountain bike out and propped it up against the side of the house.

He needed the toilet, could not wait. Not wanting to take the chance of being spotted by an early rising neighbour, he crept back into the shed, dropped his trousers and did what he had to do, apologizing silently for the mess someone would find in due course. He wiped his arse with an oily rag, dropped it on to his excrement and smiled proudly. There was a lot of it.

Then he was out, riding the bike away.

Shitting and thieving, boy, great start to the day, he thought.

Next he needed some food, so he pedalled furiously to the twenty-four-hour McDonald's on Preston New Road, opposite the KFC where he'd eaten the evening before, and cycled into the drive-thru. He bought a breakfast with orange juice, then hid around the back and scoffed the meal behind two huge metal trash cans.

It was almost seven – he'd seen a clock on the wall of the drive-thru – and he had to keep hidden for about an hour and a half before he could see the next person he had to talk to.

Katie Bretherton was now sixteen and evolving into a beautiful, willowy young woman. She had good brains, good ambitions and up until about six months ago, had been Mark Carter's girl-friend. She'd stuck with him through his sister's death and his brother's jail term, and for a long period of time after that she and Mark had a wonderful time together. They had been good mates to begin with. This had become a 'relationship' and they'd discovered sex together.

But Mark had slowly evolved. His relationship with his mother got even worse, he had no male role model to look up to, and although Katie tried to keep him on a leash she sensed he was drifting away from her, becoming wild. When he struck up a friendship with Rory Costain, she cut Mark loose. There was only one direction to go by hanging around with a Costain and that was spectacularly downwards. Notwithstanding her pleas, Mark did not listen.

That morning, as usual, she set off for school from her house on the opposite side of Preston New Road, the posh side, where she lived with her very functional family. Mum, Dad, brother, sister, dog, cat, two cars.

Mark Carter was a long way from her mind. She was looking forward to a day at school, including English, French and PE, her favourite subjects, and she excelled in them all. At her age and year, school uniform was optional, but she usually chose to wear it for most of the week, but not today. She and some mates planned to go into town after school, so she was dressed in a tiny skirt and a blouse.

She kissed her mum, patted the cat, kissed the dog – who licked her face sloppily – then she was on her way.

Mark knew her route to school well. Indeed he had walked with her there and back on many occasions. He knew she had to walk from her house to the underpass that ran under the main road, so that kids could avoid the heavy, dangerous traffic on the dual carriageway. It was a well-lit facility and well used, but it was the best place for Mark to confront her.

From the cover of a hedge, he watched her walk on to the slope leading to the underpass, then came up behind her on the stolen bike. He whizzed past and swerved in front of her, trapping her between the underpass wall and the bike.

'I need to talk to you.'

She eyed him angrily. 'You're in my way.'

'I know. Like I said, I want to talk to you.'

'Don't think so.' She started to back out of the trap.

'Katie – please.'

'Mark, I've said all I need to say to you. You want to hang about with Rory Costain, that's fine. Just don't include me—'

'Rory's dead. You must have heard.'

'What?' Her face screwed up.

'He was murdered – and I was there.'

'No surprise, then.'

'Katie – I was fucking there!'

'I'd heard some lad got shot,' she admitted, 'but I'm not interested. That world' – she pointed in the direction of Shoreside – 'has nothing to do with me. And even though you live on the estate, it had nothing to do with you, either – or so I thought. It's all about choices, Mark.'

'OK, fine, whatever . . . but I just want to tell you they're after me, the people who did it, and I'm leaving for good. I have to get out of town. I wanted to tell you.'

'Mark, you live in a dream world, guns 'n' robbers. You're pathetic. I can't actually believe we were ever together. I mean, look at you. You're a mess.'

'They killed Rory's dad last night – Billy Costain. They were trying to get me.'

'I don't believe you.'

'Check the news, I'm sure it'll be on – but of course you

don't listen to the news, do you? It's all friggin' *Mamma Mia* and *Strictly Come Dancing* to you, isn't it?' Mark kept his voice low but harsh. People were passing. Other kids on their way to school. Adults, too.

'I'm not interested in being a lout, Mark. Nor were you.'

'OK, I should've guessed you'd piss me off. I just wanted to tell you I was going and ask for a bit of help, that's all.'

'Mark, we're not even mates any more.' She shook her head sadly, wishing the opposite were true.

'But I still love you,' he blurted. His bottom lip began to wobble and big tears formed in his eyes.

She grabbed his arm. 'Don't be embarrassing.'

'Sorry, sorry,' he blubbered. 'Let's go somewhere – please.' She shook her head as if this was madness, in two minds as to what to do. A big part of her said dump him and walk away. The other part knew she still really liked him and that, underneath it all, he was a good guy.

She led him back up the slope, away from the underpass, on to her estate. The little row of shops on this estate was thriving, unlike its counterpart on Shoreside. A newsagent, hairdresser and a small bakery in which was a tiny area set aside as a cafe, about ten seats. It was here she took Mark, sat him down and ordered a couple of Cokes.

Then, with growing horror, she listened to his story, snippets of which she had heard on the news and from friends, never realizing Mark was in any way involved.

'To me, and anyone else with a brain, the answer's simple. Go to the police. You haven't done anything wrong, except rob three people.' She pulled a disapproving face at this. 'They'll protect you, it's their job. Speak to that Christie guy, the one who dealt with Beth . . .'

Mark was already shaking his head. 'No, he's a twat, they're all twats,' he spat.

'Stop swearing,' Katie admonished him with a hoarse whisper, looking around embarrassed.

'OK, OK. I'm going. I just wanted to let you know, that's all.'

'Why?'

'You know. Sorry I was a dickhead. I just wanted to let you know before I left.'

'Have you seen Bradley?'

'Yeah.' Mark ran the back of his hand under his nose. 'I let him know.'

Katie sat back and regarded him, her mouth tight.

'Look, will you do me one last favour?' he asked.

She sighed. 'Depends.'

'Use your phone, call me a taxi to take me to Preston railway station.'

'Why not Blackpool? It'll cost a fortune to get to Preston.'

'They'll be on the lookout for me around here.'

'Mark – who's they?'

'Cops, crims, killers . . . everyone. I've got enough to pay for the taxi. Preston's on the mainline, so I can go anywhere from there.'

'And what will you do?'

'I haven't worked that one out yet.'

'Have you spoken to your mum about this?'

'That bitch.'

'She's still your mum.'

'Sod her, I'm going and that's that.' He looked longingly at Katie. She was very, very pretty. 'Will you come to the station with me and say goodbye?'

And although her senses told her no, the fact was that she was still a young, romantic lass, still in love with Mark, and what could be more beautiful than saying a tearful goodbye on a cold railway platform? It was an offer her immature mind could not refuse.

Despite the time of day, busy for taxi drivers, one arrived in ten minutes, lured by the length of the journey and its earning potential. But when the lady driver saw her fares, she balked.

'You sure you have enough money?' she sneered at the kids.

Angrily Mark almost stuffed the roll of notes he'd stolen from his mother into her face. 'Does that look enough?'

'Yeah, OK, just asking,' she said defensively.

The two teenagers got into the back and their twenty-mile journey began.

At first they were silent, engrossed in their thoughts.

'My mum'll kill me if she finds out about this,' Katie said.

'Why should she?'

'Cos the school will phone her up eventually when they realize I'm not there.'

'Oh, yeah, that's what they do, isn't it? I think they've given up on me.'

'You fool, Mark, you bloody fool,' Katie said almost in the style of one of the heroine's she had just been reading about in an Austen novel.

Next thing, the two were in a clinch. Their teeth clashed, their lips mashed together and groans of ecstasy emanated from their throats. The taxi driver saw the embrace in the rear view mirror and gave them an 'Oi'.

They disengaged. Katie looked seductively at Mark and he looked lustily at her, feeling himself tight against his zipper. They sat close together for the remainder of the journey and using Katie's school bag and Mark's rucksack for cover, Mark slid his hand up her skirt and she hers down his jeans. But they fooled no one, especially at the point of climax when Mark howled loudly.

The taxi driver tutted disgustedly.

There were problems on the west coast mainline, delays in both directions and the next train, north or south, wouldn't pass through for at least another hour. Going east wasn't a problem, but Mark had set his mind on London. Homeless and hungry in Leeds didn't have the same ring to it, somehow.

'This is so wrong,' Katie breathed into Mark's ear. They continued to embrace on the platform at Preston railway station. 'Please don't go. I didn't realize I missed you so much.'

The young, virile Mark's resolve was weakening. He was hard again, his cock feeling like it was on fire, straining against his damp clothing.

'I need to disappear, otherwise they'll kill me.'

She pushed him away. 'If that's what you want.'

'You've got Bradley,' he said, hurt.

'Bradley's nice enough, but he isn't you.'

'I do want to be with you, but I can't.' He looked up at the overhead arrivals monitor. A train from Manchester for Blackpool was due in shortly.

Katie's mobile phone rang. She checked it. 'My mum, jeez. The school must have contacted her already.' She pressed the disconnect button.

'They won't know you're with me,' Mark said confidently. 'Just get on the train and waltz back into school. Say you felt ill or something – but please don't tell anyone you've seen me, or know where I'm going.'

'I won't,' she promised him. She kissed the tip of her forefinger and placed it on his lips, then turned and crossed the platform as the Blackpool train drew into the station.

'No reply. Her phone must be turned off.' Katie's mother, a mid-forties version of her pretty daughter held up the home phone to prove her point.

Henry Christie held up his hands to reassure her as he spoke. 'It'll be nothing to worry about.'

'Nothing to worry about? She hasn't missed one day of school since she was five years old. If that little brute has anything to do with this, I'll wring his neck.' Her own neck and jaw were tensed as she spoke.

'It may not be anything to do with Mark. It might not be anything to do with anything,' he stressed, ineffectually.

'Ma'am, has she seen Mark Carter recently?' Karl Donaldson asked Mrs Bretherton, pronouncing the surname as 'Carduh' and utilizing his slow Yankee twang as a soothing device. Her eyes came up to him seductively. Henry thought he heard her gasp.

'No, no,' she said, suddenly self-conscious under Donaldson's eyes. 'I know she missed him, though. Always mooning around the place. I think they've had relations,' she said timidly, 'but she never confided to me, though.'

Mrs Bretherton was wearing a fairly low cut blouse, a practical piece of clothing and not excessively revealing, but Henry spotted that her upper chest and lower neck had flushed red. She actually fanned herself by flapping hand, and blowing out. It's not that hot, Henry thought sourly.

'Are you OK, ma'am,' Donaldson inquired as though he cared.

She licked her lips, they'd gone dry, and said, 'Yes, I'm just hot all of a sudden.'

Henry's mouth curved down disdainfully at the corners.

'I'm sure there's nothing to worry y'self about,' Donaldson cooed. 'Even if she is with Mark, he ain't no danger, but we do need to trace him. And obviously we'll put our efforts into finding Katie, too. S'please, doncha worry.'

'I won't,' she said with a quiver.

The two detectives had hurried from the school on receiving the news from the head teacher about Katie's absence and gone directly to the Bretherton household. Henry would have staked Donaldson's fat pay packet on Katie being with Mark. It was too much of a coincidence. They'd once been very close and if Mark was going around saying his farewells to his mates, it was always on the cards that Katie would be on the list as well as Bradley.

'*Detective Superintendent Christie receiving?*' Henry's PR called out.

'Go 'head.'

'FYI, we've got a patrol on Pier Gardens, Shoreside, attending the scene of a garden shed break.'

'And that has what to do with me?' Henry said irritably.

'We thought you'd be interested. Looks like someone might have bedded down there for the night, then stolen a bike – and also left an unpleasant calling card.'

'Oh, right, sorry. I am interested, Get the patrol attending to take details and pass them on to the MIR please.' Henry's thumb came off the transmit button and he looked triumphantly at Donaldson and Mrs Bretherton. 'Could be where Mark got his head down.'

Mrs Bretherton's house phone then rang.

She picked it up. 'Katie, where the heck are you? I've been worried sick. The police are here . . . oh.' She looked at the dead phone. 'Hung up.'

'What did she say, ma'am?'

'That she was OK. That was it.'

'Will you ring her back, please?' Henry asked.

'And beg her not to hang up,' Donaldson said sweetly. 'If she is or has been with Mark, we urgently need to speak to her.'

'I'll try.' She fumbled with the touch-tone keypad under the gaze of the two men. Eventually she tabbed in the number, put the phone to her ear and looked at Donaldson as she waited, her eyes taking him in. Henry could see she was wondering what it would be like. He glanced at Donaldson who had that lopsided grin on his face and Henry suddenly realized that the big dumb Yank thought he was God's gift to women following his tawdry encounter in Malta. That, Henry thought peevishly, could unleash a very dangerous animal. 'It's ringing,' Mrs Bretherton said. Then it was answered as she bent forward, as if craning to hear would actually increase the volume. 'Darling, please don't hang up. I'm not angry. Please, this is very important . . .' Henry held and waggled his fingers for the phone. 'Love, please don't hang up, there's a police officer here who must speak to you.'

'Katie? This is Henry Christie . . . yeah, I thought you'd know me. Love, you're not in trouble but just tell me, have you seen Mark Carter this morning?'

*   *   *

Katie agonized over her answer. The half-filled train was heading towards Blackpool and she could still feel Mark's hand down her panties, and what he'd said about love and her promise to him not to talk almost made her say no, I haven't seen him.

But Katie Bretherton was no liar.

Plus, she could see that her overriding responsibility was above her feelings for Mark. She was a very moral girl who wanted to do the right thing. She watched the countryside blur by for a moment.

'Yes, I have seen him.'

The platform was getting busier with irritated passengers. Late trains were nothing new, but this was getting ridiculous.

Mark milled around restlessly, his eyes roving. Only when he was on the Virgin Express and the next stop was Crewe would he feel anything like safe. He checked the boards. The news was good. One minute to the arrival of the Pendolino service to Euston, stopping only at Crewe and Rugby. In less than three hours he would be at Euston Station and on the streets of London.

He was on platform three, the main one, looking north up the tracks as they curved away in the distance. The train came into view in its distinctive Virgin livery.

He heaved up his rucksack and sleeping bag, checked his ticket once more, the one he'd bought for cash at the station. Carriage D, seat twelve, forward facing.

The train was less than a hundred metres from the platform now, slowing down gently.

Mark edged to the safety line, trying to work out where carriage D would be. Fourth down from the front, or fourth from back?

He positioned himself where he thought the middle of the train might be once it had stopped.

The engine passed him. The brakes hissed. He could smell diesel and smoke. He looked for his carriage.

The train stopped and the doors slid open. Some angry-looking people disembarked. They'd been stuck somewhere out in the country for two hours, no hot drinks, no food. Sod 'em, Mark thought. Just get out of the way and let me on.

He was about to place his right foot through the nearest door when hands gripped his biceps at either side of his body and he was dragged roughly away from the train.

* * *

Henry was driving. Donaldson was in the passenger seat, grinning like a slightly woozy Cheshire cat.

'That poor woman almost had an orgasm when you talked to her,' a miffed Henry said.

'I know,' he said smugly.

'Your mojo is on fire.'

'Yeah, baby.'

Henry scowled at him. 'It's only just dawned on you, hasn't it?'

'The amazing effect I have on the opposite sex? Yuh, suppose so.'

Henry gasped with disbelief, but before he could say anything, his phone rang. 'Henry Christie . . . thanks for that.' He looked at Donaldson. 'Got him.'

THIRTEEN

Having warned Karl Donaldson in no uncertain terms not to unleash his newly discovered sexual superpowers on Kate, Henry dropped him off at his home. Then he headed down the A585 towards Preston. He'd told the plain-clothes officers who'd arrested Mark on the railway station to lodge him in the cells on suspicion of robbery and he would come to collect him personally.

Meanwhile, Donaldson settled in Henry's house and was given a cup of tea by Kate who, having known him for a long time, was completely immune to his charms. From a purely objective standpoint, though, she could have happily ripped off his clothes and pleasured herself on him, and had she not been so completely in love with Henry, that's what she would have done. A long time ago.

'Karen phoned earlier,' she told Donaldson. 'Said she'd be up mid-afternoon.'

'Oh, smashing,' he said dubiously.

Instantly the female radar honed in on something. 'Is that OK?'

'Yeah, yeah.'

She folded her arms. 'You two aren't having problems again, are you?'

'Uh, no,' he lied. It wasn't long since Kate had acted as a bit of a go-between and engineered a meeting between him and Karen after they'd been having problems following him being wounded in Barcelona. Kate was under the impression they'd weathered that storm. Maybe she'd been wrong. She could sense something was troubling Karl, who in terms of his personal life was a bit of an open book. Unlike his professional life that was shrouded in secrecy.

'You can tell me, you know.' She smiled sympathetically at him – and he almost fell for it. The man who had faced one of the world's most wanted terrorists and emerged victorious, who had hunted down bombers and violent criminals, had almost blabbed his infidelity to his wife's friend.

'Nah, it's nothing – honestly.' He held her stare sheepishly, before being forced to shrug, look away and cough guiltily.

'Fine,' she said.

'Henry said it would be OK for me to use the study. I need to do some research on the Internet.'

Henry pulled up at the new police station in Preston about half an hour later, traffic having held him up a little. He was buzzed into the building via the enquiry desk and made his way along the ground floor corridor to the custody office where he presented himself to one of the two custody officers. They were lords, masters of all they surveyed, a step higher than everyone else on a raised area that reminded Henry of a spaceship command centre, the captain's bridge. He knew the custody officer, so there was no need for introductions.

'I've come to collect Mark Carter.'

'Good, a wick little bleeder, that one. He's spat at me and pissed all over his cell.'

'Charming.'

The custody officer beckoned over a gaoler and told him to take Henry to Mark's cell, a juvenile detention room just off the main custody reception area. As the cell door opened, the strong odour of urine hit Henry.

Mark was stretched out on the bench, on his side, facing the wall. He did not move when the door opened. A pool of yellow stinking piss was on the cell floor, splashed up on to the walls also.

'He won't clean it up, so we've left him in it,' explained the gaoler to Henry.

'Do you piss everywhere you go now?' Henry said, a comment that elicited no response from Mark. 'I said . . .'

'I heard what you said,' Mark mumbled into the wall.

'Get me a mop and a bucket,' Henry said quietly to the gaoler. 'You're going to clean this up, Mark.'

'No I'm not.'

'Wrong answer.'

Mark twisted his head around and saw that his annoyer was Henry. He groaned. 'Oh no, not you. Just eff off and leave me alone.'

The gaoler eyed Henry, gave a tut, then went down the corridor for the mop, leaving Henry temporarily alone with Mark. The detective stepped carefully into the cell, avoiding the pee, and leaned over. His mouth was only inches from Mark's right ear.

'You get the fuck up, you mop up your own piss and then you're coming with me.'

'Or what?' Mark was staring intently at the wall on which was inscribed without any originality, 'Cops'r'cuntz', a sentiment with which Mark agreed wholeheartedly.

'Or I'll rub your nose in it,' Henry whispered.

Mark flinched.

Henry added, 'You know I will.'

'I've got rights. I'll sue you.'

'No one's done that successfully yet,' Henry said. He stood up as the gaoler returned with the cleaning utensils, one in each hand, reminding Henry of a soldier on latrine duties. 'Get up Mark, we have some important things to discuss.'

'Go away.'

Henry turned to the gaoler and gave him the 'look'. The man nodded and quickly sidestepped out of view. Henry grabbed Mark's arm and yanked him off the bench and before he knew it he was on his knees, one arm wedged up between his shoulder blades face to the floor. His head was being pressed down by Henry's big hand on the back of it, his nose hovering less than an inch above his urine.

Henry bent low again. 'I have no time to mess about here, Mark. Things have got very serious and you have to cooperate with me.'

'Did that bitch tell you where I was?'

'None of that matters any more. Just clean up your mess and let's get moving.' Henry ratcheted Mark's arm another inch up his back. A hiss of pain exited from between his clenched teeth.

'OK, OK,' Mark relented.

'And after you've done that, we might go and scoop up the

shit you left in some poor bugger's shed last night, at the same time as returning his bike to him, eh?'

'It's definitely Petrone,' Donaldson was saying. He had a mug of filtered coffee in his hand and was standing in Henry's back garden, looking out across the adjoining field on which sheep grazed and a pair of noisy Canadian geese pecked at the ground next to a pond. He was on the phone to Don Barber down in London. 'Confirmed with my own eyes.'

'Well, at least it's some revenge for Shark's death.' Barber said, referring to the undercover FBI agent.

'You could look at it that way,' Donaldson conceded, 'but it's one less avenue for me to get to the American.'

'Any leads as to who might have whacked him?'

'I mentioned this witness before, who they've got in custody now. It'll be interesting to find out exactly what's been seen or otherwise.'

'Where is he in custody?'

'Preston at the moment, but being brought back to Blackpool.'

'OK, keep me posted, Karl.'

'Will do, boss . . . there is one thing.'

'That would be?'

'I've decided to review all the murders between the Petrones and the Marinis that happened since the Majorca shootings, if that's OK.'

Barber hesitated slightly. 'To what end?'

'Mm, maybe nothing, just an aside the SIO up here said to me. I just want to have a look at the patterns to the killings, see if anything strikes me as odd.'

'In what way?'

'Again, not sure yet, but the SIO has a vague theory that we might not just be up against the Mafia . . . as I said, it's a vague one.'

'Don't spend too much time on it.'

'I won't.'

Donaldson chucked the last dregs of the coffee over the fence and returned to the house. Kate had been studying him from the kitchen. He handed her the cup and said thanks, but wilted under her knowing eyes.

'Please don't say you've been unfaithful,' she said, 'not you.'

Had Donaldson been accused of murder, not even the most experienced interrogator in the world, not even torture, would have made him reveal a thing. But the hurt, accusing glint in Kate's eyes turned his stomach over and he had to hold himself back from prostrating himself at her feet and begging forgiveness for his transgression.

'No,' he said haughtily. 'Can I use the study now?'

'I should bloody well think so.'

Mark Carter scowled at the remark made by Henry and rammed the mop head into the bucket.

'Finished.'

'Right, let's get going.'

He made Mark carry the bucket down the corridor to a tap and sluice sink where he poured the urine and water away, then rinsed mop and bucket.

'You had a shower?'

'Do I look like I've had a shower?'

'You look like shit, actually. Come on, now you've cleaned up your mess, let's clean up the mess that's you.'

Karl Donaldson slid his laptop out of its case, plugged it in, switched it on. It was a new one, state of the art, and was up and running in seconds. He connected to Henry's broadband system.

Firstly he checked his personal emails, then wished he hadn't.

There were four new ones, three from travel agents he subscribed to, the fourth from an unknown sender that the computer marked with a red flag warning and the perceptive words, '*This could be dangerous*'. He clicked on it, saw it was from someone called 'VanLang'. At first he thought it could have been one of the many he received from online Viagra sellers – not that he needed any – but when he opened it he found it was from his sexy neighbour in Malta.

'*Arrived home. Missing you. Can still feel you inside me. You exploded!!! Want to see you again. Can this be arranged? I can travel at a moment's notice. Husband not a problem. XXX*'

Husband? Donaldson squirmed, recalling she had mentioned a boyfriend, not a spouse. But not only that, how had she managed to get his email address? He wracked his brains for the moments when she could have got it. On reflection, she did have one or two opportunities. For a very serious moment he considered replying, but that would have compounded his stupidity and started an electronic dialogue that might get out of hand. Emails were dangerous, as many a person in power had discovered to their cost. As were texts. He pressed the delete button as though it was electrified.

'Not good, not good,' he mumbled, suddenly not liking adultery very much any more.

Next he went on to his work emails and saw he'd received forty-odd of the bastards, all with 'Read me' and 'Urgent' flags. He couldn't be bothered with any, his mood knocked for six by Vanessa's message.

Then he went on to the FBI website, logged into the staff-only section, and started his research.

From a purely investigative point of view, Henry would have preferred not to tell Mark about his mother's death – just yet. He wanted to bleed him dry of any useful information about the assassination of Rosario Petrone, and would have liked to extract this from the lad without having to deal with the additional burden of emotions that would come with telling him about Mandy's death – and the manner she'd met it.

It was a delicate balancing act, one that Henry hadn't quite worked out.

It was certain, though, that Mark had a right to know about her death, whether they got on well or not. Henry would also have to arrange for a message to be passed to Mark's older brother, Jack, presently lounging for a long spell in clink.

They were at the custody desk. Mark had showered and although he was in the same set of clothes, he looked fresher, smelled cleaner. Mark's property was in a sealed bag, but Henry took a few moments to check that the contents actually matched the list on the custody record before signing for it. He whistled at the amount of money in Mark's possession and gave him a questioning look. 'Planning on being away for a while, were we?'

'In case you're thinking – it's kosher. It's my mum's money. She gave it to me.'

'Highly unlikely,' Henry said. He signed the record and resealed the bag. 'Come on, pal, back to Blackpool.' Henry herded the crestfallen boy out of the custody office to the secure bay at the back of the police station, where his car had been moved by arrangement.

'In the back,' Henry said, opened one of the rear doors and shoved Mark into the car, then sidled in alongside him. 'Child locks're on, so don't think you can just leap out at traffic lights.'

There was a uniformed police officer behind the steering wheel of the car, who looked over his shoulder and nodded at Henry.

'Who's that joker?' Mark said snottily.

'That joker is none other that Constable Bill Robbins, our selected driver for the day, who, at great personal cost, has rushed down here from police HQ to assist us,' Henry said grandly. 'And if you do think of running away, I'll get Bill here to shoot you. Not to kill you, obviously, just wing you, because Bill's a sharpshooter who could shoot the nadger off a gnat, couldn't you, Bill?'

'Could that.'

'What are you on about, idiot?' Mark snarled.

'Show him, Bill.'

Robbins shifted on his seat and pulled something up from between his legs. A Heckler & Koch G36.

'It has one of those red dots,' Robbins explained, 'which makes it very, very precise.'

'Armed and dangerous,' Henry said, 'especially when provoked.'

Karl Donaldson refreshed his memory. He started with the shooting three years ago in Can Pastilla. This was a file Donaldson knew well, for obvious reasons, and he accessed it through the FBI database with no problems, his computer taking him there almost instantly.

Three men sat at a table. The fourth picking up a gun that had been planted for him and killing the others with deadly calm. A true professional, the only glitch being the traces left in the restroom and on a table by the slightly careless Mustapha Fazil. If the traces hadn't been found and lifted, Fazil would never have been identified and Donaldson would maybe have read his name in a crime circulation after his arrest on Malta, then filed it none the wiser.

Two of the men at the table had been real players in the Marini Mafia clan that was in dispute with the Petrone clan. They were Carlo Marini, probably number three in the Marini clan, and a guy called Paulo who was just a bodyguard. A bit player, but a clan member nonetheless.

'Bang, bang, bang,' Donaldson said to himself. Three dead

men and the start of one of the bloodiest Mafia wars in recent years. He re-read the police reports of the shooting, which he knew well.

The FBI knew the meeting was to take place because of the information supplied by Shark, the undercover agent. He'd infiltrated the Marini clan several years earlier and had won the trust of the leaders. His information had stated that they were to meet a guy from the US who had a network of retail outlets and was prepared to sell Marini products – i.e., fake goods – in the States. A good toehold of business that would have been fantastic for the Marini people. But the whole thing had been an elaborate ruse by Rosario Petrone, luring Carlo Marini out to Majorca with a promise of amazing wealth, his greed being his downfall, as much as he might have checked out the credentials of the American. The desire to be rich simply led to death.

All well and good. Except one of the three dead men was the FBI agent. And Donaldson had been tasked by Don Barber to find the killer, this 'American', a task at which he had singularly unsuccessful.

Then the reprisals began. The streets of Naples were awash with blood.

Donaldson went into another file that was basically a cut and paste job from newspaper reports detailing the murders that followed. Almost too horrible to contemplate, and he could imagine the chaos in the city.

Outraged, the Marinis struck back. A Petrone scooter boy, one of the youngsters who delivered drugs in the Petrone sector of the Naples, hunted down like an elk by a pack of wolves. He was beaten, savagely mutilated, tongue cut off, balls hacked off and stuffed into his mouth.

'Choice,' mumbled Donaldson.

Next a Petrone retaliation. The murder of a Marini lookout. Machete'd to death without finesse.

Two very obvious Mafia style murders at that level.

Donaldson tabbed down a page.

Then the Marini clan struck back.

The Petrone number two, Roberto – Rosario Petrone's cousin – mown down by a car whilst on a secret visit to Rome. A similar murder, in fact, to Rosario Petrone's in Blackpool. A quiet road in a residential area. A car running over him twice, a man jumping out and pumping two bullets into his head. Nothing unusual in that, except it was different from the two preceding murders, the feature of which had been frenzied horrific violence. Roberto Petrone died violently, yes, but in a more cold, calculating manner.

Not that the Mafia weren't capable of committing such murders, but the Camorra murders were often more bloody, as the next ones showed. A lieutenant in the Marini clan and his girlfriend found butchered in a hotel room, hacked to pieces, the room bubbling with blood and guts.

And so on and so forth. Tit, tat, murder, counter murder. Many, many killings.

And yet . . . Donaldson frowned. Some of the killings attributed to the Marini clan were of a more sophisticated, cunning nature than the others. Yes, there were the blood soaked, insane attacks in amongst them, but three were car related – knocked down, run over, shot – and three others were even better than that. Long range assassinations of major Petrone clan players.

One was by a sniper at Venice Airport, an assassin secreted almost a mile away from the target. Another was a sniper taking one out at a Naples street cafe from a position in a high tower block half a mile away from the target, and a further similar job in Rome, when a Petrone clan member on a tourist visit to the city had his head blown off by a killer hidden near the Coliseum.

Three good quality assassinations and three car related ones, four if the hit on Rosario Petrone in Blackpool was added.

Seven that did not immediately fall into the category of the others, with all the targets being well-protected high-flyers and decision makers, not gofers or street runners or soldiers.

Maybe the Marinis had brought in special people to carry out these attacks. They certainly had the money to pay for professional assassins, but it wasn't something the Camorra clans often did. Why pay for seven professional killings when they had enough people of their own willing to have a try at earning their spurs?

Donaldson could understand them bringing in one or two – as Rosario Petrone was alleged to have done by recruiting the 'American' to carry out the hit in Majorca.

And the long-range hits were something special. Not many people outside the military were capable of carrying out such hits. Donaldson had a good knowledge of such people.

He opened another file and studied the profiles of half a dozen professional killers. Two were actually in jail, another was believed to have been killed in Africa, leaving three operational. One of these was believed to be living in Thailand with young boys for company. Another was a British ex-special forces soldier who was supposed to have carried out a hit in the north of England recently and was lying low. That left one, and the chance of him being hired by the Mafia to carry out three assassinations was, whilst possible, pretty remote.

Donaldson sighed, rubbed his neck. He flicked back to his personal email and his heart lurched when he saw another message had landed from 'VanLang'. He opened it with trepidation. It read, '*Please reply. Am desperate!! XXX*'.

He wondered if he had enough money in his bank account to bring a hired assassin out from retirement.

Henry had known Bill Robbins for a long time. In the eighties they had worked briefly as PCs together, but more recently Bill had worked with Henry to help prevent the American State Secretary being blasted to smithereens by terrorists. Since Henry had become a superintendent on FMIT he had tried to get a role for Bill on the team, but the Chief Constable had blocked his efforts. Bill therefore continued to be a firearms trainer at the training centre at HQ, as well as being required to carry out regular operational duties in his 'down time'. Bill had asked to be issued with a broom so he could shove it up his arse and clean the floors as well as everything else. He had submitted the report as a joke and a broom had been subsequently issued to him by stores with instructions for use.

Henry had got permission from FB to have Bill dropped off at Preston nick, fully tooled up, to drive Henry and Mark back to Blackpool, and to provide armed protection should it be necessary.

Henry leaned forward and whispered into Bill's ear as they reached the roundabout at Marton Circle on the outskirts of Blackpool. Rather than going down Yeadon Way into Blackpool, a road that led almost directly to the police station, Bill veered left and went towards Lytham instead.

Sullen, not even looking up, Mark did not even notice the change of direction.

Henry sat back. 'You've gone off the rails, Mark. I thought you were better than that.'

'Than what?'

'Shitting in people's sheds, nicking bikes . . . robbing people.
I really thought you were something different.'

Mark eyed him. 'What's this? You a social worker now?'

'No, I'm a cop doing a job.'

'Oh, friggin' spare me.' Mark now saw they were headed
somewhere other than Blackpool. 'Where are we going?'

'Somewhere I can talk to you.'

'Somewhere to beat me up?'

'I do that sort of thing in the cells.'

'Last time you talked to me, you conned the shit out of me,
then you got what you wanted and pissed off.'

Henry reddened at the accusation.

'True, eh?' Mark rammed home his steel-tipped advantage.

Henry's lips tightened into a thin line.

Bill reached the T-junction at the seafront. A right turn would
take him to Blackpool, left towards Lytham. He went left, past
Pontins, then right on to the sand dune front at St Annes and
drew up on the car park next to the beach cafe. Bill climbed
out, stretched his legs. Mark caught sight of the holster at his
side under his windjammer, and the Glock pistol in it.

Donaldson stood up, exasperated. In his role at the Legat, he
had access to many computer files at all levels, but as he clicked
on to the ones he particularly wanted to see, this access was
denied.

'Goddamn technology,' he said through gritted teeth and paced
around the study. It had previously been a garage, but when the
house had been rebuilt following the fire, the space had been
converted into a fairly airy office. Donaldson's mind went briefly
back to the arson attack that had almost killed Kate. That had
been a hell of an experience for both of them.

There was a tap on the closed door. 'Can I come in?'

'Of course you can ma'am,' Donaldson cooed as he opened
the door.

'I heard you muttering.'

'Just annoyed at the computer. I can't access something I need
to see, but it's probably because I'm doing it from here rather
than in the embassy,' he reasoned, not really knowing too much
about such things. He used technology well enough but didn't
understand how or why it worked.

'Could you use another drink?'

'That would be fine.'

He followed her into the kitchen where the coffee-filtering machine was dripping and hissing away. He leaned against a worktop as Kate reached for a couple of mugs from hooks on the wall. It was still on the tip of his tongue to admit his unfaithfulness, but he checked himself. Telling Henry had been as far as he was prepared to go in the self-torturing stakes for one day. To reveal all to Kate, he guessed, would be disastrous. He was of the opinion that men and women were wired up differently, that the picture they saw might be the same, but each sex viewed it differently. He knew Henry wouldn't say a thing to anyone, but suspected Kate might see it as her duty to tell Karen.

She filled a mug for him and handed it over, looking directly into his eyes. 'I wouldn't say a thing, you know,' she said as though she'd read his simple mind.

A thought skittered through his synapses. If I were being tortured, water-boarded, nails pulled out, branded by hot irons, my balls wired up to the electrical circuit, I would not reveal a national secret. But this – *this* – was much worse than torture. Subtle, psychological prodding, accompanied by a beautiful face and big innocent eyes, a package designed to draw information out of him. And mind reading. Fight it.

'I've nothing to say, honest. You're barking up the wrong tree. And I need to phone my boss.'

'There's a lot of ground to cover, Mark,' Henry said turning squarely to the lad in the back of the Mondeo. He held up a hand to stop Mark's protestation. 'Let me just tell you what I know and then let me tell you something very important.'

Mark sneered, an expression that seemed permanently affixed to his face.

'First off, I know that you and Rory Costain were out on the rob two nights ago. You beat up two people and stole from them. Maybe you even did more I don't know about.' Mark opened his mouth. Henry snapped, 'Shut it. You robbed a lad in the town centre and a girl just down the road from the nick. But that's not all, is it? Tell me about the old man, Mark.'

'What old man?'

'The one you tried to rob.'

'Didn't rob no old man.'

'What did you do to him?'

'Don't know what you're blabbing about, Henry.'

'Mark, you stupid little shit. I've talked to Bradley and I've talked to Katie . . .'

'The little twats.'

'Your mates, actually. People who care about you.'

Mark's sneering expression showed he thought differently. He folded his arms. 'Nothing to say.'

'Have you any idea who the old man was?'

'What old guy?' Mark said stubbornly.

'Ever heard of the Mafia?'

'Course.'

'That old man was a Mafia godfather . . .' Henry stopped speaking as Mark sniggered. 'Put two and two together, Mark. You saw him get killed and the people who did it saw you watching. And then they killed Rory and you managed to get away . . . and they would've had you last night, but you got lucky, but Rory's dad didn't.'

'Is he dead?'

Henry nodded. 'Very.'

'So you think I'll be safe if I come and tell you what I saw? Stop taking me for a goomer, Henry. You couldn't protect anyone.'

'And you think you've got a chance by running away to London?'

Mark stared ahead.

Henry said, 'Things have changed again.'

Mark sighed. 'Sure they have.'

'These people will stop at nothing to get you.'

'Why would that be?'

'Because they think you can identify them.'

'They're wrong.'

Henry was starting to bubble crossly. 'Let me lay it down, Mark. I know you and Rory saw that old guy being murdered. You were right up at the end of the alley. I know you tried to rob him first and that he turned nasty, didn't he? Not your usual victim, eh? He turned nasty because as a matter of course he killed, or had people killed, in his line of work. He was hiding out in Blackpool from a gang war in Naples and whoever killed him is desperate not to be caught, even if it means innocent people get killed.'

'Like Billy?'

'Like Billy,' Henry confirmed. 'And someone else . . .'

*   *   *

Donaldson was back at the computer, still getting nowhere. He had phoned Don Barber to tell him of his initial findings – that some of the killings attributed to the Marini clan didn't quite fit in with their usual MO and were more professional than normal. He had even discovered a newspaper cutting relating to one of the long-distance shootings in which a Marini boss claimed they were not responsible for the hit.

Donaldson thought it was an unusual step for a Mafia boss to take – to deny a killing. Barber had sounded suitably unimpressed, then asked if there was anything more on the lad who'd witnessed Rosario Petrone's murder, but Donaldson said he didn't have any more updates, although he expected that the witness was probably back in Blackpool with the SIO by now.

'OK, keep me informed,' Barber said, ending the call just as Donaldson was about to ask him if there was any problems with the computer down at the embassy. He was about to call his boss back, but as he was about to hit the redial button on his mobile, he stopped and raised his face, looking at the 1964 picture of the Rolling Stones that Henry had put up on the study wall.

Mark climbed heavily out of the car and walked towards the beach, his eyes transfixed on the horizon. Henry walked behind him, Bill Robbins a few paces behind Henry, watchful, tense, not relaxing. Mark stopped on the edge of the sand dunes, then squatted slowly down on to his haunches, put his elbows on his knees, his head in his hands.

But he did not cry, just remained silent.

Henry moved to his side, placed a hand on his shoulder. 'I'm sorry, Mark,' he said sincerely.

'I have no one,' Mark said, matter-of-fact, glancing up. 'Best thing for me is to end up in a young offenders' institute until I'm eighteen. Then I can go on the dole, father a dozen kids and live off the state.'

'It's a plan,' Henry said.

Mark smiled and said, 'There was a camera.'

FOURTEEN

Donaldson was just about to pick up his laptop and hurl it against the wall when he glanced out of the study window to see Henry's car pulling up outside the house. He placed the computer gently down on the desk and watched, slightly puzzled, as Henry got out of the back of the car and trotted up the driveway to the front of the house. He saw a driver at the wheel, but could not make out any of his features because of the reflected light off the windscreen. There was also a dark, indistinguishable shape in the back seat of the Mondeo. He heard a muted conversation between Henry and Kate, before Henry opened the study door and leaned in.

'Got the lad,' he said breathlessly. 'On the way back to the original murder scene for a witness walk-through. Want to come?'

Donaldson was already getting to his feet, even thought he suddenly felt leaden as, because of what Henry had just said, he realized why he'd been unsettled about the conversation he'd recently had with Don Barber.

'It started here,' Mark Carter said. 'Me and Rory stood here.' He pointed to the spot in the doorway diagonally opposite the shop known as Lucio's on Church Street, Blackpool. 'We'd done the girl and the lad, and we had the girl's mobile phone with us,' Mark explained. He might have been deeply upset at the news of his mother and his own prospects for the future, but he hadn't lost his mind enough to tell Henry that he and Rory had also rolled a drunk for a fiver and a tin of cider before committing the two street robberies. His mother might've been murdered, Rory might've been murdered, killers might be on his trail, but he'd carried out three serious crimes and Henry only knew about two of them. And that's the way it would stay because Mark knew that despite all the other stuff, the robberies would have to be dealt with at some stage. There would be no weaselling out of them. 'The old man came out of that shop. It were Rory's idea to rob him, and everybody else,' Mark whined, 'because he thought he'd be an easy target.'

Henry, Mark and Donaldson were on the footpath opposite

Lucio's. Bill Robbins was still at the wheel of the Mondeo at the road's edge.

'That's his shop?' Donaldson asked. Henry nodded. 'All fake goods. They make the stuff in factories in Naples and sell it on the high streets.'

'Why don't the real manufacturers shut them down?'

'Because it suits them,' Donaldson said.

Henry couldn't be bothered to ask.

Mark went on, 'We watched him cross the road and followed him. An old guy with a walking stick, pretty rich looking,' he pondered. 'He went down there and we went after him.' He led the men along the route he and his now deceased partner in crime had taken. Down Leopold Grove, over Albert Road, then into the alley which cut north–south to Charnley Road.

Bill followed in the car like a kerb-crawler.

The evil chant, 'Vic-tim, vic-tim,' replayed through Mark's mind. Suddenly he felt very weak, but pushed on. It had been his decision to get this crap out of the way, probably manipulated by Henry, who had convinced him that time was running out to catch killers who were responsible for four deaths in Blackpool alone.

Henry, however, knew he was on wobbly ground here. In the eyes of the law, Mark was a juvenile with all the protective trimmings that came with that status. He had the right to be accompanied by an adult at all times, as Mark had rightly told him, and even getting Mark to run through something to which he was a witness was an iffy thing to do without an appropriate adult present. It was made more complicated because Mark was in custody for robbery offences and everything that happened to him should have been recorded contemporaneously on the custody record.

But Henry was in a hurry and was already working out how he'd cover his tracks if questions were asked.

Mark had now led them to the end of the alley where it opened on to Charnley Road, the scene of the murder, now clear of police activity. Bill had driven around in the Mondeo.

'Rory had a go at him here,' Mark said, 'but the guy whacked him with his walking stick, smacked his head.'

Karl Donaldson walked past into Charnley Road, looking up and down, imagining the scene. Mark went on to describe what had happened – the car, the killer – and the killer looking at the two boys in the mouth of the alley. He had looked directly at them and Rory had shouted at him, stepped forward and taken a photo on the stolen phone. Then the boys had fled.

'We ran, God did we run.'

'And the camera, the phone, whatever – where is it?' Henry asked.

'That's the problem. Rory dropped it somewhere.'

'Somewhere?'

'Somewhere between here and North Pier.'

Henry blinked. 'So there isn't a camera?'

'It could still be around.'

'Where did he drop it?'

'Dunno.'

'Did you search for it?'

'Not really.'

Henry's teeth ground grittily as he fought his disappointment and thought this through.

'I got a decent look at the bloke,' Mark volunteered.

'Mm . . . walk the route with me, the way you went to North Pier.'

'Now?'

'No – next week. Yes, now,' he said.

'I might do a runner. I know I can run faster than you can.'

'Like I said, if you do, I'll have you shot in the leg – escaping felon.' Henry beckoned to Bill in the Mondeo to get out and park up. Mark then took the men along his escape route. Back down the alley, left on to Albert Road with the south aspect of the Winter Gardens on their right, then on to Coronation Street, diagonally across into Birley Street – one of the main shopping streets – right into Corporation Street then on to Talbot Square. They had passed the exact spot where they'd robbed the Goth, done a left on to the Promenade and crossed over to the entrance to North Pier by the war memorial.

No sign of the mobile phone.

Henry's frustration boiled over and he cursed. Mark looked contemptuously at him. 'All you're interested in is getting an arrest, isn't it? You actually don't give a monkey's about me, do you? What I've been through, what I'm going through, how I feel?'

Henry picked up Mark by the lapel of his hoodie and slammed him hard against the war memorial. 'Let me make something very clear to you, pal,' he said. 'The guys who killed the old man, Rory, Billy and your mum are still out there. They think you can ID them, Mark, and just at this moment I'm the only one who can keep you alive.'

Mark was not afraid of Henry. 'Or get me dead,' he rejoined.

Henry was back in his office off the major incident room. Bill Robbins had joined him, as had Jerry Tope, Alex Bent and Karl Donaldson. Mark Carter had been booked into custody and was now sweating it out in a juvenile detention room whilst Henry tried to work out the best way forward.

'I suppose the humane thing to do would be to have a quick interview with Mark about the robberies – making sure he admitted them, of course, then bail him into the care of social services. The humane thing,' he said again. 'Then I want to get him with the e-fit people to get a face down on paper. In the meantime, I want a search team to work that route, turn over every rock and find that phone. It's vital it turns up.'

The others nodded assent.

'And then what?' Bent asked.

'Good question,' Henry admitted.

'Can I make a quick suggestion?' Bill Robbins asked.

'Go on.'

'I know it's a long shot, but –' he screwed up his face as though what he was about to propose was particularly stupid and that he would be stoned to death – 'is it worth checking the found property register for the mobile phone? Sometimes people have been known to be honest and hand in property . . . it'd only take a minute.'

'Not such a bad idea. Can you do that?' Henry asked.

'Now?'

'Now.'

Robbins rose and left the room.

The remaining officers all shook their heads. 'Not a chance in hell,' Bent said cynically. 'And if it had been handed in, it should have been cross-referenced to the crime report, so we should know if it had been.'

'Mm,' Henry said doubtfully. 'Can you check the phone's status, though?' he asked Bent. 'I'm presuming it was blocked after the robbery was reported. If it has, maybe it could be unblocked, and if it's still transmitting a signal we could locate it that way?'

'Will do.'

'Have we heard anything from Rik yet?'

'No he's at the mortuary with Mandy,' Bent said.

'The pathologist will be wanting to do Rory's PM. Ask Rik if he'll cover that for me, will you? And then arrange to get Mark Carter sorted?' Henry checked his watch. 'Social services should be here soon, so they promised.'

It was almost four p.m. as Bill Robbins sauntered through the tight, badly decorated corridors of Blackpool police station. He was feeling quite serene, having been dragged away from the drudgery of some tedious lesson planning at the training centre to come and be Mark Carter's bodyguard. Since coming to the station he had locked all his firearms in the safe in the ARV office.

He went down to the ground floor where the public enquiry desk was located and popped his head through the door behind the desk itself. As ever there was a stream of people at the desk being attended to by a harassed assistant. Bill saw the found property register on a shelf underneath the desk, reached through and took it, then stepped back out of sight lest a member of the public demanded to see a real cop as opposed to a public enquiry assistant, or PEA as they were known.

He retreated into the tiny PEA office and flicked through the book.

These days the police took less and less property from the public. When Bill had joined the job, the cops took everything. Now finders were encouraged to keep what they'd found and if they hadn't heard anything within twenty-eight days, were told that the property became theirs. This even applied to fairly large sums of money.

There wasn't much recorded in the book over the last two days. Bill would have expected that if a mobile phone had been handed in, it would have been retained by the police to cross-check with recorded crimes, pretty standard procedure for such items.

A female PEA came into the office, fitting her epaulettes. She was clearly just coming on duty, working the four-to-midnight shift, after which the police station would be closed. She was a bonny young thing, Bill thought patronizingly, glancing at her name tag: Ellen Thompson.

'Can I help you?' she asked.

'Just checking to see if a mobile phone has been handed in over the last couple of days . . . doesn't seem to be anything.'

'Mm, I've certainly not taken one in,' the PEA said quickly. 'Don't know about anyone else.'

'It would have been recorded in here, wouldn't it?' Bill tapped the red-spined found property book. She nodded. 'OK, no probs.'

The PEA held out her hand. 'Shall I put it back for you?'

'Thanks.' Ah well, he thought, another bright idea that came to nought.

Henry and Donaldson stepped out of the lift on the top floor and entered the canteen. Henry was gagging for a drink and something to eat. Donaldson was coffee'd up to the eyeballs, so he bought a mineral water and both men picked a cherry-topped raisin swirl each to go with their drinks, and took their mini-feasts to a table giving them a view across the Irish Sea.

Henry sipped his coffee and waited for the hit before biting a chunk out of his pastry.

Jerry Tope entered the canteen, got himself a brew and went to sit alone. Henry was watching him, but not thinking about him.

Donaldson winced as he tasted his water. 'Complex stuff,' he said.

'What, H2O? Hydrogen, oxygen isn't it?'

'If only things were that simple,' he frowned.

'You have a look of disquiet,' Henry observed skilfully.

'Something doesn't add up.'

'Tell me about it. You can trust me, I'm a cop, a detective super at that.'

'I've been looking at all the Camorra killings since the hit in Majorca,' he explained, 'and some don't fit the pattern.'

'In what way?'

'The hits on the senior Petrone clan guys seem much more tidy and professional than all the others. The street killings are the usual horrid mess, but the ones where the bosses are taken out are much more clinical – it's no wonder Rosario did a runner. Anyway, I don't know. Maybe it's nothing.'

'Whoever killed him also seems very keen to the extreme on eliminating witnesses,' Henry said.

'Problem is I can only access certain files at the moment. I need to look at some more detailed information that I know exists, but I don't seem to be able to get into. A glitch, I think.'

Henry nodded in Jerry Tope's direction. 'How about our resident hacker? Could he be of assistance?'

Donaldson looked around at Jerry who sipped his coffee thoughtfully and nibbled a custard cream. He knew the Intel unit detective was a skilled hacker and often searched the databases of other organizations without consent. He had once probed deeply into the FBI computer and delved much deeper than most hackers, until he had been discovered by the IT bods at Quantico and chased – in the cyber sense of the word – across the world. Donaldson had been given the task of investigating Tope and there could easily have been much embarrassing egg-on-face all around if the FBI hadn't actually wanted to recruit Tope.

So far, Henry had deflected their advances on behalf of Jerry, but he guessed that one day a financial package would come along and lure him away from Lancashire. Henry would hang on to him for as long as possible because he recognized a brilliant asset when he saw one, even if he was a glum sort of guy.

Donaldson considered him whilst eating his half-cherry. 'Nah, back burner . . . I'll go and try again. It was probably just one of those IT gremlins.'

'He's there if you need him.'

Henry and Donaldson watched Tope as he split apart his custard cream and began to lick the filling with the relish of an adolescent.

Henry dropped Donaldson off at his house, gave Kate a quick wave – who, by rights, should have been sat at an airport now – then shot back to the police station. He had about an hour, he estimated, that he would put to good use by writing up the murder book and doing a spot of problem solving.

Donaldson's mobile rang as he walked through the door of Henry's house. He answered it with trepidation as the caller ID told him it was Karen calling. Despite the caution, he tried to give his voice a pleasant lilt.

'Hi, babe, where the heck are you?'

'Love, I'm sorry, I couldn't get away from work.' Karen was a superintendent working for the Metropolitan Police but seconded to Bramshill, the grand former stately home in Hampshire now home to a broad spectrum of police training. She was head of the overseas development arm, assisting other countries to develop training packages for their high-ranking officers. She did sound contrite.

'I really wanted to see you,' Donaldson said sweetly. 'I really got sidetracked up here.'

'That's OK, hon. These things happen.'

There was something in her voice underneath the slightly syrupy tone that Donaldson picked up on.

'When can I expect you?'

'I'll try and get up for lunchtime tomorrow, now. That OK?'

'I'll still be here.' Donaldson had moved out on to the front step to take the call, looking through the front door down the hallway. Kate appeared from the kitchen wiping her hands on a towel, watching him on the phone.

'OK, bye,' Karen said hesitantly.

The line went dead. Donaldson drew the phone slowly away from his ear. He could not work out the voice. Did she somehow know about his indiscretion? Impossible, he told himself. Unless crazy Vanessa had found out who Karen was and had contacted her to reveal the lurid details of the fling. One thing of which he was certain: if Karen knew, she would not hold back. He would get a full broadside and maybe this was the sweetness before the storm. Then again – maybe she was the one seeing someone else? He gulped drily.

'Everything all right?' Kate asked.

'Yuh, think so. Karen will be coming tomorrow instead of today. Some hold up at work.'

'Are the kids OK?'

'Yeah, should be. They're with Karen's sister down in Southampton for a few days.'

'So – are you going to remain standing on the front step, or are you coming in?'

He smiled wonkily at her. 'Any chance of a shower, and maybe a sandwich?'

'I have pastrami, I have rye bread, I have crisp salad and I have mayo. I also have a power shower . . . tempting?'

'God, yes,' he gasped.

'What do you want me to do?'

Henry looked up from the murder book and his mass of notes. The bulky form of Bill Robbins was leaning on the door frame. 'No luck with found property, I take it?'

'Nope.'

'Never mind, good idea, though. Have you had something to eat?'

Bill shook his head.

'Get something while they're still open and then hang around will you? Not sure what's happening to the star witness yet.'

Bill nodded, pushed himself upright and left the MIR to catch a meal in the canteen.

Henry closed the office door, not wanting any more disturbances. Better detectives than him had had cases seriously threatened by not keeping the murder book up to date. It was sometimes difficult to do, especially when things were happening, but there was never any excuse when the lawyers came into the equation, as they always did. And at the moment, Henry's notes were in disarray. As he sat down he was immediately interrupted by a knock on the door, which opened without invitation as Rik Dean wafted in. Henry thought about saying something about manners, but bit his tongue.

'Post-mortem carried out on Rory Costain,' Rik announced brightly. 'Only confirms what we already know – shot in the head, massive brain trauma, some lovely chunks of bullet recovered.'

'We need to get them compared to the fragments recovered from Petrone, then the link will be conclusive, but I already believe it is. Can you fix that?'

'I've already got it put through Scientific Support and a motorcyclist is on his way with them to the forensic lab.'

'Good – and what about Billy Costain and Mandy Carter?'

'The pathologist will do Billy this evening and Mandy in the morning.' Rik checked his watch. 'She wants to start in an hour and said she'd like you to be there for that one.' Rik sneaked forward, bent slightly and wagged a finger at Henry. 'And not just because you're the SIO, I suspect. She spoke very affectionately about you.' He raised his eyebrows and Henry half-thought he was going to say, 'Nudge, nudge, wink, wink.' Instead, Rik said, 'You got something on the bubble with her?'

'No,' Henry said flatly, and if he could have, he would have sent Rik back to stand in on Billy's PM, but he knew it was something he had to do – professionally and personally. 'I'll be there.'

Rik did then wink. 'Just remember, pal. One day soon we may be kith and kin, you and me, so we now need to set the ground rules of infidelity.' Henry scowled at him. 'Like, if I stray and you find out – zip.' Rik pretended to zip-up his lips. 'And vice-versa . . . a family trust thing.' He looped his forefingers together and pulled, like they were links in a chain.

Henry said tiredly, 'My sister might be a doozy, but I actually think she'll see right through you sooner rather than later, or, vice-versa, you'll see through her, because she finds it equally hard to keep her panties on as you do your flies up. Don't want to be a killjoy, but if you two ever get hitched I'll show my ring-piece in Burton's window.'

'You can be very cutting, Henry.'

'The truth often has a sharp edge to it.' He looked down despondently at the murder book and closed it softly. He guessed it would be a midnight thing. 'Fancy a bite?'

Freshened and sated, Donaldson was back in Henry's study looking at the laptop. He had a small lager next to him on the desk, which he sipped. It was cold and tasted wonderful with the huge sandwich he'd just eliminated.

His fingertips rested on the keyboard, touching it lightly, but not pressing any keys. When the connection was made he went on to the FBI website and entered his password to take him on to the highly sensitive staff site. He was then asked a series of security questions to enable him to get further into the site and on to the databases he wanted to interrogate.

Things seemed to be going well.

He clicked on a folder named 'C2' and a prompt requested a further password from him, which he supplied, then hit 'enter' triumphantly.

There wasn't even a moment's hesitation before the screen flashed 'ACCESS DENIED'.

He cursed and tried again, thinking he might have entered an incorrect letter or digit, but the response was still the same.

He watched the screen for a few moments, then picked up his phone and dialled his office at the American embassy in London. Even though it was now well past office hours he had every expectation that his shared secretary, a very busty sixty-year-old career FBI admin lady named Jacintha, would still be hard at it. Her family had flown the coop, her husband had popped his clogs (as Donaldson believed they said up north when someone had died) and her life revolved around work, a tiny south London garden and four smelly cats.

'Cinth, it's me, Karl.'

'Hello, sir,' she said primly. All the men were deferred to as 'sir', whilst all the women were given short shrift.

'Cinth, I'm trying to log on to look at a file, but I can't seem to get into it for some reason. Any idea why?'

'Not in the least, sir.'

'Could you possibly do a quick check with the IT guys? I really need access. Then call me back?'

'Yes sir, no problem.'

Donaldson exited the programme and went on to his email. Two unread messages vied for his attention with little red flags, both from a Scandinavian lady who was becoming a nuisance. He knew he should really have deleted them without reading, but curiosity urged him on. The messages were actually blank, so he clicked on the attachments.

'Oh . . . my . . . God,' he said as he opened them. The photographs had obviously been taken by Vanessa herself – he hoped. They were detailed self-portraits of a particular part of her anatomy, held apart by her fingers in such a way that made him cringe.

'Not even a gynaecologist . . .' he started to say and deleted the photographs. He sat back and felt a little less fresh now. 'What have I done?' he asked himself.

His mobile phone rang.

'Karl, it's Don Barber – what's happening up there?'

'Erm . . .' he began, choosing his words carefully, 'we managed to get hold of the witness, who is now in custody in Blackpool,' he answered, trying to get his mind back on track.

'Is the lad any use at all?'

Donaldson blinked. 'Hard to say at this stage. Definitely saw the murderer, saw the killer's face and a photo was even taken on a cellphone . . .'

'What did the photo show?'

'That's a good question, Don – because the phone's missing. The witness who got murdered lost it whilst running away from the scene. So far it hasn't turned up, which is a pisser.'

'Yeah, yeah.'

'The police artist is going to spend some time with the witness tonight, so we'll see what comes out of that. Don, I can't seem to log on to some files I want to see. I wondered if you were having problems down there?'

'No, it's all working correctly far as I know.'

'Not what . . .' Donaldson started to blurt, about to say, 'I heard', but he stopped himself for some reason.

'What's that, buddy?' Barber asked.

'Nothing . . . hey, speak later, yeah?' Donaldson ended the call and sat pensively, mulling things over. He looked at his mobile phone and shook it, but his mind drifted back to the close-up shots he had received from Vanessa. 'Hell, I wonder if she wants me to send shots of me back to her?'

Henry ate a hearty tea, meat pie, chips, peas, gravy, mug of tea and another sticky bun. A real copper's feast and it tasted amazing. He had reached a stage in his life where, more often than not, he was reasonably careful about what went into his mouth, but every now and then an unhealthy meal or a fast food breakfast was just what the doctor ordered. The type of food he'd survived on in the eighties, and he always remembered having a stained tie from the juice that ran out of hot chip shop meat pies and always caught him off-guard. It was a long time since he'd eaten such a pie, but the memories lingered fondly.

He told Rik and Bill Robbins, who was still in the canteen, to hang fire, then he went down to the CID office to see how Alex Bent was faring with Mark Carter. Bent was standing at his desk, placing some paperwork on it, having just come back up from the custody suite. Henry asked him how it had gone.

He answered thoughtfully. 'OK. I've got the robbery stuff out of the way. He's having the Goth and the girl, no problems, and the attempt on the old man. And the shed break. Says he dumped the bike behind those shops near where Katie Bretherton lives. He's been fingerprinted, photographed and DNA'd, now he's just having some scran. A social worker's been with him, but he's gone out for some food, too. Told him to come back in an hour.'

'How is Mark?'

'Not good.'

'I need to get back to the mortuary, so if you can carry on with Mark, that'd be good. I take it you're getting on reasonably well with him?' Bent nodded. 'In that case, get a witness statement starting from the point where the old man gets hit by the car and up to the present, if you can. Include as much as you can.'

'I might not have time to get everything in it tonight. It'll be a long one – and the e-fit guy is here, too.'

'Do what you can, Alex. I'll pop down and see him on my way out.'

*   *   *

Mark had only ever been in a cell once in his life before, other than the one at Preston. That had been at Blackpool nick, too, and as he looked around the one he'd been placed in, he realized this was the same one. That was when he'd been locked up for shoplifting, the time when he'd gone off the rails following the death of his sister and he'd ended up running with a bad crew then. A bit like now, he thought as he looked at the sickly cream-flecked walls with obscenities carved into them along with names such as 'Kev', 'Rocky' and 'Moose ere 12/4'. Mark knew Moose, a bit of a no-brainer from Shoreside. Big, dumb and harmless, unless you laughed at him. Then he punched your lights out with frightening efficiency.

The key rattled in the door, which then creaked open. Henry Christie stood there. Mark said nothing, couldn't even be bothered to sneer at him any more. He was too tired.

'How're you doing?'

'Great.'

'I thought I'd tell you what happens now.'

'Not interested, Henry. I'll go with the flow. Big picture is that I'm going to end up in institutions until I'm eighteen – that's if I live long enough.'

'We'll discuss protection later. I just wanted to know how you were, that's all.'

Mark raised his chin and looked squarely at the detective. 'As if you give a shit.'

What stung Henry was that Mark was probably right. When he had met the lad before to investigate his sister's death, Henry had seen a good chance to use Mark to nail a big time drug dealer nicknamed the Crackman. He had played on Mark's vulnerability to get him in a position from where he could feed Henry information that would lead to the mystery dealer, and, in a skewed way, it had been a successful job. But along the way Henry had made some promises to Mark that he didn't keep, and that was partly why Mark had veered off the path and been drawn into Rory Costain's feral lifestyle.

But, like most cops, Henry shrugged off most of the guilt. There was only so much that could be done for people and, at the end of the day – a phrase Henry hated – he wasn't Mark's keeper. His mother was, and she'd failed. His big brother had a part to play, too – and he'd failed. Problem was, Mandy was all Mark had and now she was gone, so

Mark's future, particularly the next two years, looked very shaky indeed.

Henry's reassurances wafted over Mark's head. It was obvious he didn't believe a single word that came out of the detective's mouth. 'We'll look after you.' 'We'll sort you out.' 'You've nothing to worry about.' 'Honest.'

Bollocks.

Even Henry didn't believe himself.

All he really wanted from Mark was a statement and a good description of the murderer, then hopefully, if things got that far, for Mark to pick the guy out of a line-up. And then give evidence at court. If it got that far. A lot of 'ifs', the main one being 'if' an arrest was made. But the bottom line was that Mark was the main witness so far and he was expected to make a statement that would put his life in greater danger than it already was. On top of that he had to deal with his mother's murder, probably at the hands of the same person who had killed Rory and the old man. Not forgetting Billy Costain.

And Mark was sixteen. He was afraid, even if he didn't show it. He had no familial support. He did not trust the cops because they'd shafted him once before, and he was a troubled teenager with all the usual hormonal issues to deal with.

It was a very big ask for a very young boy. And, in truth, Henry wasn't completely sure how to deal with it. So after getting a very big flea in his ear from Mark, he made his way across to the mortuary where, it seemed, the bodies were stacking up. As he drove, his hands dithered on the steering wheel.

Karl Donaldson continued to try and log into the files he wanted to inspect without success, each time thinking this would be the occasion he got through. A bit like hitting the side of a TV in the hope that the picture would come back. It never did, of course.

Finally, seething, he picked up his phone again, which spookily, rang as his fingers closed on it.

'Mr Donaldson, sir, it's me, Jacintha.'

'Hi Cinth.' It was his shared secretary.

'You asked me to speak to the IT guy about your little difficulty.' The words 'little difficulty' came out and sounded like she was referring to erectile dysfunction or something.

'Yeah, I'm still struggling,' he said, as though he did have that condition.

'Well, the guy I spoke to was really shirty with me and told me it was none of his business.'

'Why would he say that?'

'I don't know. I told him I was making the enquiry on your behalf.'

'And?'

'He just said that your access had been denied.'

Donaldson's whole being missed a beat. 'What does that mean?'

'He wouldn't say.'

'Access denied?' Donaldson said, his voice rising. 'Who can deny me access to files I have a right to see?'

'Well, most files are password protected,' Jacintha said.

'I know that . . . and there are some I don't have access to, which I understand. But the ones I want to look at are, or were, available to me. Did the guy say anything else?'

'I asked him who you should talk to about it. It's obviously some sort of misunderstanding that needs clearing up.'

'Yep . . .' Donaldson waited.

'He said you need to speak to Mr Barber.'

Donaldson's mouth dried up. 'Don Barber? Why Don Barber?'

'He didn't say.'

'Right, well thanks for that, Cinth. I appreciate what you did. Can you put me through to Don, please?'

'He's not here.'

'What do you mean, not there? You mean he's gone home for the night?'

'No, I mean he isn't here. Hasn't been in the office for about four days now, sir.'

'Where is he?'

'That I don't know, Mr Donaldson, sir.'

FIFTEEN

'You didn't send your lackey this time?' Keira O'Connell said. She was scraping back her hair and fixing a dangerous-looking clip into it before fitting her surgical cap.

'A detective inspector's hardly a lackey,' said Henry, sounding tired. He had enough problems to be going on with and O'Connell's obvious annoyance at his rejection of her was starting to wear thin. 'Look, Keira,' he said reasonably, hoping that his massive male ego hadn't got things wrong or completely out of proportion. Maybe she was this cross all the time. 'I'm really flattered.' Already he knew he sounded patronizing. He wasn't good at saying no to women, not initially anyway. Only when the guilt kicked in. 'I'm trying desperately hard to make a go of it with Kate. And as much as the thought of being with a beautiful woman like you is –' his throat went gritty here as his thoughts instantly turned to what it would be like rolling around with her – oh, mama – 'incredible, I just can't risk anything.'

'Are you sure you're happily, *happily* married?' she asked simply. She picked up a scalpel.

'Yes,' he said without hesitation.

O'Connell's eyes played over his face, trying to see if there was a lie there. Her jaw line tensed and relaxed several times. 'OK,' she relented. 'Desperate woman, acting desperately . . .' She picked up a pair of latex gloves and blew into one of them, inflating it. 'Let's go and cut up our next body . . . people do seem to have a habit of dying around you, Henry,' she observed.

Billy Costain's large body had been laid out on the slab and prepared for post-mortem. A CSI was in position to record events.

Henry looked at the four bullet holes arced across Costain's wide chest, and he realized how close he himself had been to being the next body for examination. His phone vibrated in his pocket, making him jump.

'Excuse me.' It was 'Home' calling. He backed out of the mortuary and answered it, expecting to be speaking to Kate. 'Hiya, sweetheart.'

'I may be many things to you, but sweetheart ain't one of them, buddy,' Karl Donaldson told him.

'Oh, I don't know,' Henry said. 'What can I do for you?'

'You mentioned Jerry Tope, the custard cream licker?'

'What about him?'

'Can I borrow him after all? I'm still having difficulties, shall we say, accessing work. I could do with him having a look-see. And he owes me a favour for not sending him to prison for fifty years for hacking into the FBI website.'

'Which is what you want him to do now?'

'Well, yeah . . .'

'You're welcome to him. I'll have to ring off, find his number, then get back to you . . .'

'I've had a drink,' Jerry Tope said. 'Can't turn out.'

'How much have you had?'

'A pint.'

'And you can't drive after a pint?'

'I can drive after ten pints, I just choose not to,' Tope said, clearly annoyed at the interruption to his evening.

'I need your help. A computer thing. Can I come and see you?'

Tope sighed so heavily that Donaldson expected to feel a draught down the line.

'Where do you live?'

'A place called Lea, just on the Blackpool side of Preston.'

'Gimme the address, I'll find it,' Donaldson said. Tope told him, Donaldson scribbled it down and as an afterthought asked, 'Do you have a broadband connection?'

Tope tutted and said, 'No, I'm the only computer geek in the world without one.'

'Sorry.' Donaldson hung up gently, his mind in turmoil, still completely unable to fathom out why he should have been denied access to FBI files. Then another thought struck him. 'Shit, I don't have a car.'

For some reason beyond Henry's comprehension, Kate had always seen herself driving a Fiat 500. So when the model was redesigned and the opportunity presented itself, she bought one. There was no doubt about it. They were classy, cool, small – tiny – cars, and, for a woman of Kate's stature, ideal.

Not so for Karl Donaldson. Six-four and broad to match, when Kate waggled her keys at him and said, 'You're more than welcome to borrow it,' he wondered just how the hell he was going to fit into it. His own car was a spacious Jeep.

'This looks like a bizarre logic puzzle,' he said. 'Rearrange this shape –' he wafted his hand down his body – 'to fit into that cupboard. Last time I had my knees around my ears was when the doctor was massaging my prostate.'

'Far too much detail, and an image I'll be unable to wipe from my mind forever.'

'Didn't you used to have a Ford?'

'Fell to bits.' She jangled the keys and dropped them on to his open palm.

He approached the car with trepidation and like a member of a circus freak show, folded himself into it limb by limb.

As well as the luxurious transport, Kate had also provided Donaldson with a satnav into which he keyed Jerry Tope's postcode, and pulled up outside the pleasant semi-detached house some twenty minutes after leaving Blackpool. A combination of tiredness and the physical assaults he'd endured recently had made him stiffen up on the journey in the Fiat and he had to force his joints to open in order to get out of the car.

Tope came to the door to greet him, grinning at the size of the car versus the size of the man. Noticing the smirk, Donaldson said, 'I'm good at getting big things into tiny spaces.'

He shook hands with Tope, who gestured for him to enter the house where he was then introduced to Tope's wife who was emerging from the kitchen. She was a tiny, rotund ball of a lady, with thick spectacles, a serious monobrow and facial hair issues.

'Marina, this is Karl Donaldson I was telling you about.'

Donaldson proffered his hand. Mrs Tope squinted up at him as she shook his hand – and gasped as he came into focus. Tope eyed both of them and noticed his wife's reaction with a drop of his face.

'Err,' he interrupted, 'what exactly do you want me to do?'

Unwillingly, Marina Tope let go of his squeezed hand.

'Could we talk privately?' he asked Tope. He glanced at the wife. 'Nothing personal, but . . .'

'Ooh, I understand. Why don't you take him up to your room, Jezzer? I could bring a drink up for you both. Tea, coffee, something stronger?'

'Tea, milk, no sugar, would be excellent, thanks.'

'Consider it done.' She bit her bottom lip and Donaldson saw that her top set of teeth were like tombstones.

'Yeah, yeah, come on up,' Tope said. 'And I'll have a brew too, luv.' Tope steered his visitor toward the stairs. 'First on left.'

Donaldson had to duck on the stairs as he went up, then also to get into Tope's room, which was a back bedroom.

'You've got your own rumpus room?'

'Yeah . . . no kids,' he said wistfully.

Donaldson had expected an all-singing, all-dancing technology show. Instead, he found the room to have been kitted out as a study but with plenty of bookshelves and cupboards. The books on display were mainly thick, Tom Clancy type techno-thrillers, but there was a good selection about computers too. He had also expected to be faced by a barrage of computer screens and stacks and bits 'n' pieces, and satellite dishes, but all there was, was a desktop PC and a laptop next to it. Knowing what he knew about Tope, Donaldson was a tad disappointed that he wasn't looking at a room from somewhere like Bletchley Park.

'You OK?' Tope asked him.

'Yeah . . . kind of thought . . .'

'Bells and whistles? Was once like that, but truth is you don't need all that much crap these days. Just keep your machines up to date and Bob's your uncle. Although I do own an exact replica of an Enigma decoding machine.'

'I'd like to see that,' Donaldson said. 'One of those things we Yanks liberated from a German U-boat, if I'm not mistaken.' He saw Tope stiffen at the twist of history. 'Only kidding,' he said.

'Mm.' Tope sounded doubtful. 'Anyway – take a pew.'

He sat on one of the two office chairs and it creaked under his weight. He'd brought along his own laptop, which he hoisted on to the desk. 'I want you to do some hacking for me.'

O'Connell was deep inside Billy Costain's chest cavity when Henry's mobile phone rang again. He was glad of the diversion because the atmosphere between him and the pathologist wasn't really conducive to a pleasant post-mortem, if such a thing could exist. She had turned to ice since he'd snubbed her and the already chilly temperature of the mortuary seemed to have a second layer to it.

It was Donaldson on the phone. 'Need to see you urgently, Henry,' who didn't need to be a detective to detect the extremely worried tone.

'I'm up to my neck in blood and guts,' Henry told him. 'Only about a quarter of the way through a PM.'

'How about I see you there, then – half an hour?'

'I take it you've unveiled something of interest?'

'Understatement, buddy, understatement.'

'Do we need anyone else here?'

'People you trust,' Donaldson said and hung up.

Henry had backed out of the mortuary to take the call in the room where the body fridges were stacked against the wall. As he ended the call, he looked up to see a figure enter the mortuary and his heart sank a little. It was FB, the Chief Constable. Bobby Big-nuts.

Billy Costain's bullet-shredded lungs were just about to be removed when the last of the specially invited guests arrived at the mortuary and squeezed into the office. Henry had managed to find a couple of extra chairs, and space was limited. FB, of course, had claimed pole position on the largest, comfy chair behind the desk. Henry was in a plastic chair next to him. Karl Donaldson, edgy and upright, had declined the offer of a seat. There was no way he could have sat down for any length of time because he was like a caged tiger. Jerry Tope was sitting alongside Bill Robbins and Rik Dean leaned against the back wall. Last to arrive was Alex Bent, the DS who had been dealing with Mark Carter.

Henry inspected the faces. With the exception of FB, he trusted each one of these people without question. He only mistrusted FB in the area of 'Me', but otherwise he begrudgingly trusted him, too.

Donaldson chewed his nails nervously. He sighed, troubled.

FB scowled at him.

Henry nodded at Bent. 'OK?'

'Yes, sorry I'm a bit late. Just finishing up with Mark.'

'Where is he now?'

'I handed him over to social services . . . is that OK? They're going to provide him with some short-term accommodation and then we'll arrange an urgent case conference to decide what to do with him. And this is the e-fit.' He showed Henry the product of Mark's memory and a computer programme.

Donaldson looked at it as it went round the room. He did not display any reaction to the picture, but inside he went icy.

Henry's lips twisted and he shook his head sadly as he thought about Mark. There was one lad he had seriously let down and he wasn't sure how to make amends. However, that would have to wait. Henry turned to Donaldson. They'd had a rushed discussion before everyone had landed and Henry knew what he was going to say, but wasn't sure how things would be taken forward from that point. 'Karl?' he prompted.

'Uh.' Donaldson came back from wherever he'd been, 'OK.' He took a deep, unsteady breath. 'It's a tough one, this,' he admitted. 'But I think Rosario Petrone, Rory Costain, Billy Costain –' he jerked a thumb in the direction of the mortuary – 'and Mark

Carter's mother –' he pointed at the bank of fridges, in one of
which was Mandy Carter's body – 'were murdered by an FBI
hit squad.'

His eyes went from one man to the next. If he'd intended to
shock them, he'd succeeded. Every mouth had popped open,
with the exception of FB who said gruffly, 'We're listening.'

'Let me just say this first,' Donaldson continued. 'I've got a
lot of work to do on this, but I reckon this is the way the cards
are stacking. Some of you know some of the stuff I'm about to
say. However, I think I need to go over it again so everyone's
reading from the same page, as it were. Forgive me if you already
know these facts, but I'll try and keep it succinct.'

'If you would,' FB could not help but say.

The two men exchanged a scowl.

'For several years the FBI had an undercover operative who
had infiltrated one of the Camorra Mafia clans – the Marinis.
He operated at a pretty high level—'

'Sorry . . . I'm not up to speed on this,' Bill Robbins interrupted, 'but why was he there? What was he doing?'

'He was there because we are interested in the Camorra. They
have worldwide networks in place and though they remain Naples
based, they are spreading and they're rich, powerful and ruthless, as you guys know. Jerry here gave you a good background
briefing, I believe. This operative, codenamed Shark, was unfortunately murdered by a hit man known as "The American" about
three years ago. No one knew he was undercover, no one does
even now. But he was killed alongside a Camorra leader called
Marini. The hit, our intelligence suggested, was ordered by
Rosario Petrone. Our guy wasn't the target, he was just collateral
damage.

'You know of the gang war this hit sparked off – again, I
know Jerry did a great job of briefing you all on this. Marini
versus Petrone, and lots of people died . . . but that aside, I was
tasked to track down the hit man known as the American.'

'Just you?' Bill asked.

'Just me. Not a simple task, but hey, I got on with it and
didn't get anywhere until a guy called Fazil got arrested by
chance in Malta a few days ago. He was linked forensically to
the murder scene as the guy who supplied the weapon for the
American. So, I go to see Fazil, who gets killed in police custody
before I can get anything out of him.' Donaldson considered
telling them about the murder of two cops and his own run-in

with the gunman, but decided against it. He had a quick story to tell and didn't want to bog it down in peripheral detail. 'You guys with me so far?'

All nodded silently, even FB.

'Oh, sorry guys,' Alex Bent said apologetically and reached into his pocket to come out with his vibrating mobile phone. He checked the display and said, 'I probably need to get this.'

'OK, go ahead,' Henry said and Bent sidled out of the room.

Donaldson felt like his head was about to explode. He had developed a huge arc of pain over his eyes and if he had suffered from them, he would have said it was a migraine. It was staggering in its intensity, like a hammer drill boring out holes behind his eyes.

'Are you all right?' Henry asked, picking up on his friend's condition.

'Stress headache.'

Alex Bent came back in, a serious look on his face.

'Henry – the mobile phone stolen from the Goth . . . it's been switched on, the phone company's triangulating its position now, as we speak.'

SIXTEEN

Ellen Thompson had been a public enquiry assistant at Blackpool police station for just over six months. She was twenty-three years old, a single mother with a two-year-old son and lived on and off with her partner, Lee Clarke, in a rented terrace house just to the north of the town centre. She had no previous convictions, otherwise she would never have got the job, but Lee Clarke had. He was a drug user, small time thief and handler of stolen goods.

At the time of Ellen's application for a job as a PEA, she and Lee were having one of their regular splits from each other. Consequently, the rather flimsy background check on her did not reveal Lee's presence in her life. Ellen had been desperate for a decent, regular job with a bit of flexibility in it and being a PEA, whilst not massively remunerated, was good work, well within her capabilities and actually pretty interesting.

However, two months after proudly securing the job, Lee Clarke came back on the scene. A bad boy, full of charm, and try as she might, Ellen could not resist him and his bad influence.

On top of which, the fact he was the father of her son was an extra pull on her heart strings.

At first, on his return to her life he was, as usual, remorseful, brimming with positives and promises. He said he'd put his drug habit behind him, kicked thieving, kicked booze.

And she fell for it.

Then her money started to disappear and he was obviously back on the line.

Money was tight and he needed more and more to fund the habit of a lifetime.

Then they had the conversation. 'Do you get cash handed into you?'

'Occasionally.'

'Other stuff?'

'Lots of stuff, but we mostly tell people to keep what they find.'

Lee looked pensively at her, his devious mind working the angles.

He continued to steal and waste even more money.

Then, as things became tight again and desperation grew, she committed the first theft at his suggestion. Cash needed to feed a baby. Fifty pounds found by an old woman on the bus station. Ellen said she should hand it over because someone had already reported it lost, which was a lie. She entered it into the found property book behind the desk at the police station and a couple of days later, the owner's signature appeared and the cash was handed back. Apparently.

A couple of other thefts followed the same route. Only small amounts, but a great help all the same. And then a mobile phone was handed in by one of the smelly town centre drunks who was always in the station, either under arrest for being drunk and disorderly, or simply because he could not stay away from the cop shop. It drew him like a magnet and he was often escorted off the premises. His boozed up breath even made it through the security screen the day he came in when Ellen was on duty. He had obviously been imbibing for a number of hours. His words slurred loudly and he rambled on about being certain two lads had robbed him. On the other hand, he wasn't sure if he'd spent his money, but could definitely recall a dream in which two youths had been through his pockets and nicked his cash – and his cider. Later that night, he'd been staggering through the streets when he kicked something on the floor, which turned out to be a mobile phone someone had dropped.

He pushed it on to the sliding tray, then turned and rolled out of the station, waving dismissively. A drunk like him had no use for such a device.

Ellen took the phone, saw it was a good model, put it into her locker to sneak home later. The appearance of the firearms PC asking awkward questions about a phone had spooked her and she decided she had better take it home, just in case further inquiries were made.

It didn't matter if the phone had been blocked.

Lee knew someone who could unblock it, then it could be sold on and would be worth quite a few quid.

Though Ellen had only come on at four that day, she wanted an early finish. Lee had been on to her continually, calling and texting her frequently on her mobile, pleading for her to come home. Pack in the stupid job. Come home and fuck, then go out and get rat-arsed together. The kid had been farmed out to her mother, so that wouldn't be anything to worry about. He was high or drunk or both, and the problem was, Ellen wanted to be too. The quick answer was to throw a sickie. She simply told the communications room sergeant she was going home because she felt nauseous with women's problems.

She left at nine thirty with the phone in her bag. Curiosity made her switch it on as she got into her battered Ford Fiesta in the car park. The message that came up said, 'This phone is barred from use.' No surprise there.

They ran out to their cars. Henry to his Mondeo, FB to his massive four-by-four Lexus, Bill Robbins to the Ford Galaxy belonging to the ARV unit, Bent to his VW Golf, Donaldson and Jerry Tope to the Fiat 500, and Rik Dean to the Mercedes Coupe that actually belonged to Henry's sister.

Henry stopped mid-track, seeing the Keystone Kops side of this surge of manpower. 'I think this is a bit of overkill, don't you fellas?' He gestured with a shrug and his hands.

FB said, 'You guys get on with it – I don't do operational,' effectively withdrawing himself from the job, much to Henry's relief.

'Bill, Jerry, Alex and Rik – you jump in the Galaxy. Karl, you come with me.'

The relief in the American's face was evident. He had given Jerry Tope a ride to the mortuary in the Fiat 500 and the shoe-horning of the two men into it had not been a pretty sight.

'We can come back for the other cars as and when,' Henry said and they all piled into the allocated vehicles. Henry flicked open the glove compartment and grabbed his PR, switching it on. He called into comms. He told them who was in each vehicle and said, 'Please go ahead with the directions from the phone company. And I want a dedicated operator on this for the time being,' he ordered loftily. The power of a superintendent.

'Roger, that will be me,' the operator responded.

'Update, please,' Henry said.

'At the moment the phone signal is still moving northwards, still in Blackpool.'

'Roger that,' Henry said.

'DI Dean, I also received that,' Rik said over his PR on behalf of the crew in the Galaxy.

'Superintendent Christie to DI Dean, let's get moving then, please.'

The two cars sped off the mortuary car park and headed towards Blackpool.

'You OK,' Henry asked Donaldson as the Mondeo shot through a set of lights outside the hospital.

'So-so . . . shaken and stirred,' Donaldson admitted. 'I can't believe what I think I know . . . and that e-fit, hell, that made me shiver . . . the likeness. That lad Carter must have good eyesight.'

'To see and remember, and be able to describe a face in such detail . . . he must have eyes like a shithouse rat.'

'Hey, babe,' Lee Clarke slurred as Ellen Thompson entered the living room of their tiny house on north shore. She pulled off her coat and tossed it across the dining table on top of a pile of other clothes. 'I knew you'd come . . . babe, I missed you. I hate you working.'

'Well if I didn't, we'd have nothing at all, would we?' She sat down, unzipped her tight boots and peeled them off with gratitude. They were killing her feet.

Clarke was smoking a joint and Ellen sniffed appreciatively. 'Good shit,' she said and waggled her fingers at him in a 'gimme' gesture.

'Last one,' Clarke said sadly, inspecting the spliff. She waggled her fingers more urgently. 'Oh, babe,' he whined.

'Give.'

Reluctantly, he handed her the joint and she took the last drag, holding the smoke deep in her lungs, feeling the wonderful euphoria of the drug seep into every part of her body. She exhaled slowly and sat back.

'You got some dosh?' Clarke asked.

'Few quid.'

'Enough for a few pints and some more good shit?'

'Dunno, dunno.' The cannabis had made her feel out of it already.

'Nobody handed any cash in today for you to take a percentage?'

'No . . . oh, I did get something . . .' She crossed unsteadily to the dining table, rooted in her coat and found the mobile phone. She handed it to Clarke. 'You can get something for this, can't you?'

Clarke inspected it. He had stolen and fenced many a mobile phone and knew their worth. 'Found property?' he said with a knowing chortle.

'Our property,' Ellen said.

'Hey, this is a good phone,' he said appreciatively.

'How much?'

'Forty quid, I guess. It sells in the hundreds.'

'Can you get that tonight?'

'Oh, yes.'

'So we can party, party, party?'

'Oh yeah.'

She stood in front of him, still dressed in the knee length, but tight, skirt and white blouse of her PEA uniform. She hitched up the skirt and straddled him. 'Let's start how we mean to go on,' she said, slowly unbuttoning the blouse.

Clarke's eyes misted lustfully over as he reached up and grabbed her generous boobs. She leaned into him and mashed her lips on to his, forcing her tongue into his mouth.

The pounding on the door was a rude interruption.

Clarke pulled his head away and gasped. 'I hope that's not Tweedy,' he said, referring to his dealer. 'I owe him some money, but coming round here is bang out of order. Ignore him.'

But the knocking persisted in an authoritative way. Whoever it was, wasn't going to go away in a hurry.

'Shit,' Clarke said and pushed Ellen to one side, extracting himself from underneath her. She moaned with annoyance as Clarke got up and said, 'I'll piss him off.'

'How much do you owe him?'

'Dunno. Twenty, I guess. Not a lot.'

For Mark Carter it might as well have been another police cell. Out of one, into another, the only difference being this one was en-suite and the bed looked half-comfortable and inviting.

'You're lucky,' the social worker had told him on the way.

'And why would that be?' he asked harshly. The social worker, God bless him, came across as a decent kind of guy, trying his best to do a thankless job with a stroppy teenager. However, Mark had no intention of making anything easy for him.

'You're the first guest. The place doesn't officially open until next week after being refurbished. People haven't started filtering in and out yet.'

'Inmates, you mean?'

'I mean young people with serious needs.'

'So there won't be anyone else there tonight?'

'Nope – just you. But I'll be in a room down the corridor if you need anything. I won't be far away.'

'Like bumming, you mean?'

'Eh?' Then the guy got it, reddened and laughed nervously. 'We're not all raving perverts, you know,' he chuckled with a tinge of hurt.

'Well that's reassuring,' Mark said. 'I feel as if I'm being bum-fucked anyway. You might as well just do it for real. I don't give a toss.'

'Now then, Mark. We're simply interested in your welfare, that's all. You've been through a lot and we're trying to do the right thing for you.'

'Oh? And do I get to have a say in what the right thing is?'

'Of course you do, Mark, of course you do.'

Mark had been handed over to the care of the social worker after he had spent some time with Alex Bent making a witness statement and then with the police artist at the computer, compiling an e-fit of the guy he had seen murder the old man. When finished, Mark had been spooked by the likeness. It was spot on.

He had then protested he didn't need social services and could easily look after himself, and would answer bail and not do a runner. Unfortunately, by virtue of the fact he'd been arrested doing a runner was just one of the things that negated his argument. He had money in his pocket and the police thought he would probably never be seen again. He was also a juvenile who had just lost a parent, did not have any other immediate family, and there was a responsibility to ensure his safety. That meant, for the short-term at least, Mark would be put in a home.

Had Mark known anything about stereotypes, he would have sneered at the social worker's car. A completely knackered old Citroen with a gear lever coming out of the dashboard, which was built as flimsily as a paper house in Japan. Instead, he sat glumly in the front seat, his mind in turmoil.

'Is my mum really dead?' Mark asked at one point.

'I'm afraid so, Mark.'

'Whatever.'

They drove up the promenade, passing the Norbreck Castle Hotel on the right, until they came to Little Bispham where the social worker pulled the car across the road into the wide driveway of a large detached house opposite the tram stop at Melton Place. It was a big, old, imposing building, erected some time between the world wars, called Cleveley House.

'Here we are.'

Mark eyed the place and sighed. 'This isn't secure accommodation, is it? I mean, I don't have to stay here if I don't want to.'

'In theory, Mark, you can walk out anytime.'

'Which means I can't, obviously.'

'It means that if you do, next time you will end up in a secure home. You see, there is a bit of trust needed here. We know you're a sensible lad and that you know it'd be silly to walk away because of the consequences.'

'Some bloody situation.'

'Come on, let's make the best of it. Let's get you settled in, then let's go out and get a takeaway, my treat, then come back and watch TV for a while and try to chill our beans. There's satellite TV on a forty-two-inch screen in one of the lounges, so we could either watch a film that's on, or hire one for the night. Up to you.'

'Tch.' Mark shook his head.

'I'm Barry, by the way.'

'Whatever.'

The social worker unlocked the front door of the house and they entered a grand hallway, with a central staircase that split either way on the first floor. He showed Mark to a bedroom at the end of a long corridor up the stairs.

'This is yours. If you want to get a shower, then maybe come down to the kitchen at the back of the house?' The social worker, Barry, nodded reassuringly as he spoke, trying to be infectious in his positivity. 'There are towels and soap and stuff. No change of clothing yet, but I'll sort that in the morning.'

And that was something Mark had not really thought about. Tomorrow. He sat on the bed, brooding, his brain churning. Part of him wanted to walk out, another part craved the security that this place, and Barry, offered. He also needed to sleep. Tiredness overwhelmed him. A night in a coal-hole and a shed hadn't really been all that comfortable. He decided to forego the shower and go straight for the food. He fancied a Chinese. He was famished and very thirsty all of a sudden. Wearily, he stood up and sauntered back along the corridor to the top of the stairs. He paused here, wondering if he really wanted to spend any time with the good-natured Barry. There was every possibility he would drive Mark mad. Maybe being alone would be the best end for the day. Let it all roll and tumble through his mind.

But he was still starving and the thought of a Chinese chicken curry was appealing, and things would feel so much better on a full stomach.

He placed his foot on the first step down – which is when he heard the crash from the kitchen at the back of the house.

'Are we sure this is the one?'

'Down to three metres, or so I'm told,' Henry said to Donaldson. 'This was the location of the last pulse before the phone signal went dead.'

'Are they ever gonna answer the door?'

Henry pounded on the front door of the house to which the phone company had directed them. They had been standing outside the terraced house on Cornwall Avenue in North Shore for a couple of minutes. Henry's car was at the kerb, as was the Galaxy driven by Bill Robbins, containing the others.

Henry was getting impatient, thinking the occupants could have seen who was knocking and decided not to open up. He rattled the door, but it was firmly locked.

Then he regarded Donaldson and said, 'I am about to exercise my power of entry.'

'Which power is that?'

Henry could have reeled off the many he knew that gave him

the right to burst into peoples' homes unannounced, but just said, 'I'll think of one that fits.'

He took a step back, braced himself, then flat-footed the door just underneath the Yale lock. It was a powerful, well delivered kick, but only rattled the door in its frame. He repeated the action, but it still held firmly.

'Lost my touch,' he muttered angrily. 'Getting old.'

Donaldson elbowed him out of the way. 'Allow me.'

His first mighty kick almost took the door off its hinges. He stepped aside and allowed the English detective to enter the vestibule, shouting 'Police' as he barged in, through the inner door into the narrow hallway where he almost tripped over the body that lay diagonally across the floor, slumped half against the wall. Henry just managed to stop himself from pitching head-long on to the floor.

Lee Clarke had a neat bullet hole in the centre of his fore-head. He'd obviously been standing when shot, answering the door, facing the person who had killed him. The bullet had entered his skull an inch above the bridge of his nose and removed the back third of his cranium. He'd probably stag-gered a couple of steps, spiralled and fallen. The remaining pieces of his brains had dribbled out underneath him and he was now lying untidily in a thick, disgusting pool of blood and other matter.

Donaldson peered past Henry. 'You know this guy?'

'No – but I know her.' Henry was looking into the living room.

Still in her PEA uniform, Ellen Thompson was as dead as her drug-addled boyfriend. The crimson flowers of blood on her white shirt were still blossoming and the fingers of her right hand were jerking spasmodically in after-death. She had been shot at the door to the living room, maybe coming to see what was going on in the hall, only to be greeted by a gunman who had stepped over Clarke's body and killed her just as mercilessly. She had fallen back and was sitting upright on the settee, arms and legs splayed at wide angles and, despite the twitching, dead.

'Shit,' Donaldson said. The eyes of the two men locked as they both had the same, dreadful thought. The witness, Mark Carter.

SEVENTEEN

Henry Christie moved into gear, excitement and fear coursing through him, coupled with the experience of thirty years as a cop responding – occasionally – to life and death situations. Of course, there was nothing to say that Mark Carter's life was really in danger, but at that moment Henry was furious with himself for just allowing the lad to be handed over to social services without adequate protection. Like everything else in the police, it was usually better to do things over the top than to look stupid and investigate a death that might have been prevented. Henry kicked himself for underestimating the ruthlessness, cunning and resources of the people who had killed Rosario Petrone and any witnesses to their crime.

Somehow they had been able to beat the police in tracking the mobile phone signal. Whether that was through the unguarded way in which the location of the pulse had been transmitted via radio communications, or because they too had access to mobile phone companies and tracking equipment, Henry could not be certain. But from what he knew of Karl Donaldson's suspicions, he guessed it was both, which made him even more irate at himself. How could he have forgotten the lesson he learned that resulted in the death of Billy Costain? How could they possibly have known that the radio transmissions were about the mobile phone that had been used to take the photographs of the murder taking place? Henry was sure that was never mentioned over the air, but he would have to listen to a recording of it to make sure.

It put them ahead of the police in time and distance.

If they could locate a mobile phone signal, if they could listen into encrypted police radio messages, then it would be simple for them to track down and kill the last witness whose only protection was a social worker.

Henry and Donaldson raced out of the terraced house and up to the Ford Galaxy in which sat Bill Robbins at the wheel, with Alex Bent, Rik Dean and Jerry Tope alongside and behind him. He yanked open the passenger door and spoke hurriedly.

'Alex, Rik, Jerry – you need to cover this scene.'

'What scene?' Rik said. He was in the front passenger seat alongside Robbins.

'They got here before us. Two bodies, both shot to death. You guys cover the scene.' He handed Rik his car keys. 'Bill, you, me and Karl are going up to Cleveley House just to make sure Mark Carter is safe and well.'

'Got it,' Robbins said.

'Alex – do you have the phone number of Cleveley House and the social worker who took Mark with him?'

'No, but comms should have Cleveley House in their records and the social worker's mobile number is on Mark's custody record.'

'Right . . . I'll sort them.' Henry glanced at everyone's face as no one seemed to want to move. 'Come on, let's get shifting . . . lives at stake, here.'

Mark reached the foot of the stairs in silence and could hear raised, angry voices from the kitchen, furniture scraping on hard floors. He moved along the hallway, edging along the wall, passing the TV lounge, then a door with a toilet sign on it, until he was a few feet short of the kitchen where he flattened himself tight, back to the wall, and steeled himself to peek around the door. That was when he heard the social worker scream, 'Mark – run.'

At the age of forty, Barry Philips had come late to social work, and actually wasn't really anything like the stereotype of the profession. He'd ended up there through the path of redundancy than through any great desire to help people, but found that he loved the job. Working with teenage boys was the area he got the most out of. He found them fascinating and a great challenge, and although he had only just met Mark Carter, he could see a lot of good in a boy who was fundamentally decent and intelligent, but had experienced major traumatic events in his life. Because of Mark's age, Philips knew the reality was that he wouldn't be spending much, if any, time in care, but Philips was determined to do everything he could for a lad who had definitely been given the shit end of a prickly stick.

Philips already knew Mark would give him a rough ride, but he was looking forward to giving him a settled night in Cleveley House. Maybe at some stage there would be the chance of an exploratory chat about the future and what Mark saw, although he also guessed it would be a difficult subject to broach as the immediate past had yet to be dealt with properly.

In some ways, Cleveley House would be a blessing. Just the two of them, no interruptions. On the other hand, as comfortable as he would be, the night would be a lonely one for Mark once he was in bed.

However, under the circumstances, nothing could ever be perfect for someone who'd just lost their mother in horrific circumstances, as well as a friend, and had witnessed others being murdered. But Philips still relished the possibility of helping Mark to deal with these things . . . if only Mark would allow it to happen and would not clam up.

At least he had got Mark as far as the home, then into it, then up to the bedroom. Philips had had kids jump out of his car at the first set of traffic lights before now. But Mark was obviously shell-shocked, Philips had thought as he left him in the bedroom and went back to the kitchen.

The house had been well renovated and was due to be opened properly for business the week after. Philips had only managed to get Mark into it because everywhere else in the area was full to bursting. There was an overnight space in a home in Rossendale, but Philips had argued with his boss that a forty-mile journey was out of the question. His boss had relented when Philips had volunteered to stay over with Mark, and had let him use Cleveley House.

The kitchen was big enough to fit a small dining table and Philips sat at it, and opened his laptop and diary and placed his mobile phone on the table next to him. He needed to catch up on his notes before doing anything else. He was conscientious like that. There was a lot to write about Mark and he wanted to do it whilst it was still fresh in his mind.

He was so engrossed in it, working hard with his head resting on his left hand as he wrote, that the next time he glanced up, the three men had already entered the kitchen from the back door.

Each was wearing a balaclava ski mask, all dressed in black, two carrying handguns and one a large hunting knife. It was this one who, even before Philips could rise or even utter a gasp, moved behind the social worker with a roar of warning, dragged his head back to expose his neck and had laid the blade of the knife across the windpipe, the kitchen chair scraping the floor as it moved.

'Where's the boy?' one of the others shouted, stepped forwards and held the muzzle of his gun against Philips's temple.

Philips swallowed, his eyes wide in terror, feeling his throat ripple across the knife blade. Yet in spite of the predicament and his own personal danger, Philips still believed his first duty was to protect the life of the boy he had been put in charge of.

'What boy?'

The man with the gun bent to his face. 'Don't be a dick, I know he's here,' he said savagely. 'I've just followed you from the police station. Where is he? Tell us, save time, save anguish.'

'This place is empty except for me,' Philips said bravely.

The man stood upright. His eyes flicked sideways to the man who had the knife at the social worker's throat.

'Kill him.'

There was a moment of hesitation, a millisecond that Philips took advantage of and he screamed, 'Mark – run!'

Then the man behind him pushed his head forwards and at the same time drew the knife across his throat. Not tidily, not a nice slice, but roughly gouging and riving the blade into the larynx, pulling hard, pushing the head down, sawing, grinding, finding the carotid, then swiping the knife free as Philips, clutching desperately at his torn throat, fell off the chair. Everything twitched. He gagged horribly, gurgled, spat blood, which also pumped out of his neck via the severed artery. Then he no longer clutched at his neck, but for something above him. His fingers tensed and contracted as they seemed to reach for the light above. Then the gushing eased, his hands relaxed with no strength left in them, and flopped to the floor. The jerking of his feet slowed, became less urgent, gentler as though he was walking in his sleep, then ceased altogether.

'Find him, quickly,' said the only man who had spoken, ripping the telephone off the wall as it began to ring, then scooping Philips's mobile off the table and stamping on it.

'You know where we're going?'

Bill Robbins nodded, and as he did a quick shoulder check, accelerating away from the kerb, said, 'Used to be a bail hostel, as I recall.'

'What firearms have you got?'

'Glock on the waist, H&K, baton launcher and Taser in the safe. The usual.'

Henry nodded, then used his PR to call in, interrupting a

two-way conversation between two other patrols. 'Detective Superintendent Christie to Blackpool, urgent, repeat, urgent.'

'Patrols stand by,' the operator came in who was the one running the mobile phone location incident. 'Go ahead, sir.'

'Carrying on from the previous job, please send all available patrols to Cleveley House in Little Bispham. No one to enter the premises and I want everyone to RV at a point of your choosing, comms. I want the ARV down there . . . suspect armed individuals could be at the address intending to cause harm to a boy called Mark Carter. I'm en-route with one armed officer – don't ask – ETA maybe one minute.'

'Affirmative . . . RV point to be Little Bispham tram stop on the promenade opposite Wilvere Drive – received?'

'Received,' Henry said. 'Know it?' he asked Robbins, who nodded.

'Only two patrols available to attend at present, though, sir, both in South.'

'Send them,' Henry ordered. 'What about the ARV?'

'On refs.'

'Turn them out immediately, get back to me when you have and I'll give you more instructions and details.' Henry squirmed to look over his shoulder at Donaldson. 'I was half-hoping that if the bad guys are monitoring us, the massive response we deployed would be enough to make them think twice. As it happens, it's pathetic. Two patrols miles away and the ARV stuffing butties down their necks.'

'Not sure anything would make much difference,' Donaldson said. 'They're ahead of us anyway, they move fast and there's every likelihood they've already dealt with him and gone.' He clicked his fingers as though this was all a waste of time.

'Come on, Bill, get this tug moving.' Henry smacked the dashboard.

'I am, but this is a police owned Ford Galaxy, not a Maserati – and where did you get an ETA of one minute from?'

'Bit of an exaggeration?'

'By about four minutes, not counting traffic,' Bill said as he careened on to the roundabout at Gynn Square and gunned the vehicle sluggishly around it, blue lights on and a weary two-tone horn sounding as they hit the promenade northwards in the direction of Bispham.

'Blackpool – Superintendent Christie.'

'Receiving.'

'ARV en-route.'

'Thanks for that . . . now call Cleveley House and see if you can contact a social worker called Barry Philips. He should be there. Also contact the custody office. This man's mobile phone number should be in Mark Carter's custody record. If you can't get a response from Cleveley House, call the mobile. It's imperative we contact this guy, as he's the one with Carter.'

Mark heard Barry Philips scream out the warning and for an instant he could not move. He could not even begin to imagine what had happened in the kitchen, around the corner, probably less than a dozen feet away from where he was standing. He'd heard the shout, then what? Maybe the sounds of a struggle, the thump of something heavy – a body? – hitting the floor and a horrible gurgling, gagging sound.

Then he moved. He spun away from the wall, taking two long paces, pivoted into the TV lounge, his eyes searching for a hiding place. There wasn't much choice. The furniture consisted of one L-shaped sofa pushed up into one corner of the room, then a couple of mismatched armchairs and, of course, the 42-inch TV that Barry Philips had boasted about, which was screwed to the wall.

Basically nowhere.

Panic overwhelmed him momentarily before he scrambled over to the settee, pulled it away from the wall and crawled in backwards behind it, like some crustacean reversing into its shell. He stretched himself out as long and as thin as he could and tugged the settee back up to him. He had to grind his teeth together to stop them chattering. He tensed every muscle tight and hoped he didn't emit some wimpy squeak of terror or fart of fear that would give away his position.

'No reply from either number,' the comms operator informed Henry.

'Keep trying, please.'

'Will do.'

Henry and Donaldson exchanged a worried look. 'Doesn't necessarily mean anything,' Henry said.

'No, you're right,' Donaldson said.

Neither man meant it.

Robbins performed a dangerous swerving overtake through a set of traffic lights, finding the narrow channel between the vehicle to his nearside and the oncoming one. He saw the driver of that one, who seemed to have big, wide eyes and an expression of horror on his face. He powered on, the Galaxy having picked up momentum, a bit like a container ship.

'We're probably about thirty seconds away,' Bill said, flicking off the lights and siren.

'Pull in here,' Henry instructed him, pointing to a spot at the roadside. Robbins braked sharply and veered into a halt.

A few beats passed.

'What the hell're you doing?' Donaldson demanded.

'Waiting for back up. This is the RV point – Wilvere Drive.'

Donaldson screwed up his face at Henry. 'You kidding me? We need to get in there now, otherwise that kid's dead and they've gone for sure. There's no time to sit here with thumbs up our asses waiting for cops who might not get here. How far away from the house are we?'

'Just beyond that slight bend,' Bill said, pointing. 'Just out of sight.'

Donaldson and Henry looked at each other again. 'You know I'm right. Two patrols coming from the south, the ARV only just jumping into their vehicle in the garage. If we hesitate, he's dead. These guys don't mess around. And if we're wrong, then let's have red faces. I don't mind lookin' stoopid. We need to get in there now – and this talkin' is just a waste of time.' He reached for his door handle.

Henry nodded. 'You're right.'

'Give me a minute,' Donaldson said and opened his door. 'I'll go around the back of the place, then you hurtle in through the front door.'

'You have no weapon,' Henry reminded him.

'I'll improvise if I have to,' He touched Henry's shoulder, trotted diagonally across the road, leapt over a garden wall and disappeared.

'Let's hope he bowls into the right place. There's lots of old biddies in these houses along here,' Henry said. 'Time to go.'

The first of the men stepped into the TV lounge, checked it quickly. Across the hallway, the second man opened the door of another lounge opposite.

'Clear,' the first man said, backing out of the TV lounge, his gun held combat style, an isosceles triangle formed by his arms and chest, the gun held in his right hand, supported by the left.

'Clear,' the second man echoed, coming out of the other lounge. He was the knife man, but now he was armed with a pistol, the knife wiped clean and sheathed at the small of his back.

The third man, clearly the leader, had waited in the hallway for his colleagues to do his job. He said quickly, 'Upstairs and check the bedrooms. I'll wait here. If you find him, bring him to me alive. I want him to look me in the face and ID me again before I kill him. Go.'

The two men sprinted down the wide hall, moving silently as they went, and took the stairs just as quietly and began a well structured, swift search of the bedrooms on the first floor.

Donaldson clambered over the brick wall and slithered down into a patch of damp soil. He moved quickly behind a rhododendron bush and inspected the rear aspect of Cleveley House. There was one door, which he guessed was a kitchen door, three ground floor windows and a patio door. On the first floor there were four windows, one with the lights on.

Keeping low, he stepped out from cover and, crouching, ran across the width of lawn, then over a paved area, to the back of the house, flattening himself up to the wall. He edged to the door that he now noticed was slightly ajar.

The man in the hallway, the leader, remained stock still, listening for any movement. He also had an earpiece screwed into his left ear, wirelessly attached to the radio on a harness at his waist. The police transmissions had stopped for some reason, but he wasn't too worried. He estimated his team had about four minutes before the cops came in their size tens, by which time he and his men would be gone and the boy would be dead. He was certain of his skills and abilities.

He remained in a crouching position, weapon drawn and ready, constantly looking, evaluating, listening, reassessing. Upstairs he heard a door being kicked open. He backed up slightly, his eyes rechecking the two downstairs lounges that had been declared empty.

The one on the left, then the TV lounge on his right.

And then he saw it, and computed it, and instantly realized that the room wasn't empty because he saw the L-shaped settee move ever so slightly – and knew exactly where the boy was hiding.

*   *   *

Bending low, Donaldson ran his left hand across the kitchen door and very gently put some pressure on it, pushing it further open by one inch. He waited for the creak that did not come. But it was a brand new UPVC door, so why would it creak? He opened it an inch further, then wide enough for him to step into a tiny vestibule, with an inner door six feet ahead that opened into the kitchen itself. Donaldson took a silent stride to this door, held his breath, opened it.

He was definitely in the kitchen. There was a sink, cooker, refrigerator, shelves, cupboards, work surfaces, a small dining table and a dead body with a horrendously sliced open throat, lying in a sea of thick, deep-red blood.

There was no time for sneaking about. The man crossed the TV lounge and dragged the settee away from the wall, revealing the stretched out, terrified form of the boy lying prone behind it.

Mark stared up at him as he tore off his balaclava and pointed his gun at Mark's head.

'Remember me, sonny?'

Mark did. He knew this was the face of the man who had killed the old guy on the street in Blackpool and who had probably killed Rory and Billy Costain. And also, his mother, Mandy Carter.

Mark was determined to show no fear.

'I know you, you murdering bastard.'

'Good, because I'm the last face you're ever going to see.'

He placed the muzzle of the gun against the crown of Mark's head. The boy shut his eyes tightly and at that moment, fear did overwhelm him.

Donaldson stepped over the blood to the kitchen door, braced himself for an instant before looking into the hallway and catching a glimpse of the back of a black-clad figure entering the next room on the right.

From upstairs he heard the clatter of doors being kicked open.

'Henry, you should be here by now,' Donaldson murmured under his breath.

The man curled his fingers around Mark's collar and heaved him one handed out from behind the settee, keeping the gun jammed against his skull. He dragged him out as though he was a dog about to be put down.

Karl Donaldson stepped into the TV lounge doorway, his wide frame filling the gap. He'd wanted to say some profound words at that point and if he'd been in a movie, that's probably what he would have done. He would have explained why he could not allow the killing to happen and the gunman would have had the opportunity to say his piece, too. But there was no time for such niceties. Explanations were rare in real life. If Donaldson had said something, even given a warning, the gunman would simply have turned and shot him, then the boy, because Donaldson knew what the man was capable of.

Instead, Donaldson had to act immediately.

Taking full advantage of the fact that, for the briefest moment in time, the gunman had his back to him, he charged across the room, powering low and hard into him, bowling him over, breaking his grip on Mark's clothing. The collision sent both of them crashing into the back wall and into a radiator underneath the window.

They fell into an untidy heap, but the man was very fast and strong, and highly trained. Donaldson held him in a massive bear hug, his arms wrapped tightly around him as they hit the wall. But the man managed to unpin his left hand and punch Donaldson hard on the side of the head. It was a blow that, despite travelling only a short distance, connected accurately and powerfully and with great effect. The strike of a man familiar with hand to hand combat. The knuckles smashed like brick into Donaldson's temple, just above his jaw hinge. A shock wave surged through his brain, sending him sideways, and although he tried hard to keep hold of this extremely dangerous man, his whole body just went loose as the message relay system from brain to function crashed for an instant.

The gunman broke free and rolled away.

Donaldson sagged on to his hands and knees, his eyes watering from the blow, vision blurring.

In a flowing motion, the man contorted back to Donaldson, his gun arcing around.

Just as quickly as they'd deserted him, Donaldson's senses returned like power being flicked on at a fuse box.

Using his arms as pivots, he spun his legs through ninety degrees and kicked upwards at the man like a break-dancer. His right foot caught the barrel of the gun with such force he could not keep hold of it and it was banged from his grasp.

Donaldson bounded up on to his feet and the two men faced each other, crouching low like wrestlers, both breathing heavily.

The gunman smiled – but Donaldson had no time for that. He knew he was in a fight to the death and had to take the man down without hesitation or conscience. They went for each other, coming together like two stags in a contest that was evenly matched and brutal.

Henry and Bill Robbins reached the front door of the house. Robbins had his MP5 strapped diagonally across his chest from left shoulder to right hip, ready for use. The Glock was in a holster at his hip. He also wore his chequered police firearms baseball cap. Henry, not wanting to feel naked, had grabbed the Taser as a security blanket.

The door was open, led into a wide, tiled, vestibule, then through an inner door into the hallway, facing the central staircase.

As they stepped side by side, Henry on the left of Robbins, through this second door, the two men who had been searching the first floor appeared on the landing at the top of the stairs. Their guns came up.

Robbins forced Henry away with a sweep of his left hand, and brought the H&K round into a firing position and screamed, 'Police, drop your weapons.'

The man on the right fired his pistol. Henry jumped to one side, whilst Robbins returned controlled fire with the machine pistol. Two bullets slammed into the man's chest and he windmilled backwards, as Robbins' aim shifted across and he took down the second man with a burst of fire.

It was a ferocious fight. The two men, both large, powerful, hard and determined, came at each other with a fighting style that combined brutal street battling – fists, headbutts, knees to groins, gouging and biting – with more refined, but equally violent, martial arts – chops to the neck with the side of the hand, throws, powerful short blows, thumbs to pressure points. Each man vied for supremacy. They both tired quickly and it would be the one who could just get the slight edge that would be the victor.

Donaldson fought clinically and dispassionately, landing punches, some better than others, taking what the man had to offer and he felt he was coming out on top.

For the men, the fight seemed to go on forever, even though it lasted less than a minute. Donaldson began to feel confident he would win as they clashed and tumbled across the lounge floor, toward the fireplace, but he slipped, his knee gave and the man was on him. He punched Donaldson hard on the side of the head again and the blow caught him perfectly. Everything suddenly gave up as the man pounded Donaldson's head on the side of the marble hearth.

Suddenly – amazingly – the man screamed, jerked and writhed and no longer held on to Donaldson, who rolled away and back up to his knees.

His opponent had been Tasered by Henry Christie and was having fifty thousand volts of electricity pumped into him through the probes discharged by the gun-like device in Henry's hands. He was experiencing what was described by the Taser manufacturer as neuromuscular incapacitation. It lasted for only a few seconds, after which he would immediately regain all his functions. This was a fact that Donaldson knew. He waited for the spasms to cease then leapt on the man before he even knew he had recovered, flipped him on to his front and forced both his arms behind his back and yelled, 'Could do with some cuffs, here, pal.'

Henry went over to him and handed him the pair he'd brought in with him, which Donaldson ratcheted on tight and turned the man back over.

They made eye contact.

'What the hell, Don, what the hell?' Donaldson said breathlessly.

'Had to be done, pal.'

Henry watched the exchange, then turned to Mark Carter who was still crouched by the end of the settee. He rose on unsteady legs and Henry went over to him, said, 'C'mere pal,' and drew him tenderly to him and held tight.

EIGHTEEN

'You know I won't have a choice on this one,' FB said. 'It'll be taken completely out of our hands. The IPCC will have a field day with it, as will the press, and we'll just have to hunker down and take it on the chin.'

'We have nothing to hide,' Henry said. 'It was a fast moving scenario, two people had been murdered and another life was at risk, and from all accounts a third person, the social worker was murdered trying to protect that person. I'll go with it and take the flak about procedure and processes. It's not about doing things right, it's about doing the right thing and I'm happy we did the right thing. My concern is about Bill Robbins at this point. He needs complete protection here.'

'I have no choice but to suspend him from firearms duties,' FB said firmly, 'including the delivery of firearms training and related matters. He won't even be allowed to pick up a gun until all this has been dealt with.'

'I know that, he knows and accepts that, but he still needs our support.'

FB nodded. 'You have my assurance. We'll be behind him all the way,' he said without conviction.

'In the meantime, I'd like to have him transferred on to FMIT, temporarily.'

'Done.' FB said without hesitation, surprising Henry with this move, although this was tempered when FB said, 'I'd been wondering where to dump him.'

Henry breathed out and looked sideways at Karl Donaldson. It was gone midnight, the raging fires of the initial incidents had died down slightly and there was a slight calm in the proceedings. The three men had decamped to the office of the Divisional Chief Superintendent at Blackpool police station, which they had commandeered. They were trying to work out how best to handle the situation. The best idea they could come up with was to tell the truth. FB had taken up a lofty psychological position behind the Chief Super's desk, separating him from the other two, as though he wanted to distance himself from the mess of three dead bodies in a children's care home, two of which had been shot by one of his firearms officers. *And* two other bodies in a terraced house in the town, one of who was a police employee who had possibly been a thief in uniform, living with a known druggy, and had unfortunately stolen the item that got her killed, a mobile phone. There were going to be uncomfortable times ahead for the force.

'And you, Mr Donaldson,' FB said, turning sardonically to the American. 'It looks as though your speculation that an FBI hit squad was involved in numerous killings was correct.'

'It does.' Donaldson remembered the slightly disbelieving remark FB had made in the earlier briefing Donaldson had started, but not finished, the one rudely interrupted by the fact that the mobile phone signal had been reactivated. However, Donaldson's reply did not have any hint of triumph in it. He was completely and utterly devastated by what had happened and who was involved.

'So, you'd better pick up where you left off – and then bring me up to the point as to why two FBI officers have been shot dead by one of my officers, and another one is in custody on suspicion of murder.'

Donaldson stirred uncomfortably, pursed his lips and said, 'I'll try my best, sir.'

FB raised his eyebrows. They went up in an inverted U-shape. It was the first time Donaldson had ever called him sir.

Fortunately for Henry, because everything had happened within the confines of Cleveley House, it was a relatively straight-forward task, not an easy one though, to control the scene. Two bodies at the top of the stairs, another in the kitchen, one prisoner in the TV lounge, one terrified witness – and lots of resources on the way.

The first job was to keep a calm head and save life and limb, even if it meant compromising any evidence at the scene, but when it became obvious that three people were definitely dead and no one else was about to die, next on the agenda was securing the scene. There were many simultaneous things Henry had to think of.

The living prisoner, once secure, was the first to be dealt with. With his face swelling like a distorted balloon, he had been held firmly down until reinforcements arrived, and then dragged bodily out and thrown head first into the cage in the section van. He'd been thoroughly searched before this, by Henry and a Support Unit officer who'd been one of the first to arrive on the scene.

'Don't trust him an inch,' Donaldson had chirped in as he watched the search. He was exhausted by the exertion of the fight and had stood well back when the uniforms came in, although the prisoner continued to look dangerously at him through his good eye. Once satisfied he'd been searched and everything that needed to be taken off him was, two burly SU officers took him to the van. He hadn't put up any further resistance, but Donaldson had thought his warning was necessary, considering the prisoner's background. He had followed the officers out of the house and watched his boss, Don Barber, being hurled into the van.

He tugged Henry to one side. 'I want to go with him.'

'What do you mean?' Henry's face scrunched up.

'I want to go in the back with him.'

'Not a good idea.' Already Henry was thinking how he would explain a dead body in the back of a police van. He had enough to deal with, without a death in police custody. He knew Donaldson was eminently capable of doing something like that.

'I won't touch him.' Donaldson held up his hands. 'Honest – and he needs to have someone in with him. Getting out of those cuffs will be a doozy for him if he isn't supervised. And as well searched as he was, I wouldn't be surprised if you find more weaponry on him when he gets searched again. He's ex-special forces.'

'I'll need to put someone else in with you.'

'I need to talk to him, ask him why,' Donaldson persisted.

'Someone else has to be in there – and no funny business,' Henry insisted.

Donaldson nodded. Henry turned to the support unit officer who'd assisted him with the body search. He looked a useful lad and he had already earwigged the conversation. 'You up for this?'

'Sure, boss.'

Henry gave Donaldson a meaningful look, then jerked his head to the back of the van, hoping to hell he wouldn't regret this. 'Everything off the record between you – and no thumping him.'

'You have my word.'

The van pulled away. Henry watched it with trepidation, then went back into the house where he found Bill Robbins at the top of the stairs inspecting the two bodies he'd shot. Donaldson had looked at the deceased men, but had been unable to identify them – neither, surprise, surprise, carried any ID – although he pointed to the unmasked face of one of them which was very swollen underneath an eye. Maybe a broken cheekbone from a fight in Malta?

Robbins looked distraught. Only to be expected, Henry thought sympathetically. His mind must be in a dreadful state. Henry was keen to get Robbins off-scene, both for evidential reasons and also to get him into the clutches of his firearms bosses, for a debrief and perhaps the start of the counselling process. 'Bill, you OK?'

Robbins glanced at Henry, who then found out why his old

friend was looking so put out. Not, it transpired, because of the 'Oh shit, what the hell have I done; what the hell's going to happen to me and my pension?' thought. Or the 'I'm so deeply affected by having killed two people that I'm going to have post-traumatic stress,' thought either.

Robbins said, 'All that friggin' training and it comes to this.' He pointed disparagingly at the bodies of the two men. 'I aimed for their chests, their body mass, their hearts. I intended to get two bullets into each of them, but looking at this – pah!' He threw up his hands in disgust. 'This one, not too bad. Chest shots, I'd say, one in the heart, the other a lung shot . . . so, so, but the grouping leaves a lot to be desired. But this one! Jeez – a neck and shoulder shot. What is that? Just plain bad shooting. It's a wonder he's still not breathing.'

Henry blinked at him in astonishment. 'You're bothered about your aim?'

'Well it's what I train for, innit? If I shot like this on the range, I'd suspend myself.'

His eyes were malevolent, yet dead. As he sat back with his cuffed hands uncomfortably behind him, he kept them un-waveringly on Donaldson sitting on the steel bench opposite, virtually knee to knee in the tight confines of the cage. They rolled with the movement of the police van as it slowed, rounded corners and accelerated. The tough-looking constable accompanying them sat tucked in one corner, watching the dangerous prisoner for any sudden moves.

Blood dribbled out of Donaldson's nose. He wiped it away with the back of his hand.

'Talk to me off the record. Tell me why, Don. It's over now and you've nothing to lose.'

Don Barber, Donaldson's boss, tilted back his head on to the cage wall and continued with the intimidating stare. Then his mouth curved into a smile and, as often happens with prisoners caught in the act, he said, 'Nothing to say and you've got it all to prove buddy boy.'

The smile mocked Donaldson who, still with adrenaline pulsing through him, held back the urge to pound his fist into the face of the man who, he was certain now, had taken the law into his own hands and murdered people purely as an act of revenge. 'And anyway, why are you so bothered? You and me, we're just the same. Wolves in sheep's clothing.'

'No, you got it wrong there, Don. My actions are always authorized and necessary and right, or they protect the lives of others in immediate, life-threatening danger.'

He snorted. 'Wrong, you fucking simpleton.' Barber laughed harshly and shook his head.

Donaldson regarded him in the darkness of the cage. The streetlights ran continuous bars of yellow across his face as the van travelled. Then he sat back. 'I will prove it all, Don,' he declared. 'From the moment Shark was killed because he was in the wrong place at the wrong time, through every revenge killing you and your little team carried out. Right up to here.' Donaldson's index finger jabbed downwards. 'To this point where you went beyond all comprehension and started to kill innocent people simply to protect yourself, and would have killed another boy just because he saw your face.'

Barber shrugged confidently. 'I'll be protected.'

'No, you'll be thrown to the wolves,' Donaldson said. 'No one will come near you with a cow-prod, even.'

'We shall see.'

The van slowed, turned and pulled into the yard at the back of the police station. The momentum caused the two men to rock forwards and for a moment, their faces were an inch apart.

'So getting into the van was a waste of time?' FB said, annoyed at having been denied a punchline. 'He admitted nothing?'

'Yeah – nothing.'

FB looked worriedly at Henry. 'But the stuff here, on our patch, we can prove that?'

'Yes.' Henry was certain. 'When everything's bagged together, so long as we do it all slowly, methodically and professionally, we have him. From the moment he killed the old man to the point where he held a gun to Mark Carter's head, and everything in between. We'll match clothing, fibres, firearms and vehicles. We found a Volvo saloon on false plates in a street behind Cleveley House and that'll be a treasure-trove for the scientists, I suspect. There'll be bits of the old man all over it.'

'Good – make bloody sure,' FB said.

'I will,' Henry said.

FB rolled his heavy body up to his feet and emitted a sigh. 'Looks like you've got a hell of a lot of shite in your organization.'

Donaldson took the remark silently, but it hurt him badly and he fumed as he watched the Chief leave the room. As the door closed and he was certain the man had gone, he said, 'Hate that guy.'

'He obviously touched a nerve,' Henry said, feeling slightly defensive of FB for once and not enjoying the sensation, so he added, 'but I get your drift.'

'Jeez.' Donaldson touched his battered face gingerly. 'He didn't half hit hard. I have a horrible feeling he would've beaten me if you hadn't turned up and zapped him. I owe you one. You are a bit of a Taser expert, I take it?'

'Never used one in my life,' Henry admitted. 'Lucky I didn't electrocute you.'

Donaldson shook his sore head and chuckled.

'Coming back to the subject, I take it that it was the computer thing that put you on to him? You haven't really had chance to explain . . .'

'Yeah. Nothing else, no suspicions whatever. Until I couldn't get on to files I knew I had the right to access. These were the ones with detailed information about the Camorra killings, with weapon details and everything. I'd looked at the general stuff that anyone can access and noticed, as I said, there were some that didn't seem quite Mafia-like. Truly professional hits. I told Don I was looking into the patterns, which he didn't seem overly keen on, and that was probably when his radar started shitting itself. There was something else, too.'

'What?'

'I never told him the witness you had was a teenage lad. I never described the witness at all, but he let it slip that he knew the witness was a lad. Are you counting the number of times I said the word witness?' Donaldson paused with a grin. 'Anyway, when he said this initially, I didn't pick up on it straightaway, it just kinda seeped into my brain. I assume he may have realized he'd made a blunder, too. Because he'd seen Mark, of course.

'I guess if I hadn't had access to Jerry Tope, I still wouldn't be sure about anything. But Jerry hacked into the authorization emails that Don had sent to the IT guys, telling them to deny me access to these files. Then I found Don himself wasn't at the embassy. All the time I'd been talking to him on his mobile, I'd assumed he'd been in London. *Wrong*. We also found emails booking three rooms at cheap hotels in the Blackpool area . . .'

'Which we'll have to search,' Henry said. A phone desk rang.

Henry scooped it up. He listened, said a few yeps, hung up. 'He wants to talk.'

Don Barber was in a white paper suit and matching slip-on boots. His skin had been carefully swabbed and hair combed by a crime scene investigator. Samples had been taken, he'd been photographed, fingerprinted and a swab of saliva taken for DNA purposes. He was sitting in an interview room, still handcuffed, guarded by the same officer who had accompanied him and Donaldson in the back of the van.

The detective and the FBI agent walked in. Henry gestured for the constable to leave, then he sat opposite Barber whilst Donaldson remained standing. Henry placed two sealed packs of tapes on the table, together with associated paperwork.

'Off the record,' Barber said.

Henry shook his head. 'No, not now. You had your chance, blew it. No more off the record unless I say. You are well and truly in police custody and we're not playing games. You want to talk, that's fine, but it'll be on tape, audio and video. If you don't want to, that's fine too, we still go through the motions. Your choice, but either way I'd recommend you talk to a solicitor – lawyer – so you know exactly where you stand.'

Barber took it in. 'I want these off.' He raised his manacled hands. 'I want a drink, I want to see a lawyer, I want to see a doctor and I want my phone call, and I want some people telling of my arrest.'

'No phone call, no one to be informed or your arrest yet.'

'I have a right.'

'Which has been temporarily suspended. Authorized by the Chief Constable.'

'That means I'm being held incommunicado. That's illegal.'

'For the time being, that's how it is. Until I'm satisfied no one else is in danger from you and that all outstanding suspects have been arrested. Your choice.' Henry held up the tapes and waggled them enticingly.

Four hours later, Donaldson looked up as Henry entered the Chief Superintendent's office where he had been waiting. He had not been allowed to stay as the two detectives – Rik Dean and Alex Bent – chosen by Henry, had interviewed Barber.

He stood up warily. 'Well?'

'Rik and Alex have just briefed me,' Henry said. He checked

his watch. 'Unfortunately, we've had to get the police surgeon out to him, who has told us he needs to be taken to hospital. He's suffering from head pains, apparently. Feels faint. Sorry. Fancy a coffee?'

'Whatever.'

Henry led the American out of the station and down on to the promenade. It was a chilly dawn, the tide was way out, but the sky was clear. They walked to the McDonald's on the promenade where Henry bought two black coffees. They sat in the deserted restaurant.

'There's a long way to go,' Henry said apologetically. 'He's talking, but he's not forthcoming, if you know what I mean? He has to be pinned down before he'll admit anything and even then it's not great.'

'Where exactly are you, then?'

'He blames the other two guys, the dead ones.'

'Has he identified them?'

'Says he doesn't know their names but it was all their idea.'

'He's lying.' Donaldson churned inside, like the rumblings of a volcano about to erupt.

'We'll keep on at him.'

'You know I need to speak to him – alone.'

Henry nodded – his insides now churning.

'I may have to visit him in hospital.' Donaldson held Henry's gaze until Henry broke off. 'I won't kill him – but I need my answers. Without them, it's all speculation. Why did he want me to track down this, this American hit man? Why kill Fazil? Why did he let me live, then change his mind? How did he know Petrone was in Blackpool?'

Henry took a sip of the bitter coffee. 'Because tracking down a professional hit man is hard, but killing a few Camorra Mafia dons who you suspect of ordering the murder of an undercover agent is more straightforward. My guess is that once you found and identified the American, he'd have been taken out, like Fazil was. Fazil only died after you confirmed to Barber that you were sure he was the guy who delivered the gun in Majorca.'

'And he had someone waiting, ready to strike.'

'Maybe one of those two dead guys, the one with the broken face? Given time, we'll find out. As to how he found Petrone,' Henry shrugged deeply, 'who knows? Intelligence reports? Someone blabbed somewhere?'

'Speculation, Henry.'

'Can *I* speculate on something?' Henry looked down his nose at Donaldson. 'Would I be right in thinking the FBI can listen into encrypted police radio transmissions?'

Donaldson said nothing, but tried to look innocent.

'Which accounts for the very state of the art radios found in their possession?'

'Obviously, we'll want them back.'

'And mobile phone triangulation?'

'Goes without saying. I'll be able to backtrack everything he did in that respect, but don't expect the FBI to admit to very much . . . and what became of *that* phone?'

'Not found, as yet. Probably down a grate somewhere.' Henry finished the coffee. 'I need to get back, there's a lot of shit to sort out and I don't want to cock anything up. And I need to sort out Mark Carter. He's been sitting in a waiting room for the last few hours, getting his head down.' He stood, but leaned on the table. 'Don't do anything silly, Karl. I know you're upset with the guy, rightly so, but we have him now. We'll delve and delve and turn over all the shitty rocks necessary. Let justice take its course.'

'Lecture over?'

'And out.'

'You might need these.' He dropped a set of car keys into Donaldson's hand. 'My Mondeo – on the car park in front of the nick.'

Donaldson had a coffee refill for free, just by giving the young lady behind he counter one of his best smiles that, even so early, completely made her day. He sat back down alone at a window seat, and gazed across the promenade to Central Pier.

His mind was full of Don Barber. He hated what the man had done and yet Donaldson could see where he was coming from. Revenge was a very forceful emotion to contend with. Shark had been his responsibility as well as an old friend. And his over the top reaction had been his response to his death. Blood for blood. Donaldson had been there, however much he had denied it to Barber – who didn't know half of what Donaldson had done over the years.

He fished out his phone. It was early, but he still called Karen's mobile, knowing that she would be in bed and unable to take the call. He didn't call the home phone because he didn't want to wake her, but he wanted to leave a message she'd find when she got up because she always left her mobile down in the kitchen.

He walked back to the station, jiggling Henry's car keys and thinking about what he would say to Barber. As he crossed Bonny Street, his mobile phone rang and he was surprised to see it was his home number.

'Karen? I didn't wake you, honey, did I?'

'No, I was already up.'

'You OK?'

'Yes – how about you?'

'Oh, it's been a busy few hours, but I came through.'

'Good.' She sounded shaky.

'You sure you're all right?' He was already wondering if she had found out about the Scandinavian sex-fiend he'd screwed.

'I am, just feeling queasy, that's all.'

'Heavy night?'

'No, not really . . . been sick that's all . . . look, Karl, I'm really sorry if you think I've been a bit off with you for a few weeks. It's just . . . look, I don't really know how to put this.'

His heart was already sinking. He said nothing, expecting the worst.

'It's just, I didn't know for certain, but I went to the doctor yesterday and he confirmed it.'

'Confirmed what?'

'Do you not listen? I've been sick this morning, yeah. Does that not tell you something?'

'Are you saying you're pregnant?'

'Duh – yes, you big, dumb, wonderful Yank.'

Donaldson was speechless for a few moments, as his jaw dropped and he took in the news.

'I wanted to tell you face to face, but seeing how you phoned this morning and declared your undying love to me in a voice-mail, I thought I'd tell you so you can prepare yourself for when I get up there this afternoon. Maybe flowers at the ready? Chocolates? An expensive present of some sort?'

'You're pregnant?'

'Yes . . . impregnated by your gallant sperm.'

'When? How?'

'About a month ago, I guess. How – I'll draw you a diagram this afternoon, then tonight we can do a re-enactment if you like? But more to the point, how do you feel about it?'

Donaldson caught a sob in his throat. 'Fantastic,' he said, his eyes moistening. 'Utterly, utterly, fantastic. What about you?'

'Great – sick, but great. Just more icing on our cake.'

'I love you, babe.'

'Love you too.'

The conversation degenerated into several minutes of cooing and lovey-dovey words designed to make any eavesdropper poorly, before they hung up, desperate to see each other later in the day.

In the blink of an eye, Karl Donaldson's world had a renewal of perspective. Suddenly, he was no longer bothered about Don Barber and what he had to say to him. He could wait for the answers now. They would come as he and Henry investigated the man. The two other men would be identified in time – and no doubt turn out to be FBI operatives with military backgrounds who both knew Shark. And as for the hit man known as the American, so what? He was still out there, plying his dirty trade, but again, so what? One day, Donaldson, or someone like him, would take the bastard down, but for the moment, he could stay out there. His time would come, probably in a hail of bullets.

Donaldson could not wipe the stupid grin off his face. He did an about turn, trotted across the promenade to the seafront and gazed at the horizon, his chest bursting with pride, almost unable to breathe, swallowing back his tears. This is what real life is all about, he thought. Sperm and babies.